Praise for Michael A. Black's

Melody of Vengeance

"Black has created a pulp action hero right out of the forties. The characters come to life as if leaping off of a old movie serial screen. When you pick up this book, make sure you clear you schedule first, because once you start reading you won't want to stop. This is a perfect homage to the work of Walter B. Gibson, Lester Dent, and Henry W. Ralston. Reading this book was pure fun."

–Jon Jordan, *Crime Spree* Magazine

"In Doc Atlas, author Mike Black has created not just another Doc Savage clone but the best in modern pulp excitement that harkens back to the glory days of pulp adventure, but has real heart, soul, and meaning for today's readers. You're in for a real treat with this one!"

–Gary Lovisi, Edgar nominated writer
and editor of *Hardboiled Magazine*

"In this action-packed thriller, adventurer Doc Atlas is up against a mob of killers, the mysterious masked vigilante The Wraith, and a hidden mastermind. This is a novel you won't be able to put down!"

–Tom Johnson, author of the Jur series
and editor of *Pulp Fiction Magazine*

"Whether he's twisting a tale of mystery or bringing pulp heroes to life, Michael A. Black's flair for storytelling and his powerful prose win new readers every day. Pick this book up and you'll become a Michael A. Black fan for life."

–Julie A. Hyzy, author of *Deadly Interest*,
the second in the Alex St. James series

"Michael A. Black writes with a talent and an energy that cannot be contained by any single genre. Whatever he takes aim at, he nails dead-on. Readers are sure to be clamoring for more of Doc Atlas."

–Wayne Dundee, author of the Joe Hannibal series

Books by

Michael A. Black

Echelon Press Publishing

Melody of Vengeance

Five Star

Freeze Me Tender

The Heist

Windy City Knights

A Killing Frost

To Rose Jones —
Thanks for all that you're
done for my dad and me.
Take care
Mike

A Doc Atlas Adventure

MELODY OF VENGEANCE

By

Michael A. Black

Michael A. Black

Echelon Press
Publishing

MELODY OF VENGEANCE

A Doc Atlas Adventures

Book One

An Echelon Press Book

First Echelon Press paperback printing / January 2007

Cover and illustration © Tim Faurote

Final titling © Nathalie Moore

2004 Ariana "Best in Category" Award winner

Echelon Press

9735 Country Meadows Lane 1-D

Laurel, MD 20723

www.echelonpress.com

ISBN 978-1-59080-497-1

1-59080-497-X

Library of Congress Control Number: 2006928975

PRINTED IN THE UNITED STATES OF AMERICA

10 9 8 7 6 5 4 3 2 1

To my best friend, Ray Lovato,
with whom I've shared many an adventure since we first ran up
that dirt hill so many years ago.

Introduction

A Hero for All Ages

Growing up, we all look for heroes to emulate. And as kids, many of us spent hours in our rooms, eyes wide with excitement, turning page after page of a well-loved book. What were we doing, but living vicariously through our favorite heroes' exploits? We *became* these heroes, trailing bad guys, getting into life-or-death situations, and feeling that incumbent exhilaration when evil was foiled forever–or, at least, until our next adventure.

Novels, comic books, and magazines were our vehicles of choice, and we devoured them, ravenously. Even today, despite the plethora of athletes on television, and stars in movies, there's still nothing quite like opening a book and stepping into a *real* hero's adventure.

Melody of Vengeance brings great pulp stories back to vivid life in the character of Doc Atlas. Known as The Golden Giant, Doc is a 1940s icon–a wealthy, selfless superhero who operates out of a New York skyscraper, catching criminals and fighting evil wherever it inevitably crops up. And although Doc's feats are as original as they are incredible, clever readers will nonetheless catch author Michael A. Black's homage to the earliest pulp greats.

Black, who's made a considerable name for himself in the mystery genre with his Ron Shade Private Investigator series

(*A Killing Frost–Windy City Knights–A Final Judgment*), and with thrillers (*The Heist–Freeze Me, Tender*), has captured the energy and verve of the original pulp superheroes, and in *Melody of Vengeance*, he's taken the thrills to new heights. Doc Atlas has a team of three trusted colleagues, two of whom are Ace Assante and Mad Dog Deagan. The third, Penelope Cartier, is a modern woman and Doc's love interest. Her presence adds an essential element of sexual tension that many of the original pulp stories lacked.

When I was a kid, I missed out on the wonderful world of pulp fiction, spending my time instead buried within the yellow spines of Nancy Drew books. For me, she epitomized all that a female hero should be, and I longed to be just like her when I grew up.

I eventually did grow up, of course, and Nancy's adventures now seem "quaint." For years, however, I wished I could find some series that would bring back that feeling of vicarious exhilaration, a series that would transport me to another place, another time, with heroes I could root for, live through, and cheer with.

I discovered all that and more, in Doc Atlas. To me his adventures are like Nancy Drew…only better. *Melody of Vengeance* takes me back to the days when I couldn't pull myself away from reading, not even when my mom ordered me outside to play. Every time I read *Melody* I'm unable to put it down. I always promise myself, "Just one more chapter," but I wind up finishing in no time at all. I arrive at the words: "The End," satisfied, yet sad that the excitement is over, for now.

But just as *Melody* provides me the chance to revisit the pure joy of reading for pleasure–like I did as a kid–it does so in a way that engages my adult sensibilities. The story is multilayered with nuanced characterization and subtle interplays. With author Black establishing the tone and hitting every note perfectly, the story's title becomes even more apt. In this tale of revenge and vigilantism, this exquisite melody truly is one of vengeance.

Doc Atlas's adventures are, quite simply, the best in entertainment. With their unbeatable combination of fresh stories with a retro feel, they will delight pulp fans and new readers alike.

So, to all you pulp readers out there, sit back and enjoy. It's been a long time since you've encountered an experience like this, and I promise you–you're in for a marvelous treat.

And, to a new generation of enthusiastic readers, I envy you. For the adventure is just beginning…

Welcome to *Melody of Vengeance*.

–Julie Hyzy

1

Only by Death...

THE light from a single, dangling bulb cast a garish glow over the small room as Davis 'Butchie' Cole sat behind the big desk, licking his thumb every few seconds while he counted the stolen money. He was a big angular man whose dark eyebrows and sloping forehead gave him an almost simian appearance. His left cheek sported a long keloid, the remnant of a prison knife fight, which had left Cole scarred for life and his two adversaries dead. Two swarthy figures sat across from him in the small office, neither as big as Cole, but both were equally sinister looking. The smaller of the two took a couple of nervous puffs on his cigarette then stubbed it out. Standing, the hood strolled over to the front of the desk and eyed the large stacks of bills, each of which Cole had placed into an open black valise after completing his count.

"Pretty good haul, huh, boss?" the little hoodlum said.

Butchie glanced up briefly, his dark eyes flashing his displeasure at being interrupted. When the other man's fingers strayed across the top of one of the stacks, Cole growled, "Don't touch nothing, Weasel."

'Weasel' Phipps withdrew his hand as if a flame had seared him. He walked back to the wall and looked out the glass-framed window next to the door. Beyond the room lay the dimly lighted hallways of the huge factory. It had once been one of the largest icehouses in the city, but with the advent of the refrigerator, the company had eventually gone out of business. Now an obscure company rented the dilapidated shell for storage, but it also served as the favorite hideout of the notorious Cole Gang.

"Sit down, Weasel," the second man said. His name was Floyd Calson, and he, too, sported numerous scars on his face. But his were strange looking, like mottled flesh, starting along his jaw line and descending beneath his collar. The scars were the result of a quickly done skin graft that a fledgling doctor had done in a prison infirmary after a vengeful inmate had managed to start a fire in Floyd's cell. Calson hadn't been expected to live, with severe burns over seventy percent of his body, but he'd surprised everybody and pulled through. Months later, the man who purportedly started the fire was killed after slipping over a fifth tier banister. His death was ruled accidental chiefly because witnesses recalled that Calson, the man with the best motive, had uncharacteristically volunteered for kitchen duty that night. Coincidentally, Butchie Cole had been conspicuously absent from his assigned duties, claiming to have been ill in his cell.

Calson took out a pack of Luckies and shook one loose. The Weasel grinned at him and held out his hand. Calson tossed him a cigarette and then flicked his thumbnail over the end of a large wooden match. The brightness of the flame illuminated his coarse features.

"What's the matter with you, Weasel? Or should I say, Rodney?" Calson lighted his smoke and then held out the match. "You got ants in your pants or something?"

"Nah," the Weasel said, twirling the end of his cigarette in the yellow flame. "Just thinking that I'm gonna use my end of

2

the cut to buy a brand new 'forty-seven Caddie. Then I'll be able to get all the broads I want."

"Ya dummy," Cole said, setting down another stack. "The new 'forty-eights will be out in a couple more months."

"Besides," Calson said, the lines of his uneven skin buckling as he smiled. "A Nash is more your style."

The Weasel frowned, inhaling deeply on the cigarette.

"So we gonna get to the broad pretty soon?" he asked. He grinned, letting the smoke seep out from between his uneven teeth. "She's a looker, ain't she?"

"Yeah, well, maybe the boss don't want her messed up," Calson said. "You ever think of that?"

"Huh?" the Weasel said, his mouth losing its smile. "That ain't true, is it, Butchie? The boss didn't say that, did he?"

Cole's face twisted into a grimace as he slammed the stack of currency down on the table. "You damn little idiot. Ya made me lose count. Just for that you ain't even gonna get to touch her until me, Floyd, and Tuterrow have had our fill."

"Aw, come on, you ain't even seen her yet," the Weasel started to say, but Butchie's big palm lashed out, slapping across the smaller man's face. Despite it being only a slap, the Weasel staggered backwards. He recovered, his mouth gaping, his fingers massaging his reddening cheek.

"In fact, we're gonna bring her into this very room, and all you're gonna be able to do is sit and count this money," Cole continued. His big index finger jabbed at the Weasel's face. "And if I find out you made even one mistake…" He paused to watch the other man's reaction, then licked his lips. Cole told Calson, "Go down and get the dame," then turned back to the Weasel. "Now get in that chair and start counting. And remember, I'm gonna check your pockets afterwards."

The Weasel went around the desk and sat, the stacks of money in front of him seeming to mesmerize him. Cole took a long stiletto out of his pocket and began cleaning his fingernails. The quick flash of the blade made the Weasel jump slightly, and he quickly picked up a bundle of bills from the large open burlap bag next to the chair. Cole expertly flipped the knife so it stuck in the center of the table right in front of the Weasel. Cole laughed as the other man's head jerked back.

The laugh died in his throat as the door opened and Calson and another man came in, each holding the arm of a slim, dark-complected young woman. Calson's hand pulled her raven black hair back from her face. Her brown eyes flashed with a frightened, desperate look beneath her long lashes. Cole's brow furrowed in disgust.

"What the hell did you do, you dumb son of a..." he said. "She's a spic. I told you the boss wanted a white girl for this."

"What the hell's the difference if we're just gonna cut off her ears and throw away the rest?" Calson said. "Besides, she had a better shape to her than the rest of them broads when we hit the bank."

Cole snorted through his nostrils. "Well, I guess we can always go out and get us a hooker or something, if we need to," he said slowly. His eyes swept over the girl's body, checking out each delicious curve. She had full breasts, a narrow waist, and hourglass hips. Obviously, Cole liked what he saw because he clapped his hands together loudly. He reached behind him and grabbed the knife from the desk, rotating it slowly, the blade shimmering under the garish light of the dangling bulb. The girl turned her face away, but Calson twisted his hand in her long hair again, forcing her to look at the gleaming blade.

"Don't cut her face just yet, Butchie," Calson said. "Not till we had some fun."

Cole reached out and grabbed a handful of the lush black hair himself. Then he traced the blade around her ear, letting it sweep slowly down her neck to the top of her white blouse. She stiffened as Cole leaned close and whispered hoarsely, "What's yer name?"

"Maria," she said, rolling the R with the Spanish inflection.

"Maria, huh?" Cole said. He belched in her face and the others laughed. His breath smelled rancid. "We're gonna play a little game now, and how nice we are to you is gonna depend on how nice you are to us. Understand?"

When she didn't respond, he let the point of the knife sink into the flesh of her neck, leaning forward to flick his tongue at the tiny crimson stream.

"Weasel, clear off the desk," Cole said. "I don't want to get dirty."

The little man, who had been watching with a rancorous smile, quickly removed the stacks of bills and placed them in the large black valise. Once they'd cleared the desktop off, they dragged Maria over to it. The Weasel wiped at it with his sleeve, his foul breathing expelling in excited little pants. She tried to squirm away, but the two hoods pressed her arms closer together. As she cried out in pain, Cole took his knife and slowly cut off each of the buttons securing the front of her blouse. He pulled it open, exposing her brassiere and a thin chain, which had a small gold cross attached to it. Cole crudely pawed at her as the others looked on hungrily. Calson and Tuterrow roughly pulled Maria back onto the desk. She tried to pull away, but Calson backhanded her across the face, bloodying her lip. Pinning her arms down on the hard wood, they reached for her legs.

Cole nodded toward the Weasel.

"Take off her skirt," he said.

"No! No, please," Maria bit her lips and tasted blood, as the Weasel's small hands began to probe her. "Please. Don't."

Her voice rose to a scream as he found the catch of her skirt and pulled at it. Seconds later the little man bent over and tried to force his tongue into her mouth. Cole snatched a hank of the Weasel's hair and pulled his head back.

"You wait till all the rest of us are done, understand?" he said.

"But Butchie–" the Weasel started to say.

"Shut up." Cole twisted his wrist, forcing the Weasel to the floor. He leered down at the girl, slipping the thin blade under the chain and lifting it with the blade. "This real gold?"

Maria's eyes darted down toward the knife.

"Well, is it?" Cole hissed. When she didn't reply he laughed. "I think you like me so much, you gonna give it to me, ain't ya?"

She closed her eyes and began reciting something in Spanish. From the cadence, Cole figured it was a prayer. He ripped at the chain, flinging it across the room, then moved the point of the blade lower, hooking it under the front of her brassiere. He drew the knife upward in a quick, slicing motion and when he saw Maria's eyes open, he held the blade up over her face. With a sly grin, he twisted his hand downward, stabbing the point into the desktop next to her face.

Her scream echoed in the room again, louder and more shrill this time.

Cole and the others laughed, and the big man leaned close once more and said, "Go ahead and scream. Ain't nobody gonna hear ya."

He straightened up and unbuckled his belt, letting his trousers fall to the floor to expose a pair of filthy blue-and-white boxer shorts. Cole leaned forward again, grabbing Maria's hair and licking his lips. Suddenly he stopped.

"Hey, what's that?" he asked.

"What?" said Calson.

"Don't you hear it?" Cole said.

The other men cocked their heads as a slight whistling sound traveling up the musical scale, drifted into the room, its melody tuneless, yet familiar at the same time. Then it grew stronger, fuller, more recognizable. It was a song. A song they all knew.

Cole twisted his head toward the door where a dark shadow was visible though the frosted glass. The door flew inward, striking the wall with such force the glass shattered. A hand rose up next to the doorjamb, and Cole saw a flash of light. A millisecond later he heard the thunder as the hard punch of the round struck his back. Another round hit him in the side as he twisted toward the floor. He was vaguely cognizant of seeing Tuterrow's hand fumbling for his gun inside his coat, then three red flowers blossomed on the front of the hood's shirt. Cole sank to his knees in time to see Calson sagging before him, a neat round hole between his eyes, and then everything faded to blackness.

The Weasel managed to scurry forward and grab the knife from its perpendicular position on the desk. He crouched beside Maria, his left arm snaking around her slim neck. He managed to pull her back toward him as he stood, holding the blade against her throat.

"Hold it," the Weasel snarled. His eyes flashed like a frightened animal's. "I'll stick her. I swear I will. Don't come no closer."

Slowly, a large framed man dressed in a loose fitting black shirt, dark pants, and combat boots stepped completely into the room from the other side of the doorway. He wore a translucent ebony silk screen over his face, strangely obscuring the features beneath it. Atop his head he wore a black Australian-style bush hat, and from his gloved hand, a Government Model Colt .45 extended, the smoke still rising from the end of the barrel.

"Look," the Weasel said. "All's I want is to get outta here. Me and her are gonna get up and walk out, and if you try to shoot, I'll jam this damn knife into her throat. I'll do it. I swear I will."

His voice was a plaintive whine. The dark man did not move, his pistol still pointing forward.

"Hey, you can keep that money over there, see," the Weasel continued. "It's all yours. And I'll let her go as soon as I get out of here. I promise ya I will."

"Only through death," the man in black said, "can you escape my wrath."

Before the Weasel could take another breath, the forty-five roared, sending a heavy round through the hoodlum's right eye. The knife twisted from his numbing fingers as he slumped to the floor. Maria gulped in a breath of air, then, as if suddenly aware of her nakedness, crossed her arms over her breasts. When she looked toward the door again she saw the dark man stooping downward. He straightened up and strode over to her.

"I believe this is yours," he said, extending his hand. Her cross and chain dangled from his gloved fingers.

"Who are you?" she asked.

The masked face looked down at her. "I am called the Wraith."

2

A One-Man Wrecking Crew

BRIGHT, mid-morning sunshine shone through the thick glass windows of the skyscraper, spilling into the lavishly furnished room. It was filled with a luxurious sofa, a long mahogany table with matching chairs, and a large ornately built radio/phonograph. In the corner sat one of those new television sets. Two men were in the room. One, tall and elegant-looking in a navy blue three-piece suit, leaned against the edge of the table and twirled an ebony cane as the other read haltingly from a newspaper. The man doing the reading paused while he traced the story from the front to the interior pages. He was short and had a rough-hewn look about him. His long, sinewy arms sprang from the sawed-off sleeves of a tan chambray shirt. His trousers were blue work pants.

"And the police subsequently arrived to find the victim shivering in a corner, the bag of money still on the floor where the hoodlums had left it, along with the customary question-marked card that has become the eerie trademark of that mysterious masked crime fighter known as the Wraith," Thomas 'Mad Dog' Deagan read, before putting down the newspaper. He looked up with a triumphant smirk, as if proud of the job he'd done reading aloud. "Sheesh, that Wraith guy's a regular one-man wrecking crew, ain't he?"

Vincent 'Ace' Assante shrugged in mock disgust.

"He's just some crazed, masked vigilante, as far as I'm concerned." Ace Assante stood over six feet tall, his body lean, and his face darkly handsome. His well-trimmed mustache gave him a rakish cast, making him a dead-ringer for movie actor Errol Flynn. The red carnation in the lapel of his tailored blue suit further enhanced his insouciance. "The poor chap's probably been mentally warped by listening to too many episodes of *The Shadow*."

"Hey, that's why I like him," Deagan said. "That's my favorite show. Kind of reminds me of myself."

Ace grinned broadly. The thought of the short, stout Deagan dressed up in the garb of his fictional hero, a black cloak and hat, topped off with a red scarf, struck him as positively ludicrous.

Although Deagan was undeniably powerful, with broad shoulders, massive biceps, and huge forearms, his sandy hair noticeably thinned at the crown. At best, his features could only be termed rugged looking. Having spent most of his adult life in uniform, he'd risen to the rank of Lieutenant Colonel during the last war, a fact that Deagan never failed to bring up to the former *Captain* Assante. But since Deagan's retirement from the army, he'd preferred to dress casually, in work jeans and plaid lumberjack shirts, even for formal occasions. He'd once shown up at one of the city's official citizens' award banquets, held in honor of Doc Atlas and his crew, wearing a faded wool shirt, a worn tweed jacket, and a garishly designed iridescent necktie. Ace had laughed so hard he could barely keep a straight face when the ceremony finally got underway.

Assante, on the other hand, was always immaculately attired in tailor-made suits, which fitted his reputation as one of the most successful lawyers in New York City. He'd gotten the nickname 'Ace' from his days as a fighter pilot during the War. Although nowhere near as massive and powerful as Deagan, Assante's slimness often resulted in his strength being vastly underestimated. His lean body moved with the fluid grace of a panther, save for the noticeable limp in his right leg. Once a superb fencer in college, Assante had even competed for an Olympic berth before the rapacious dreams of a madman from Austria had lead the world into a second 'war to end all wars.' A blast of German shrapnel had ended Assante's ability to deliver the quick, rapier-like thrusts with a foil, and made him partially dependent on the ebony cane. It was only through the surgical genius of Doc Atlas that Ace Assante was able to use the leg at all.

"Ahh, you're just worried 'cause at the rate he's going, he just might eliminate the need for any more shyster lawyers like you," Deagan chided good-naturedly. His face split into a grin showing large, evenly spaced teeth. "In fact, if we could get a couple more just like him, and turn them loose on this city while you, me, and Doc took an extended vacation, we probably wouldn't have any work to do when we got back."

"You're partially right," Ace shot back. "You wouldn't have anything to do, but I, on the other hand, would be very busy because this Wraith fellow would want the very best lawyer to defend him."

"Ha, that'll be the day," Deagan said. "The guy looks unstoppable, the way he keeps mowing down the crooks."

"And that's exactly why we must apprehend him very soon, Thomas," a third voice said.

Their heads swiveled toward the door on the west wall. Doc Atlas stood there, clad only in his workout clothes. Whereas Assante could be described as handsome, and Deagan as ruggedly powerful, mere words seemed almost inadequate to describe Doc. He stood a few inches over six feet, broad shouldered with golden hair and piercing amber colored eyes. His superbly proportioned body, now uncharacteristically visible in this state of reduced dress, resembled powerful coils of wire mesh tightly bundled under his tawny flesh. Having just finished one of his daily workouts, he was covered with a fine sheen of perspiration. With his superb physical skills, he surely could have surpassed most of the standing Olympic and world athletic records, if he'd chosen to compete, but Doc Atlas marched to the beat of a different drummer. Having been trained since early childhood by his obsessively brilliant father, Doc's value system held little regard for the accolades of sociological accomplishment and notoriety. Instead, he had dedicated his life to one all-encompassing cause: the eradication of evil.

"Huh?" Deagan asked. "Whatcha mean, Doc?"

"I think," Ace said, "our next quarry has just been revealed."

"Exactly." Doc dried some of the sweat from his face with a white towel and leaned against the door that separated his huge gymnasium from the rest of his quarters.

The recreation room, in which they had gathered for the moment, made up only a

Michael A. Black

small portion of the immense space that Doc rented in the skyscraper. His capacious apartment, as well as a fully furnished set of temporary quarters for Deagan, Ace, and several other guest rooms lay beyond the gym. Doc's medical laboratory and a small, but fully furnished medical clinic, were adjacent to his scientific research center and a miniature theater for private screenings. His office area was in one of the front rooms, preceded by a foyer that opened into an area by the elevators. Although the massive building officially boasted seventy-three elevators, only one stopped at Doc's floor. The ultra new and experimental cab required no manual control. An exclusive positioning transducer automatically lifted the passenger box to Doc's floor once a special key had been inserted to activate it. The elevator could also be activated from the office area. It had a unique gearing system that raised it at terrific speed.

Additionally, Doc leased the entire floors both above and below his facility. He'd filled the lower floor with his immense clerical staff, which spent the days retrieving, cataloguing, and collating information on a myriad of topics related to his scientific and crime fighting efforts. He employed a large staff of young women, all of whom were trained in the latest keypunch techniques. The material collated by this distaff army was then fed into an immense, prototypical computer Doc had built using his own experimental design. Because of its advanced capabilities, the Federal Government, state and local law enforcement agencies, and private industry frequently called upon Doc with requests for its use. He was very selective in granting these requests, however. The floor above, he kept vacant and partially altered to allow for the special structural requirements of Doc's gymnasium section, which had lengthy ropes for climbing, and a tower for rappelling. It also served as a safety zone so no one could enter his headquarters by drilling through the floor above.

Their eyes went to the alarm monitor that suddenly rang, signaling the elevator's ascent.

"That would be Penelope," Doc said. "I asked her to stop over with some information about last night's story, which you were just reading, as well as some other items about the Wraith

from the newspaper's morgue." He turned and started thorough the door. "Please make her comfortable while I bathe."

"Doc?" Ace asked quickly.

The golden giant turned.

"What are we going to do with the Wraith if we catch him?"

"He'll be transported to the clinic for the operation, of course," Doc said. He turned and left the room.

Doc, a brilliant surgeon, was considered a world-renowned expert in several fields of medicine and science. The "operation," was Doc's euphemism for the delicate brain surgery he performed on notorious criminals in his clinic in upstate New York. It was one of his more controversial endeavors, but remained unknown outside his small group of associates. But as of late, it had become a constant source of friction between him and Assante, especially after two of Doc's more celebrated efforts had turned out less than perfect. Glenn Derbey, known as the Manhattan Stalker, had been the most daring cat burglar of the thirties and forties. But after his capture, the operation had rendered him a drooling idiot who now worked in the kitchen of Doc's clinic. Bugsy Mandrel, a well-known embezzler, had stolen millions while acting as chief accountant for a large metropolitan hospital. Now Mandrel ran one of the most successful newspaper stands in the city, having only an occasional problem making change for bills of large denomination. Still, both men, as well as a host of others, had volunteered to undergo the surgery to avoid serving in prison. These agreements had been set up as part of elaborate plea bargains that had been principally engineered by the legal expertise of Vincent Assante.

Ace compressed his lips as he thought about the two men whom he had represented. Had he made the best choice for them? An argument that they only got what was coming to them would be Deagan's reply, but the shuffling creatures never strayed far from Ace's thoughts. Especially lately.

The sleek electronic blue doors slid open with a whoosh and Penelope Cartier walked in wearing a blue and gold summer dress that showed the obvious curves of her lush figure. She held a large brown valise to her chest like a schoolgirl weighed down with homework. A small handbag dangled from her left hand. She had jet-black hair set in a fashionable permanent wave, flowing back from flawless skin. Batting the long eyelashes above her blue eyes, she drew her lips together into a mocking pout as Ace and Mad Dog jumped up and rushed through the metallic arches of the gated foyer to grab the heavy brown case.

"Where were you two gentlemen when I needed you three blocks ago?" she asked, the playfulness in her tone told them she was kidding.

"Allow me, ma'am," Deagan said, reaching for the valise with his huge hand.

"It's all yours," she said, but held onto her purse. "I can carry this one."

"Too bad," Ace said. "The color complements his pants perfectly."

He smiled at her, and their eyes locked for a moment.

Penelope, or Penny, as she liked to be called, was the star reporter for the *New York Daily Guardian*. It was the most prestigious paper in the city, owned by powerful industrialist Randolph Grantman. Grantman's ancestors had come to the United States from England and founded the paper shortly after the War of 1812. Penny had started out as a stringer, but during the War her writing talent, natural inquisitiveness, and tenacity had won her a position as a full-fledged reporter. She also had phenomenal luck, and had risen to the position of star reporter by her early twenties. Her work had taken her into the middle of some of Doc's greatest adventures, and her series of articles detailing his exploits had won her a Pulitzer Prize. Her beauteous looks had caught Doc's eye, and although it wasn't well known in social circles, a passionate romance had blossomed. But no one, except for Doc's inner circle, knew the extent of the relationship.

Another alarm bell sounded and Penny looked around with a perplexed expression.

"What's that?" she asked.

"A new safeguard alarm system Doc just installed," Ace said. "Just like they have in jails. It sends out an electronic signal that sets off a bell if it detects any metal object large enough to be a weapon."

"Must be set too low," she said, digging in her purse. "The only metal I have is my keys and my cigarette case."

"Maybe you're wearing too many bobby pins," Deagan said with a wry smile. "Anyway, Doc's orders. We're gonna have to search you."

"Oh, really?" Penny's eyebrows rose in mock indignation. "And what's Polly going to say about that?"

Deagan's mouth twisted into a self-conscious grin, of sorts, as a reddish blush crept up from his collar.

Ace grinned at Mad Dog's burgeoning embarrassment. "Perhaps we can just ask Doc to adjust the frequency this time. Since we know you." He held out his hand, ushering her forward.

"Did Doc tell you we're going after the Wraith?" Deagan asked, moving along beside them with the case. He clucked his tongue. "Can you believe it?"

"I gathered that from the stuff he wanted me to bring," Penny said. She glanced around. "Where is the big guy, anyway?"

"He's in the shower," Ace said, quickening his pace to keep up with the fast-walking Deagan. "He just finished his workout."

"Well," Penny said, withdrawing a Lucky Strike from her cigarette case. "I guess I have time for a smoke then."

Deagan used his free hand to pat his pocket, but Ace's hand shot up holding a gold-plated lighter, which he snapped open. Penny stopped, grasped his hand somewhat tenderly, and guided the flame to the end of her cigarette. Their eyes met briefly, sharing a possible look of things past, but not totally forgotten. She drew on the cigarette and, as its red ash glowed, nodded a thanks. From the look that lingered in his dark eyes as he closed the lid of his lighter, it was obvious there was still one more torch that had yet to be extinguished. Deagan pulled open the door for Penny, then, grinning, slipped in between her and Ace.

"You better put that out before Doc comes back," Deagan said. "You know how he feels about people smoking."

"And if we'd forgotten," Ace said, "I'm sure you'd remind us." He flipped a wall switch that activated a series of small wall fans positioned around the room. They began blowing the lingering smoke toward a specially installed suction hood.

"No need to remind me, Mad Dog," Penny said, blowing out a cloudy breath as she walked into the recreation room. She pulled out one of the fine mahogany chairs and slipped off her high-heeled shoes. After dropping into the chair, she began massaging her toes.

"Jeez, my dogs are killing me," she said. "You men don't know how lucky you are to be able to wear shoes that don't brutalize your feet."

"That's the price you pay for looking so swell," Ace said.

"Hey, want me to get you a pair of paratrooper boots?" Deagan placed the valise on the table in front of them. "I helped design 'em you know, and I made sure about 'em, feeling good, too. What soldier is gonna be happy if his feet hurt?"

"Maybe I'll take you up on that," Penny said, taking another drag on her cigarette. "Now, why don't we get some of those articles out so we can get right into this?"

"Sounds good to me," Ace said.

"So you know much about this Wraith guy?" Deagan asked, popping open the valise.

"Not a lot," Penny said. She smoothed her dress over her legs and smiled at Deagan. "I covered a couple of his crime scenes. Pretty brutal stuff. I mean, this guy comes on like gangbusters and pulls no punches."

"Sounds like my kind of guy," Deagan said, grinning. "Sorta like Joe Louis. I ever tell you guys about the time I sparred with him in the Army? Real swell guy. Ray Robinson, too."

"I'm sure the Brown Bomber was equally happy to lay some leather on a mug as obliging as yours," Ace said, his voice gruff. "Now, do you mind if we stick to the topic at hand?"

"What's eating you?" Deagan asked. He accepted more papers from Penny and placed them in a stack next on the table.

"When exactly did this Wraith first appear?" Ace asked.

"From all accounts, about two years ago," Penny said. "His first known crime was shooting a bunch of hoods at the waterfront. A pair of characters named Boggs and Webber. Remember?"

"That's right," Ace said. "They were suspects in the Casper bombing, weren't they? Has it been two years already?"

"Almost," Penny said.

"Well, if you ask me," Deagan said, "those two punks deserved it. Anybody who'd blow up a car and kill a woman and a little baby…" He shook his head.

Ace looked at him sternly. "Regardless, let's not forget they were still innocent until proven guilty."

"That's the problem with you shyster lawyers," Deagan said. "Always spouting off about that beyond a reasonable doubt crap, even if there ain't none." He shook his head. "Shakespeare had a point."

"Shakespeare?" Ace said, grinning skeptically. "Your propensity for uttering non sequiturs never ceases to amaze me."

"Non-what?" Deagan's brow furrowed as he looked at Ace.

"Non sequitur," Penny said. "Something that does not logically follow."

Deagan's frown deepened.

"Oh yeah? How about Henry the IV, Part II." He counted off the numerals on his big fingers. "Act four, scene two, line eighty-six. And I quote: 'The first thing we do, let's kill all the lawyers.' I couldn't have said it better myself." His jaw jutted out with a triumphant smirk.

"It figures that you would quote a play featuring Falstaff." Ace leaned back and smiled slyly. "And now that you've obviously recited the only line you know, why don't we all get back to work?"

"Now, now, boys," Penny said, patting each of their arms. She removed the cigarette from her lips and blew a cloud of smoke up toward the ceiling. "The Wraith's been implicated in at least twenty-five gangland slayings since then. Most of them have been in Brooklyn and Manhattan. You know about the black outfit, the mask, and his trademark. The special card that he's left at each of the scenes?" She held up a clipped article with a picture depicting one of them. It looked to be the size of a playing card, blank except for an oversized question mark on its surface. "The cops have never come close to catching him.

There's even speculation by some that he's got supernatural powers."

Deagan frowned. "Nah, he's just a man. I can remember when one of them rags tried to say that about Doc, too." He drew his chin up toward Ace. "And remember the time when they tried to say that Doc was really the Wraith in disguise?"

"An accusation for which they paid dearly in the form of a retraction and a hefty settlement," Ace said, holding his thumb toward his chest. "Thanks to my legal brilliance."

"Hey, be careful," Deagan said. "You might strain your arm patting yourself on the back."

Penny took a deep breath and cleared her throat. "Shall we get on with the most recent sighting?" She looked from one to the other of them. Both men nodded.

"Okay. The Butchie Cole gang knocked over the Greater Briscol Savings and Loan yesterday at about five," she said. "Shot two people, the bank president and the guard. Killed execution style, by the way. They forced all the employees to lie face-down on the floor." She paused to take another drag on her cigarette. "One female employee, Maria Hernandez, was abducted by the gang."

"So how'd they know where they were?" Deagan said.

"Will you let her finish?" Ace said.

"Guys, let's see if we can get through this without another one of your arguments, please." Penny raised her eyebrows. "Detective Hal Roland got an anonymous tip they were holed up in an old factory on east Forty-Second Street. But when the cops got there, all they found was the girl sitting, half-clothed, in a corner with all the stolen dough. The entire Cole gang had been wiped out."

Deagan's face cracked into a wide grin. "Like I told ya…a

one-man wrecking crew."

The door suddenly opened and Doc Atlas strode in, wearing a light gray gabardine suit, which was in contrast to his usual brown work shirt and pants. All of Doc's clothes had to be specifically tailored to fit his powerful physique. As his hands adjusted a necktie to a perfect knotted position, Penny cast a glance his way, obviously thinking his attire made him look particularly elegant. She saw his nostrils flare and as he detected the lingering odor of her cigarette and she immediately stubbed it out in a nearby ashtray.

"Jeez, Doc," Deagan said. "You look like you're going to the opera or something. I thought we was gonna formulate a plan on catching this Wraith guy?"

"I've already been working on that problem, Thomas." Doc held several sheets of paper up. "I've been feeding all the information available into the computer, calculating probabilities, sightings, locations, and factoring in personality characteristics. I've come up with this list of potential suspects. I took the liberty earlier of having Polly prepare this copy for your edification." Doc handed the list to Penny. "If you three would be so kind to conduct some preliminary interviews, we could meet later and discuss your suspicions."

Deagan gently took the list from her fingers and began paging through it.

"Aww, Doc, come on," he said. "Frasier Clark? I mean, I like his politics, but I've seen him in person. He's a bigger blimp than the Hindenburg was."

"You like his politics?" Ace said. "That man's nothing but a demagogue."

"Says who?" Deagan shot back.

"Says me." He and Deagan glared at each other, but

before either could speak again, Doc's calm voice broke in.

"When dealing with a social malcontent as clever as the Wraith, Thomas, we can't afford to be swayed by physical appearances." Doc was one of the few people Mad Dog Deagan allowed to call him by his given name.

"That is absolutely correct," Ace said, smiling and unable to resist a parting jab. "Who, for instance, would believe that you once sparred with the great Joe Louis, from the looks of you?"

Deagan started to respond when Penny laid her hand on his arm.

"Hold on. Doc, you're not coming with us?" she asked.

"I intended to, but unfortunately, another matter of extreme urgency has arisen." Doc's expression turned grim. "A short time ago, I received a call from Governor Dewey, on the private line, requesting my assistance."

Deagan whistled. "Must be a big one, then."

"It is," Doc said. "It seems Randolph Grantman's daughter has been kidnapped."

"Oh my God," Penny said, raising a hand to her mouth.

3

The List

ΛFTER Doc left, Penny sat down at the large table and opened the folded papers he'd given them. Ace leaned over her left shoulder and Deagan her right. Both couldn't help but notice the pleasant fragrance of her perfume.

"Let's see," she said, running a glossy nail down the names on the paper. "We might as well do a preliminary survey then set up the best itinerary."

"Frasier Clark," Deagan laughed. "Like I said, if he turns out to be the Wraith, I'll hang from my feet off the torch on the Statue of Liberty."

"It would be almost worth it to bribe that obese windbag into saying he's the Wraith just to see that." Ace held up his hands, as if framing a picture. "Imagine a boatload of new immigrants arriving on Ellis Island and looking up at Miss Liberty... The next minute they'd all be screaming to go back where they came from."

Penny reached over and smacked Ace lightly on the arm.

"Hey, this is serious stuff, guys," she said. "If Doc's right, and one of these Tom, Dick, or Harrys is the Wraith, I could be looking at my second Pulitzer." She stole a quick look at her watch, then tapped the first page of the papers. "Hmmm, maybe we can catch good old Frasier at the radio broadcasting station. It says here he records his weekend addresses on

Thursdays."

"I'll have Polly check," Deagan said with a smile.

Polly was Doc's chief secretary, as well as Deagan's girlfriend. He straightened up and quickly walked from the room. Ace glanced after him with a glint of sarcasm. "He'll probably be down there for an hour now."

Penny frowned at him. "Oh, Ace, quit being such a grouch, and help me go over the rest of these names."

He sat down in a chair across from her and for a moment looked into her eyes, then sighed.

"Okay," he said. "Who comes after Frasier?"

Penny glanced back at him for a moment. Her eyes looked down. "Wayne Morrison. I remember the story of his parents' murder back when I first started thinking about becoming a journalist."

"That was back in the late thirties, wasn't it? Back before the War. I vaguely remember it too."

"It happened when young Wayne was away at prep-school," she said. "Some burglars broke into the Morrison mansion and ended up killing both Dr. Morrison and his wife."

Ace shook his head. "How old was the kid then?"

"Around fourteen or fifteen, I think" Penny said. "That would make him about twenty-five now. Certainly old enough to put on a mask and run around at night shooting crooks."

"Wasn't there something else regarding that story?" Ace asked. "I seem to remember him coming home and discovering the bodies or something."

"Right. He'd just been picked up at the train station by the family butler."

"Any kid who sees something like that certainly has the potential to become mentally unbalanced," he said. "Maybe even a right to."

"Don't let Mad Dog hear you say that."

He smirked and took out his cigarette case.

"Okay, now we're getting into your area of expertise." She tapped her finger on the next page. "These next three names are all connected to the judicial arena. Ward Casper, Hamilton Vernon, and Paul Milton."

Ace raised his eyebrows.

"I've know Paul for some time," he said, "and he hardly seems the type. Plus, he's one of the best lawyers in the state. What motivation could he possibly have to become a vigilante?"

"You could say the same thing about Hamilton Vernon, couldn't you?" Penny asked. She reached over and grabbed a cigarette from his case, and smiled. Ace smiled, too, and pulled out his lighter, snapping it open. He flicked the wheel, igniting the wick and held it toward her. She moved her hair away and stuck the end of the cigarette into the flame. "Isn't our illustrious Brooklyn D.A. being touted as the next democratic candidate for governor?"

"He'll certainly never beat Dewey," Ace said, lighting his own cigarette. "But Hamilton does have a promising political future. As far as being the Wraith, why would he jeopardize it by sneaking around at night, dispatching people?"

Penny shrugged. "Why do any of us do the things we do? Sometimes we take risks, make mistakes."

Assante inhaled sharply on his cigarette, looked into her eyes, then blew the smoke through his nostrils.

"I suppose we do, at that," he said.

"Wasn't he some kind of Olympic teammate of yours?" she asked.

"Actually, he did complete in the 'thirty-six Games, in the decathlon," Ace said. "We were training for the next one when I met him, but then the games got cancelled."

"Well, his supporters always talk about his war record," she said. "That, coupled with his athletic prowess makes him a viable suspect, don't you think?"

I think you're beautiful, Ace thought. But he knew better than to say those words out loud to someone who was now engaged to the man Ace respected more than anyone else in the world. Instead, he asked, "Whom did you say was next?"

"Judge Ward Casper."

Assante raised his eyebrows again. "Perhaps he might be the most logical choice so far. He's a genuine war hero. Served as a paratrooper with Darby's Rangers in Europe." He drew on his cigarette one more time and stubbed it out in an ashtray. "And after what happened to his wife and infant son, who could blame him if he did go a little bit crazy?"

Penny nodded, recalling the sensational story of the mob-land bombing of the judge's automobile outside his New Rochelle home. The investigation of the blast, which authorities conjectured had been intended for Judge Casper, himself, instead of his family, had yielded two suspects. Both of them were assassinated before being brought to trial. Their murders believed to be the Wraith's first gangster executions.

"Anybody else?" Ace asked, watching her stub out her cigarette.

"Two more," she said. "Detective Sergeant Hal Roland."

"Him I could believe," Ace said with a grin. "That guy's shot enough crooks on duty that polishing off a few more when he's off probably wouldn't bother him in the least."

Penny smiled. "And get this. The last one is Father

Antonio Gisseppi."

"Oh come on," Ace said. "The Saint Francis of the Bowery? There was time when they said he'd be the next Cardinal, before he ruined his chances by getting on his 'help the poor and downtrodden' bandwagon."

"Not a very politically astute move for a potential Cardinal candidate," Penny said. She set the papers down and looked into Assante's dark eyes. "So, how've you been, Ace?"

"Meaning what?" he said, reaching for another cigarette. "How have I been since you dropped me for Doc and broke my heart in the process?"

She reached over and rubbed the back of his hand softly.

"I'm sorry," she said. "I know things turned out…badly. But I want you to know that I never meant to hurt you."

Before Ace could reply they heard a loud whooping in the hallway and the door burst open. Deagan entered, carrying Polly in his arms. He stepped inside, doing a modified pirouette, and placed her on the table. Polly was a comely lass of twenty-six with freckles and red hair, which she usually worn in pigtails. She blushed self-consciously as the others looked at her.

"Ain't she the prettiest little thing you ever done seen?" Deagan said loudly. "And she's smart too. She already had an appointment for us to see Frasier Clark at ten-thirty at the Billington Building today." He looked at her and smiled broadly. "That's my girl."

Polly blushed again and said, "I just figured it would be the logical place for you to start, since it was so close." Her blush deepened under her fair skin. "I made it under Penny's name so he'd think it was press related."

"Swell," Ace said, smiling as he glanced over at Penny.

"Good job, Polly. We'd better get started if we want to get the majority of the interviews done today."

Penny reached in her purse for another cigarette, but this time Ace only fingered his lighter in his pants pocket. His thoughts flashed back, far away, but not so long ago...

The big Nazi in charge of the squad fingered the lighter, testing its wick and flame as he lighted one of the American cigarettes he'd taken from the crew. He said something in German and grinned, making a show of placing it into his shirt pocket. Ace wondered how much prestige the Kraut would gain by saying he'd taken the lighter from a downed American flyer whose plane had crashed behind enemy lines. The rest of Ace's crew was dead, the broken and wounded men shot without mercy. Why they decided to him alive was anybody's guess. The Germans tied his arms to a thick piece of wood,

 then marched him along that muddy road. As they passed through the village where the American planes had wrought so much havoc, he almost expected it when they pushed him against the fractured wall of a bombed out house and then forced him to his knees. The three Krauts raised their rifles toward him.

So much for honor in war.

He closed his eyes, feeling a momentary shame that he couldn't bear to face his death with the noblest of gestures: looking into the faces of the enemy. But four quick shots later, when, in amazement, he did open them, he saw the most picturesque man he'd ever seen standing over him, cutting his bonds. The flood of relief and elation at being alive surged through him, and the memory indelibly etched into his every waking moment since he'd heard Doc Atlas say, "Come on. There's another German patrol nearby. I'm with a special ranger squad and we've found a place where we can hole up until we can get back to our lines."

MELODY OF VENGEANCE

4

The Transcendental Prophet

D°C took his two-seat Auburn Boat Tail speedster convertible for his trip out to Randolph Grantman's estate. He did this for several reasons. One, he wanted to leave the larger, less conspicuous Cadillac for Ace, Penny, and Deagan to use because of its size and comfort. Second, Doc wanted to cover ground fast and get out to the estate as quickly as possible. And lastly, he simply enjoyed driving the vehicle. The 1933 Auburn had been a gift from his father when the younger Atlas graduated at the top of his class from Harvard medical school. Doc loved the speedster's power and mechanics, but he had seldom driven it of late. During the late 1930s the Depression had turned the car into a symbol of elitism, and Doc was conscious of not appearing too aloof. Then the War had interrupted everyone's life, and the Auburn was placed in storage until Doc's return from the military.

After the War, he had it resurrected, but he recognized that, as one of the most conspicuous public figures of the day, it was not appropriate for him to be seen racing through the streets of New York in a sporty roadster. Hence he had purchased several regular cars, among them a Buick, a LaSalle, and a Chrysler so as not to alienate the now burgeoning middle class. But in his heart, he still longed for the times when he could get in the Auburn and race along the country roads with the top down, shifting through the familiar sequence of gears, and feeling the wind rippling over the windshield and through his hair.

He hadn't intended to let anything distract him from his new mission to capture the Wraith, but he could hardly refuse a request from the governor. And Randolph Grantman was a powerful man in his own right. His great-grandfather had come over from England shortly after the war of 1812 and settled in New York. Once there, he quickly amassed enough wealth to start *The New York Daily Guardian*. By the time the paper was handed down from father to son, shortly after the turn of the century, it had been syndicated in virtually every major city in America, swallowing up many smaller papers and businesses along the way. Not only had the *Guardian* become a powerful entity, the elder Grantman had enough foresight to invest heavily in industry and transportation, making the prominent family one of the richest in the country, if not the world.

This was particularly evident as Doc pulled off the

winding highway and onto the private drive that extended into the Grantman Estate. The road, a myriad of crushed pebbles mixed with cement, was flanked on either side by rows of symmetrically planted pear and apple trees. A small army of men worked busily, pruning and shaping them as Doc rode past. The drive curved around in a semi-circle in front of a palatial mansion. The house was enormous, the various levels each supported by majestic pillars and replete with balustrades and elaborate gables. In the center of the circular drive stood a large fountain sending a high spray of water gurgling in the late morning sunshine. Several other cars, all official police vehicles from the look of them, were parked on the far edges of the drive.

Doc parked the Auburn and strode up to the front doors. After ringing the doorbell, Doc's excellent hearing picked up the musical chimes that rang far inside the house. Presently, the door was opened by a caramel-colored maid who looked somewhat startled at Doc's massive frame. But she recovered nicely after he introduced himself.

"Right this way, sir," she said. He followed her into a large den, adjacent to the elaborately furnished foyer, filled with well-stuffed sofas and chairs. The mounted heads of numerous big cats and various breeds of bear hung in a row above the far wall, separated in the middle by a huge glass case containing several rifles. Long tables of the finest wood, their surfaces so highly polished they seemed to be reflective glass, stood at either end of the room. A group of men was clustered at the edge of the closest table. Two of them were jacketless, their shirtsleeves rolled up as they worked feverishly on a large recording box next to the telephone. They'd been engaged in a conversation when Doc entered, but everyone stopped talking as the maid announced him.

A heavily jowled man of about fifty, with thinning gray hair, rose and approached Doc.

"Dr. Atlas, thank you for coming," he said, extending his hand. "I'm Randolph Grantman."

Doc shook Grantman's hand, surprised at the firmness of the handshake despite the flaccid look of the man's face and body.

"These men are from the police," Grantman said, indicating the two men in somewhat shabby dark brown suits seated away from the others. "And they're from the FBI." He indicated the two men near the phone. "Special agent Efrem's in charge, although I've received a personal call from J. Edgar assuring me that his men will do everything in their power to

see that my daughter is returned safely." He drew his lower lip up tightly. "But I felt that the more expertise we have, the better, hence my call to Governor Dewey requesting your assistance." Grantman took out a handkerchief and wiped his forehead. "I have also availed myself of the services of Mr. K.C. Edgar."

He turned slightly, sweeping his open palm toward two more figures seated at the far end of the room. At Grantman's gesture they both stood. One, a small, wiry looking man with steel-gray hair and a longish beard, was dressed in a conservative navy blue suit. The man beside him was a swarthy giant whose head was covered with a tightly bound turban. His full black beard seemed to make his head appear more massive than it was, and as he drew himself up to his full height, Doc noticed the man stood close to seven feet tall.

"Doctor Atlas, I presume," the smaller man said. "I'm Kenneth C. Edgar. A pleasure to meet you." As he and Doc shook hands, Edgar turned slightly and cocked his head toward the giant. "And this is my trusted assistant and bodyguard, Khan Rahman."

The giant made no move to shake hands, but instead bowed his head slightly and placed his palms together.

"*Salaam aleikum*," he said.

Doc repeated the gesture as expertly as the larger man.

"*Aliekum salaam*," he said.

Edgar seemed impressed.

"Have you been to India, Dr. Atlas?" he asked.

"I passed through Bombay several times during the War," Doc said. "I take it Khan is a Sikh?"

"Yes," Edgar said. "I see you're familiar with the warrior class and its customs, as well as the traditional *namaste*, or greeting." He clasped a hand on the giant's arm. "I met Khan on one of my many trips to the region to study the country's religions. You are, of course, familiar with my reputation?"

"K.C. Edgar, the Transcendental Prophet," Doc said. "I must admit I found myself quite interested in your writings on the lost continent of Atlantis. An associate of my father's was quite taken with them also, but I would be more interested in discussing your current medical claims."

Edgar smiled. "Hopefully at a time more suited to leisure

than distress." Before he could say anything more, another man ambled over, lighting a cigarette as he walked. He was broad through the shoulders, and around average height. His face looked somewhat craggy, and his nose jutted out at something less than a straight angle. "Ain't we got enough amateurs gumming up the works already?"

Grantman's mouth twisted into a scowl.

"Detective Roland, I fully intend to report that remark to the Commissioner," he said.

Roland smirked slightly and blew twin plumes of smoke out his nostrils.

"Report anything you like, Mr. Grantman, but all I'm concerned about is getting your daughter back safe and sound." He took the cigarette from between his lips. "My point is, we're professionals, so let us do our jobs without involving amateur adventurers and eastern mumbo-jumbo."

"I have no problem with you doing your job," Grantman said, his face darkening. "But let me make one thing perfectly clear. I shall leave no avenue unused to assure the safe return of Bonnie. And I expect you to do the same."

Roland licked his lips. "Ain't that two things?"

Doc stepped forward and extended his hand. "Detective Sergeant Hal Roland?"

"That's right, Atlas," Roland said, taking Doc's hand.

Feeling the other man was trying to demonstrate his grip strength during the handshake, Doc exerted a bit more pressure than usual. Roland's lips compressed into an O shape as he grunted, "Glad to meetcha." He shook his hand slightly, flexing his fingers when Doc released him, then turned and abruptly walked back over to the two FBI agents. He glanced at Doc over his shoulder as he flicked some cigarette ashes on the floor.

"A most impertinent man," Grantman said. "If I hadn't been assured by the commissioner that he was one of the very best in the department..."

"Now, Randolph," K.C. Edgar said, a slow grin spreading over his face. "It's best not to concern yourself with trifles." He sniffed quickly and Doc took a longer assessment of the man. He appeared to be in his mid-to-late forties, but the gray hair made him look older. His sun-darkened face had wrinkles with web-like strands branching out from his bushy eyebrows and aquiline nose. Doc also noticed the dilated pupils, pungent body odor, and yellowish teeth. Although the tobacco stains on Edgar's fingers indicated a heavy smoker, the man's sour smell also suggested something else to Doc.

"Why don't we retire over to the other end of the room and I'll finish my reading of the situation?" Edgar said, laying a hand on Grantman's arm. "Perhaps you'd like to listen also, Dr. Atlas?"

"Certainly," Doc said, following behind the lumbering Khan. They went to the far side of the room and Edgar sat on the sofa. He picked up several articles of women's clothing, and brought each item to his face. He closed his eyes and rubbed the clothing vigorously. Soon the clothing slipped from his hands and he dropped back in repose. For a time he sat very still, then began jerking around like a marionette manipulated by a drunken puppeteer. The jerking grew so violent that Grantman reached forward to try to steady him, but Khan's big hand shot out between them.

"No, Sahib," the big Sikh said. "He is entranced. He will return shortly."

Edgar's face began twitching. His head bobbled almost

uncontrollably and a deep flush spread across his cheeks. With a sudden shriek, he sat bolt upright, his eyes completely open now, his breathing quick and shallow.

"Does he need your assistance, Doctor?" Grantman asked.

"I think not," Doc said. He turned and saw Hal Roland watching them, his hand on his hip, a grin stretching across his wide face.

Khan immediately went to a nearby pitcher and poured Edgar a glass of water. After he'd drunk it down, Edgar looked up at Grantman.

"She's alive," he said, "but in grave danger."

"I'm sure glad we've got that info nailed down now," Roland said, strolling over to them as he lit another cigarette.

"I will not tolerate you mocking this man," Grantman said. "His reputation is impeccable. Something that certainly cannot be said about yours. And I won't have any of your flippancy toward anything that might get my daughter back safely."

Roland looked about ready to say something, but he shrugged and headed back to the other side of the room.

"Yes, Mr. Edgar," Grantman said. "Please, go on."

Edgar exhaled heavily before he spoke.

"I'm afraid it's worse than anyone thought," he said. "I sense a great evil at work here. Someone foul and perverse."

Grantman's face blanched.

"I see," Edgar closed his eyes. "Wait. There's a figure lurking in the shadows.... I can't quite see..." He held his hand to his eyes and bowed his head. "It's becoming more clear now. Yes. Clearer."

"His face," Grantman said. "Can you see his face?"

Edgar shook his head again and opened his eyes. His mouth twisted downward.

"Randolph," he said. "I'm afraid your daughter is a prisoner of the Wraith."

"The Wraith." Grantman suddenly appeared visibly shaken. He moved stiffly to one of the large chairs and sat down heavily, placing his hands over his face.

Out of the corner of his eye, Doc watched the two FBI men slip on their coats, conversing in hushed tones with the plainclothesmen. One of them approached Grantman.

"Sir," the agent said. He was a man in his early thirties with the requisite military-style haircut and conservative suit. "If you feel up to it, we'd like to show you how to operate the recording machine."

"What?" Grantman said, looking up. Then he recovered a modicum of his composure. "Oh, yes, of course." He rose from the chair with considerable effort, his face flushed, and walked with a defeated gait to the telephone.

The other agent gave him a brief, but thorough, explanation of how to activate the machine. "It's extremely important that you record any ransom demands, and you contact us as soon as the offender calls if we're not in the immediate vicinity."

Grantman nodded.

"And what do you intend to do about Mr. Edgar's information?" he asked.

The agent looked at his partner who said, "We'll take it under advisement, sir."

"In other words," Roland cut in, "all hocus pocus aside, we're just gonna have to wait for the kidnappers to call."

Grantman's mouth compressed into a thin line and he stuck his finger a few inches from Roland's nose.

"Let me tell you something," he said. "I fully expect that

every lead will be investigated to the fullest degree. That includes Mr. Edgar's conjectures as well as those from Dr. Atlas. Is that clear?"

"Perfectly," Roland said, staring back into the other man's face. He hadn't flinched in the slightest, despite the waving finger.

Grantman slowly lowered his hand, then turned to Doc.

"What do you think is the best course of action?" he asked.

"I believed Detective Roland has a valid point," Doc said. "I realize this is very difficult, but we have no other choice but to wait for the time being. There is one thing I'd like to do, however."

"Anything," Grantman said. "Name it."

"I was told your daughter had been living in the city when this incident occurred," Doc said.

"She had…" Grantman answered. His voice cracked slightly. Edgar came forward and placed his hand on Grantman's shoulder.

"It's all right, Randolph," Edgar said. "You might as well tell him everything."

Grantman seemed to draw strength from the other man's touch. He breathed deeply and spoke again.

"I'm afraid my daughter is something of a distaff libertine, Dr. Atlas. Her mother and I are divorced, and, quite frankly, these last few years she's been somewhat hard to control." His lips stretched into a grimace. "She insisted on living away from home, in the city. A few weeks ago she came home and told me she was engaged." He paused again, looking up at a life-sized portrait of himself hanging above the fireplace. "I was both shocked and surprised. Then I found out she had been living with a man. I mean, it was bad enough that she was living in sin without the benefit of clergy, but she saved the best for last." His lower lip drew upward and a sudden fury flashed in his eyes. "Oh, yes, she relished telling me all about it. Especially that this…person she was involved with…an unemployed college student. Someone obviously well below her social standing, and…." His voice lowered to a low whisper as he added, "a Jew." Grantman leaned forward, as if the telling had drained him. Edgar patted his back slightly.

"I'm afraid we had a bit of a scene," Grantman continued. "I threatened to cut her off without a single cent if she went through with it. She left in a huff. If only I could have convinced her to come back home. I'm partially to blame."

"There, there, Randolph," Edgar said. "You mustn't blame yourself. We'll get her back."

"Do you have any children, Dr. Atlas?" Grantman asked.

Doc ignored the question, as was his custom whenever anyone made inquiries about his personal life.

"Perhaps if I could interview the young man she was seeing," he said. "I've heard he was with her when the masked gunmen forced their way into the apartment."

"Yeah, he was," Roland said, stepping forward. "But we already interviewed him. He got beat up pretty bad."

"I've often been successful at drawing out new information with my hypnosis techniques," Doc said. "I'd like very much to attempt this on the young man. What did you say his name was?"

"Bloom," Roland said. "Ira Bloom. But like I told ya–"

Before he could finish Grantman jumped to his feet.

"I demand you allow Dr. Atlas to hypnotize him," he said, his voice descending to a low growl.

Roland looked at him and shrugged. "Okay. Why not?"

"Oh, yes, Father," an epicene voice said. "Why not, indeed?"

They all turned toward the source of the voice and saw a thinly built man in his late twenties entering the room with a shuffling step. He was clad in a blue silk bathrobe and slippers. A water glass, half full of amber liquid, hung loosely in his hand. The sallow color of his face was emphasized by the deep lines that etched their way from his nose and mouth, and by his long, unkempt hair.

"Then perhaps I can get on with my life and get rid of Abbott and Costello here." He gestured at the two plainclothesmen who had followed him in. The gesture was carelessly done, and some of the liquor sloshed from his glass onto the plush carpet.

"Gentlemen," Grantman said somewhat hesitantly, "this is my son, Warren." He straightened his posture self-consciously and moved toward the younger Grantman. "Son, the guards are for your own protection. After what happened to Bonnie, we can't afford to take the chance that—"

Warren walked away from him and toward an ornate liquor cabinet set against the west wall.

Grantman scowled and said, "Get hold of yourself, for God's sake. We have guests."

"Not guests, Father," Warren Grantman said. "More hired help. And I'm so sorry I haven't fulfilled your high expectations for the almighty Grantman name." He took out a bottle and filled his glass, spilling a good portion of it in the process. "You see," he said, addressing the group, "we come from a long line of kingmakers." He spoke in a sarcastic tone and glared at his father. "I'll be in my room, as usual," he said.

The slippers made a whispering sound as he shuffled over the lush carpet. The two guards followed.

"He and his sister are very close," Grantman said. "The stress of this incident has had a devastating effect on Warren."

Roland smirked. He turned and walked to the table and grabbed his hat. "If you don't mind giving me a ride back to the city, Atlas, my partner's gonna stay here a little longer with the feds."

"Certainly," Doc said.

"Oh, by the way," Roland added, "we got that Bloom guy stashed at the Lexington Hotel in Brooklyn with a couple of dicks guarding him. I'd better call and let them know we're coming. You got another phone I can use, Mr. Grantman? That one's set up with the recording equipment."

Grantman nodded and gestured toward the other room.

"Melissa will show you where it's at," he said. "Now, if you don't mind I'm going to retire for a bit. This whole incident has drained me."

They watched as he slowly walked out of the room.

Doc approached K. C. Edgar, who was standing by the sofa.

"I would like to contact you later to discuss your insights into this matter," Doc said. "May I have one of your cards?"

"Certainly." Edgar smiled, and reached into the inside breast pocket of his jacket and removed a small, gold-plated case. He snapped it open and removed a standard-sized business card. Doc thanked him and carefully placed the card in the side pocket of his jacket.

Outside, Roland's eyebrows rose slightly when he saw the Auburn, but he said nothing as he got into the passenger seat. The low canvas roof knocked off his hat and he set it on top of his bent knee in the small sports car.

They rode in silence down the long, winding drive and turned onto the highway. After running through the shifting pattern, Doc glanced at Roland, who was still silent.

"I sense a good deal of resentment on your part, Detective," Doc said.

"Not at you, Atlas." Roland reached in his pocket and took out a package of Chesterfield Kings and shook one out. As an after-thought, he held the pack toward Doc who shook his head.

"I'm sorry," Doc said. "Would you mind not doing that?"

Roland's head turned as he removed his lighter and lit the cigarette. "Doing what?"

"I'd prefer you didn't smoke that in the confines of my automobile."

"Yeah, but I'd prefer I do," Roland said.

Doc's hand flashed in front of his face and Roland didn't realize the cigarette had been plucked from between his lips until he saw Doc tossing it out the window. "What the hell?" His words came spilling out with an angry lilt.

"If you insist on smoking," Doc said calmly, "I'll pull over and let you stand by the side of the road."

"Nah, we're in too much of a damn hurry to stop." His face reddened now, and his words held controlled fury. "But you need to get some manners, Atlas."

"Just as you need to gain control over your tobacco addiction. I am experimenting with a scientifically proven hypnosis technique, if you're interested."

Roland snorted. "I'll think it over."

They rode a few more minutes in total silence, the only sound being Roland continually flipping open the lid of the stainless steel lighter emblazoned with a military emblem.

"You were in the marines?" Doc asked.

"Yeah, Guadalcanal." He blew out a breath. "How about you?"

"I was in the Army," Doc said. "Although I did work with the marines several times in certain operations in the Pacific."

Roland cocked his head. "I thought I read you were in the ETO?"

"Actually, I served in both theaters of operations."

This seemed to impress Roland, who raised his eyebrows. "How about if I agree to blow the smoke out the window?"

Doc shook his head. "How much credence do you place in Edgar's theory that the Wraith is behind this?"

"You're kidding, ain't ya?"

When Doc didn't reply Roland chuckled softly.

"That SOB's the biggest flim-flam artist around," he said. "All he's doing is feeding that rich idiot a load of horsecrap."

"How so?"

"Like I said before," Roland continued, "that guy would be playing three card montie in the subways if he hadn't stumbled into that Transcendental Prophet crap." He shook his head and sucked at his lips angrily. "This ain't the Wraith's style. I been cleaning up dead bodies after him for going on two years now, and I ain't never seen him go after some innocent person, much less hold some rich broad for ransom."

"Perhaps he felt angered at her disdain for conventional matrimony," Doc said.

"Nah, the only people he goes after are punks and gangsters," Roland said. "You know, the ones that really deserve it. The Wraith ain't gonna care if some rich broad is living in sin with some guy, even if he is a Jew boy." He said the last words with particularly sarcastic emphasis. Then, turning to Doc, he said, "I don't know about you, but I think that Grantman guy is a real jerk. Upset because his little daughter is in love with somebody with a different religion. I thought that was one of the reasons we was all over there fighting." He stuffed the lighter back into his shirt pocket. "I served with a Jewish guy named Irwin Mishoulam. One of the bravest guys in my outfit. We lost him on one of those stinking little islands that no one even remembers the name of anymore." He shook his head. "I wonder if Randolph Grantman ever sweated with a pack on his back or a rifle in his hands? Man, his son's sure a souse, ain't he?"

"You seem bitter."

"Like I said, Atlas, don't take it personal. I ain't got nothing against you. In fact, I always wanted to meet you. I know about all them major criminal investigations that you helped to crack, and how you let the department take all the credit. Of course, that was before I knew you didn't let nobody smoke in your car."

"Seeking accolades is not one of my inducements," Doc said. "If you don't feel the Wraith is involved in this, whom do you feel is the responsible party?"

"Hard to say," He started to take out another Chesterfield, but thought better of it and replaced the pack in his shirt. "Efrem seems to think it's a mob snatch, and I kinda agree with that. Word is they're looking to expand into politics and all sorts of other legitimate enterprises to funnel in their vice-money. With Grantman's status as the political kingmaker, maybe they wanted to put some heat on him to back somebody or something. Nobody'd miss that Warren, so they grabbed the girl instead." He inhaled deeply. "Grantman's been paying people off for years to get that little worm out of jams." He coughed slightly. "I heard he even used his clout to get his kid some kind of cush assignment as a general's aide during the war. But that was only after he forced the kid to enlist because the plan was to get him elected to public office when he got home." Roland leaned his head back and laughed. "Funny, a guy with all his dough and so much political say-so that he dictates things to Tammany Hall, and he can't even control his own kids. Musta really rubbed him the wrong way when he found out his prissy little princess was playing hide the salami with a kosher dill pickle."

"He did appear to be under a great deal of strain," Doc said.

"Yeah, well, that's the roughest part of these kidnapping cases. You just gotta sit and wait for the perp to make his move." He leaned back in the seat and placed his hat over his face. "Then you gotta hope you're quick enough to nab him when he does."

5

Sentinels of Liberty

"AND lest we forget," Frasier Clark's rich baritone voice said over the speakers, "the job's only half-done. You did the first part by buying War Bonds, but now let's all chip in and bring the boys back home. Every Victory Bond you buy, ladies and gentlemen, will help do just that. And it will also give our veterans the finest medical care."

Penny, Deagan, and Ace watched the big man through the glass window as he stood by the radio console and read the rest of the commercial. The sound engineer had allowed them to stay inside the recording studio only if they promised not to say anything. To that end, Deagan winked and grinned broadly as Clark finished his spiel on the Victory Bonds. Ace merely drew his lips into a tight line as Penny smiled and turned from one to the other with her index finger extended up in front of her lips.

Frasier Clark raised a starchy, white handkerchief and wiped off his face as he spoke into the circular mike on the desk. He was huge man, but not in any sort of athletic way. His blond hair had receded badly in front, which made his attempt to disguise this fact all the more obvious as he smoothed his hair forward with his hand. Clark's jacket had been slung over the back of his chair and huge circles of sweat had soaked through the underarms of his shirt.

"This is Frasier Clark, Sentinel of Liberty. Now that all the parades have finished, my fellow Americans, and as we start to get back to the business of getting this great nation of ours back to normal, I have to ask you, did Johnny come marching home just to stand in the unemployment line?"

Clark deftly wiped his upper lip, taking a moment's pause while he turned to page two of his script.

"Now, I'm not trying to scare anybody into thinking that we're headed for another depression like we had during the last decade. But let's be realistic, ladies and gentlemen. Our president admits that things could be better in this great land of ours. The land of the free, where Communists are free to stir up domestic unrest in the form of labor strikes that are paralyzing our nation's recovery."

He used the handkerchief to wipe off his forehead again.

"The coal miner's strike in the Midwest is but one example. Our own dealings with organized labor right here in New York is another. I ask you, are these things actually happening in America? Does anyone think Joseph Stalin is sitting over in Moscow doing nothing, now that half of Europe is under his big, red thumb, while our president is content to sit and watch as Stalin's agents stir up trouble in this country to keep us occupied? They're knocking on China's door now. Tomorrow it may be yours.

"And to this point, I'd like to remind everyone of the Democratic fund raiser being held tomorrow night right here in our fair city. None other than labor's number one friend, Congressman Vito Marcantonio will be there, along with the mayor and the rest of the Democratic lackeys. Oh sure, you Roosevelt-lovers, I know what you're going to say. Congressman Marcantonio ran as a Republican in 'thirty-eight, and I'd say to you, the moral courage shown by our great governor should be a model for President Truman. The clear fact is that Governor Dewey flat out told the Republican Party not to endorse Marcantonio in nineteen-forty. So what did this American Labor Party representative do? He simply donned his Democratic cloak and was handed the congressional seat on Truman's coat tails. Let's look at his record."

Clark glanced over at the engineer's booth, somewhat surprised at the three people watching him. He held up his hand and made a cutting motion under his chin, then stood and ripped the earphones off his head. Deagan broke into applause as he watched the heavyset man waddle toward the window. As Clark opened the door, Deagan shoved his big hand out and said, "Mr. Clark, that was real inspiring. Especially that part about the Victory Bonds. I listen to your program all the time. It's swell."

"Thank you," Frasier Clark said, tentatively shaking Deagan's hand. "And you are?"

"Lt. Colonel Thomas Mad Dog Deagan, sir," he said. "This is Miss Penelope Cartier of the *New York Daily Guardian*, and this is Vincent Assante, but you can call him Ace." Deagan turned and winked. "He's a friend of mine and was hoping to get your autograph, but he's kinda shy, so he asked me to ask you for him."

Frasier Clark reached out and shook Ace's reluctant hand.

"I'll certainly see that you're mailed a copy of one of my photos," he said, grinning. "Just leave your address with my secretary." He turned to Penny and raised the wattage of his smile. His teeth were very small and slanted inward, making his face seem much rounder than it was. "And to what do I owe this distinct pleasure, Miss Cartier? Is the *Guardian* planning a story on me?"

"As a matter of fact, we are considering a special feature," Penny said, flashing a stunning smile of her own, "but I can't divulge its exact subject matter at this time."

Clark grinned. "Of course. I understand."

"However," she said demurely, "if you care to answer a few questions, I would do my best to make sure they got the attention they deserved, Mr. Clark."

"Please," he adjusted the knot of his tie under the dollop of his double chin, "call me Frasier. Fire away."

Penny smiled again. "That's a very appropriate term, Frasier, because the questions I'm going to ask concern the Wraith."

Clark's brow furrowed. "The Wraith?"

"Yes. Are you aware he rescued a girl being held hostage by a gang of thugs last night?"

"I think I heard something about that," Clark said. His mouth hung slightly agape. "But what's that got to do with me?"

"Why, I'm curious as to what you think the masked avenger's motives are."

"I…um…I'm at a loss for words," he said, licking his lips. "If you'll give me a few moments I'll go through my notes."

"Maybe this will refresh your memory," Penny said. "A month ago, in one of your broadcasts, you mentioned the Wraith as an inevitable manifestation of the police department's ineffectuality."

Clark considered this, then smiled broadly.

"That does sound like my verbiage," he said.

"And three weeks before that," Penny continued, flipping up a page on her steno pad, "you blasted Mayor O'Dwyer for not acting fast enough to curtail the growing crime wave. This was after the Wraith called and told the police where to pick up Machine Gun Grimes' body. You even hinted that the mayor might have ties to organized crime."

Clark's brow furrowed slightly.

"Well, I may have said that…"

"Perhaps you'd have seen it differently if it were discovered the Wraith was a registered Democrat," Ace said.

Clark's eyebrows raised suddenly, then he squinted at Assante.

"Say, I do know you," Clark said. "You're Doc Atlas's crew, aren't you?" He stabbed a finger at Penny. "Who are you? His girlfriend?" He moved his ponderous bulk closer to her. "So what are you really here for? Is Atlas going to declare himself as a political candidate?"

It was obvious she could feel his hot breath on her face. She leaned her head back. Ace stepped between Clark and Penny, holding his arm out protectively.

"Back off," he growled. "We can smell the onions you had for lunch, pal."

"Hey, Frasier, just a minute," Deagan said, looping one of his big arms over the heavy man's shoulders and looking at his two friends. "Maybe Mr. Clark would feel better if I asked him the questions. You know, one veteran to another. Where'd you serve, by the way?"

"Why, I tried to enlist the day after Pearl Harbor," Clark said quickly, "But an old college football injury to my knee prevented me from active duty."

"So what'd you pull? Stateside duty?" Deagan asked.

"No, I…worked politically during that time, but I wholeheartedly supported the war effort as a civilian."

Deagan stopped smiling and withdrew his arm, staring at Clark in disbelief.

"You mean the Sentinel of Liberty was a damn Four-F'er?" he asked.

Ace's chuckle punctuated the ensuing silence. Clark reddened, then ran his tongue over his lips.

"John, I believe we have to finish the recording of tonight's show, do we not?" he said. The sound engineer nodded vigorously. Clark turned back to Penny. "I'm afraid I'll have to ask you to excuse me, Miss Cartier. My attorney will be contacting your editor to discuss your use of any remarks taken out of context during this conversation. If you have any further questions, I suggest you call my secretary for an appointment. All of your questions will have to be submitted in writing, and," he looked at Assante and Deagan, "next time leave the goon squad at home, please."

"Goon squad?" Deagan said, his jaw hanging open slightly.

"We certainly will, Mr. Clark," Penny said, pushing Deagan toward the door. Ace fell into step with them, but glanced over his shoulder and winked at the Sentinel of Liberty as they left.

They heard the sound of Frasier Clark's angry shouting as the elevator doors closed behind them. Deagan looked totally downcast as the cage descended. His silence persisted until they got to the LaSalle. After opening the door for Penny, and sliding in behind the wheel, he turned the key and pressed the starter button.

"Nuts," he said, "I still can't believe it. A damn Four-F'er."

"Not only that," Penny said, "but Doc's computer printout

shows that before the War, Clark worked for LaGuardia as a speech writer in 'thirty-eight through 'forty."

"He was a Democrat?" Deagan asked.

"Yep," said Penny. "So when O'Dwyer ran in the mayoral primary against LaGuardia in 'forty-one and lost, you can bet that Clark wasn't on Willie boys' list of favorite people."

"Hence his transformation into the Sentinel of Liberty," Ace said, "the bastion of stalwart Republican idealism."

"Well, that cuts it," Deagan said, shifting the car into gear. "I ain't listening to that windbag's program no more." He shook his head. "A damn Four-F'er. That guy ain't nothing but a big, fat phony."

"For once you and I agree on something," Ace said.

"And you can take it to the bank that he ain't the Wraith, neither," Deagan said. "Somebody that would go to the extremes of dressing up in an outfit to go hunt criminals ain't the type to float with the political wind streams."

"Now I'm really starting to get worried," Ace said with a wry grin. "We've agreed on two things in the past five minutes."

"Well, now that we've eliminated fatso from our list," Penny said, "who do we interview next?"

"Go to the King County criminal courts building," Ace said, tapping Deagan on the shoulder. "Maybe we'll be lucky enough to catch Judge Casper, Ham Vernon, and Paul Milton all in the same court room. And remember," he added after a moment. "We'll be in my arena there, so let me do the talking."

"As if we could stop you," Deagan said with a grin.

Fifteen minutes later, they walked up the marble steps to the second floor courtroom of Judge Ward Casper. As they moved down the hallway, Ace touched Penny on the sleeve and nodded slightly. Then he smiled warmly and extended his open hand to the man walking toward them.

"Paul Milton," Ace said. "How are you?"

Milton paused and smiled. He was as tall as Assante but much broader through the shoulders and arms. In fact, the girth of his upper arms appeared to rival Deagan's for sheer bulk. His face was exceptionally handsome. He had brown curly hair, swept back from his forehead, and stunning looking teeth. His speech had an unmistakable British quality.

"Ace Assante. How is the second best lawyer in New York?"

"You ought to know," Ace shot back. "This is Miss Penelope Cartier and her chauffeur Thomas Deagan."

Mad Dog winced at the introduction, but said nothing.

Milton shook hands with Penny, saying he was glad to meet her and that he regularly followed her column. When he turned to Mad Dog, he smiled. "Charmed."

Deagan looked at his hand after Milton released it.

"So, you here on a case, Paul?" Ace asked.

"Just making the rounds," Milton said. "I'm doing mostly civil work nowadays. More money, better clientele, but I'm still doing some pro bono stuff. Just got appointed to represent a man who tried to rob the Bowery Mission, by the way."

"Too bad the Wraith didn't find him first," Ace chuckled. "Save the city the cost of a trial."

"With what they used to pay me as a prosecutor, they're not saving much," Milton said with a grin.

"What's your opinion of the Wraith, Mr. Milton," Penny asked suddenly. "From a defense attorney's point of view?"

"Well," Milton said, "he obviously harbors a great

antipathy for the criminal element, and he's certainly going to need a brilliant lawyer like Ace or myself once they catch him."

Assante laughed.

"But what do you think of his methods?" she persisted. "I mean, aren't there times when you get fed up with the long delays and ineffectiveness of the court system?"

"My dear Miss Cartier," Milton said. "That's like asking you if ever get tired of the smell of newsprint. And," he said leaning close with a wink, "I'm usually the one promulgating those long delays and ineffectiveness. That's how I make my living."

He straightened up and told them he had to go. After shaking hands all the way around again, they watched him stride down the hallway.

"Well, guys, what do you think?" Penny asked.

"Judging from his weak handshake," Deagan said, "I'd say he's lavender. It felt almost like a broad's."

Ace laughed. "Paul's anything but lavender, believe me. In days of yore, I used to see him in the company of some pretty nice looking women."

Deagan shrugged. "Yeah, he's got a pretty decent build. Looks like he exercises."

"Plus, I think Paul would be more inclined to do things within the letter of the law," Ace said. "I've known him for a number of years and he seems much too subdued to do anything rash. It's not his style. He's methodical and thorough."

"Did I imagine it or does he sound like he's from England?" Penny said.

"Sounded kinda like Limey to me," Deagan said.

"Nevertheless, I believe he's American," Assante said. "But come to think of it, he may have dual citizenship."

"Well that cuts it," Deagan said. "It ain't him. Them Limeys don't know nothing about guns. Don't even let their damn coppers carry 'em."

"Ohhh," Penny said, rolling her eyes at Mad Dog's remark. "Let's go see the judge."

"Ya really mean it?" Deagan said feigning ecstasy and looping his arm through hers. She smiled her beautiful smile and they marched down the hallway. Assante looked after them momentarily, then followed.

They went down to a series of large doors. Outside of each were wooden benches, upon which sat scores of uniformed officers, plainclothesmen, and ordinary citizens. Ace led them to one of the rooms and pulled open the door. He peeked inside, then motioned for them to follow. The courtroom was full of people sitting in the rows of wooden benches behind the ornately sculpted banister. In front of the divider stood several more individuals. Two attorneys argued over some legal point. A woman dressed in black sat at one of the front tables. At the opposite table two men in dark suits sat impassively. Beyond them, a uniformed bailiff stood, arms crossed on his chest, surveying the courtroom. The immense bench was finely polished dark wood, and elevated above the rest of the occupants of the room, sat a dark-haired man.

The man's dark brown hair was brushed back away from his face, which was long and leonine. Even though more than half of his body was concealed by the bench, the broad shoulders spanning from under the judicial robe gave him the aura of an athlete. The bronze plaque on the left hand corner of the bench stated: The Honorable Judge Ward Casper. His eyes flashed as Ace and the others entered the room, and a flicker of a smile appeared. The lawyers stopped arguing, and the judge glanced from one to the other.

"I'll take the matter under advisement in chambers," he said, tapping his gavel lightly. "Fifteen minutes recess."

"Please remain seated until the judge leaves the bench," the bailiff called out.

Penny and Deagan followed Ace down the center aisle and through the hinged gates. He continued walking through the same doorway the judge had gone through. It led into a long carpeted corridor with rows of doorways on either side. Ace paused outside one of them and glanced at Deagan and Penny.

"In here," he said, in a confident tone. The door opened into an office in which a secretary sat at a desk typing. She looked up at them as they entered and asked if she could help them.

"Could you tell Judge Casper that Vincent Assante would like to see him, if he has a spare moment?"

The secretary started to get up, but the door to the office beyond her opened and Ward Casper, clad in a white shirt and striped tie, stepped out.

"Ace, I thought that was you," he said, moving forward with his hand extended. "What brings you to Brooklyn? I thought you were doing most of your work in Manhattan for Doc Atlas."

"I am, Judge," Assante said, stepping around the desk to shake Casper's hand. "But we were in the area and I thought I'd stop by and see how you were doing."

The Judge glanced at Penny and Deagan and smiled benignly. Up close his large stature was impressive. His broad shoulders tapered to a slim waist, and he wore his shirtsleeves rolled up over muscular forearms, and his hands dangled from thick wrists. Perhaps his only facial flaw was his nose, a trifle too long, but it gave his face an exceptionally masculine cast.

"Come in," Casper said. "Sit down for a moment."

They followed him into his chambers, which were furnished quite nicely. The walls were covered with wood paneling and sunken bookshelves, crammed with thick volumes of law books. The shelves extended around the room. On the center wall opposite the door, a display of various law degrees hung directly in back of the large desk. To the right were several framed photographs. One of them showed a somewhat younger looking Judge Casper in an Army uniform, standing with four other soldiers in front of a big B-27. Next to it was a picture of an exceptionally beautiful woman's face, her blonde hair cascading around her shoulders. The tones and hues had been colored, giving the photo an almost ethereal look. Below it hung another photograph of the same woman, dressed in a black evening gown, standing next to a concert piano. Ace introduced Penny and Deagan. Mad Dog remained standing, his long arms crossed at his chest.

"Penny is doing research for an article on vigilantism and wanted to know if you'd be so kind as to speak with her," Ace said.

Casper glanced quickly downward, then looked at her. "Of course, Miss Cartier." His eyes swept over her body. "What would you like to know?"

"Well," Penny said slowly. "I realize this subject must be very painful to you, considering everything."

"You mean about my wife and child?" he said. "Yes, it is indeed. That's one of the reasons I was re-assigned to civil proceedings. The chief judge felt I might no longer be an impartial trier of the facts." A trace of a smile graced his lips.

"Is that your wife?" Penny asked, pointing at the photograph on the wall.

"Yes. Her name was Ellen. My son's name was Alex. He was barely six months old."

"I'm terribly sorry," Penny said. "It must have been awful. She was so beautiful."

"Yes," Casper said wistfully, "she was."

"Is that one of her also?" Penny asked, pointing to the evening gown picture.

"Yes. That one was taken immediately prior to the benefit concert she gave at Carnegie Hall," Casper said.

"Ellen was a tremendously talented concert pianist," Ace said. "I've never heard anyone play "The Moonlight Sonata" the way she could."

"Yes," Casper added smiling, "that was one of her favorites."

"She liked the classics, then," Penny asked.

"Actually, she played a variety of things." He smiled. "One minute she'd be playing Beethoven, and then she'd launch into a Gershwin or a Cole Porter tune, or something."

"You sound as if you still miss her a great deal," she said.

The smile vanished from his lips. "I do. Every day of my life."

"So, how do you feel about the Wraith?" Penny asked quickly, trying to gauge the judge's reaction.

"The Wraith?" he said quizzically. "Why do you ask?"

"I mean, isn't it general knowledge that he killed the two men accused of the crime against your family?"

"I must say," Casper said slowly, "that this is a little too personal for me to answer. Naturally, as an official of the court, I can not, and will not, condone any sort of vigilantism."

"I see."

"However, it may also be concluded that the Wraith's actions against the two accused trigger-men impeded the investigation into my wife's death. Because they were killed before the trial, we'll probably never know for sure who was responsible for ordering the atrocity."

"Whom do you feel was responsible?"

He sighed. "The conjecture was that it was an attempt on my life in retaliation for the Garbonne trial which I prosecuted some time ago." Casper's lips compressed into a thin line. "Back when I was with the D.A.'s office, before I was appointed to the bench."

"I thought Garbonne took a plea for a reduced sentence." Penny said.

"Well, he did," Casper replied. "But he was stabbed to death at Attica one week after his entry. There were obviously some disgruntled mobsters who held me at least partially responsible."

"*Hmmm*, that's interesting," Penny said. "I was working as a stringer at the time, but I seem to remember Leo Burke was trying to edge Garbonne out of the picture. Wasn't Garbonne considered too much of a liability because of his mental state? He had tertiary syphilis, you know."

"Yes," Casper said. "I do recall that, but, as I said, I'm afraid it's a moot point."

"Do you still feel in personal danger?" Penny asked.

"Show her your gun, Judge," Ace interjected.

"Gun?" she said incredulously, raising her eyebrows.

"I'm the only judge who has a concealed weapon permit, if

that's what you mean," he said with a smile. He went to his large closet and pulled open one of the oak doors. Beside his black judicial robe hung a brown leather shoulder holster with the butt of a huge pistol sticking out.

"Say, mind if I see that baby?" Deagan asked. The judge considered him briefly, then withdrew the gun. With practiced ease, he pressed the magazine release button and let the magazine drop into his palm. Then he racked back the slide, catching the forty-five round as it popped out. He strolled across and handed the gun to Deagan, who studied it admiringly.

"Colt Government Model," Deagan said. "Packs a helluva wallop. How's she shoot?"

"Like a charm," Casper said. "Carried this one in the War. I shot a German with it during D-Day."

"Yeah, I heard you were a paratrooper," Deagan said. "Me, I spent a lot of time in the European theater too. Went in with Patton."

The judge accepted the gun back from Deagan, reloaded it, and returned it to his closet.

"Naturally I don't carry it when I sit on the bench," he said with a smile. His gaze seemed to linger on Penny, as if trying to read her thoughts. "Perhaps we could discuss any more questions over dinner, Miss Cartier?"

"Thank you, but I have a previous engagement," Penny said, standing. She extended her hand. "I appreciate your time, Judge Casper."

"Oh, please," he said, taking her hand in both of his, "call me Ward."

Casper then shook hands with Deagan and Assante, who asked if he could use the judge's phone.

"Certainly," Casper said.

Assante picked it up and dialed an abbreviated number. When the other party came on the line Ace asked if Hamilton Vernon was in his office.

"Well tell him Vincent Assante is on his way down to see him," he said with a smile.

As the trio left the judge's chambers, Casper's piercing gaze trailed after them.

"So what do you think?" Penny asked secretively as they descended the white marble staircase.

"I took a look at them bullets in that magazine," Deagan said. "They were dum-dums."

"Dum-dums?" Penny said.

"Bullets that are specially flattened out to do more damage when they hit," Ace said. "Also makes them harder to match up through ballistics."

"But if he were the Wraith, surely he wouldn't show us his gun, would he?" Penny said.

"Ace knew he had a pistol," Deagan said. "I imagine it's pretty common knowledge, but I'm sure he ain't gonna use that rod to shoot any crooks. No law against a man having more than one gun. At least not yet, anyway."

"You and your western cowboy mentality," Ace said. "When are you going to wake up and see that this is nineteen forty-seven and not some damn John Wayne cowboy movie?"

"Hey," Deagan said with a grin, "smile when you say that, pardner,"

One floor below the courtrooms were the offices of various county officials, including that of the District Attorney. Since the position was an elected one, the D.A. was more of an administrator than a working prosecutor. As the top law enforcement lawyer in the county, his time was divided into various tasks, many of them dealing with public relations and the inevitable political backslapping of whatever party was in office. Hamilton Vernon, star athlete of Harvard Law School and decathlon competitor in the 1936 Olympics, was regarded as one of the up-and-coming young Democrats.

As they walked into his impressive office, Vernon stepped around the desk and warmly shook Assante's hand.

"Ace, how are you?" he said. He had black hair swept back from his face, with high cheekbones, almost like that of an American Indian. His body still showed the lean trimness of a world-class athlete.

"These are my friends, Penelope Cartier, from the *New York Daily Guardian*, and Lt. Colonel Thomas Deagan, U.S. Army, retired."

"Glad to meet you," Vernon said.

"Same here," Deagan said with a grin. "I remember you from the Olympics back before the war."

"Oh, yeah," Vernon said, turning to gesture at a framed picture of the Olympic rings hanging on the far wall opposite the door. Taped to the bottom of the frame was a piece of notepad-sized paper with the number 1.79 written on it. "Missed the bronze by that much," Vernon said. "I keep the paper there to remind myself not to miss any more points.

"Please, come in. Make yourselves comfortable, but excuse the mess, okay?" He proceeded into the office and leaned against the front of his large mahogany desk. "I'm right in the middle of preparing a speech for tomorrow night's Democratic fund raiser."

"I heard about that one," Ace said. "Congressman Marcantonio's coming, right?"

"Right," Vernon said slowly. "But how did you know that, Ace? You're not thinking of throwing your hat into the political arena, are you?"

"Hardly," Assante smiled. "We happened to catch Frasier Clark's musings about it, earlier."

Vernon broke into a hearty laugh.

"I'm sorry," he said, trying to regain control of himself, "but I was just thinking about doing a parody of old Frasier by referring to us local democrats as Sentinels of Liberty. That ought to really get him teed off."

"Is that guy Marcantonio really as much as a liability as Clark says?" Ace asked.

"Nobody's as much of a liability as Frasier says," Vernon said. "Besides, politics makes strange bedfellows, and the essence of a successful politician is being able to get into bed with somebody and not hating yourself in the morning." He grinned again, gauging their reactions. "As long as Tammany Hall wants him on board, he's in like Flynn. But there is a rumor that they're considering a certain judge for a run against him in the primary next year."

"So where do your own political aspirations fit into the

grand scheme of things?" Penny asked.

"Well, let me see," he said slowly, turning to face her. "Let's just say it depends, and leave it at that. Anyway, it's really up to the kingmakers to decide who they want to run for what."

"Spoken like a true politician," Ace said. "Miss Cartier's researching an article on urban vigilantes and she wanted to get some comments from you on the Wraith."

"The Wraith?" Vernon repeated slowly.

"You have come out against him somewhat vehemently in the past, Mr. Vernon," Penny said, flipping open her pad. "On July fifth of last year you called for the formulation of a special unit to track down and capture the Wraith, calling him 'the bane of modern society.'"

"I said that?" Vernon replied with mock incredulity. "Has a certain flair to it, doesn't it?"

"What is your opinion of him?" Penny asked. "Should a special unit be formed?"

"Well, I certainly can't condone his taking the law into his own hands," Vernon said, lapsing into his standard political voice. "No public official could. The danger here is that the man's developing into something of a folk hero. People tend to see him as some sort of modern-day Robin Hood instead of the vicious killer that he is."

"But so far, the type of people he's killed have been killers and criminals themselves," Penny said.

"So far, they have been," Vernon said, directing his somewhat penetrating gaze directly on her. "But what happens when he inevitably steps over the line? Then people will be clamoring for him to be brought to justice."

"And you'll be on record as having advocated that all

along," she said.

"Succinctly put," he said, "but accurate. And at least I won't be hating myself in the morning." His face stretched into a wry grin. He pointed to the display of Olympic rings on the wall with the hand-numbered paper. "Remember, missing a couple of points can mean the difference between those who get the gold, silver, or bronze and those who don't."

6

Jurisdictional Disputes

Doc parked the Auburn down the street from the Lexington Hotel, and he and Roland stepped onto the sidewalk. Roland turned and looked admiringly at the sleek contours of the speedster. He took in a deep breath, then blew it out pursed lips before taking out his pack of Chesterfields again and held them up.

"I assume, since we're not in your car anymore…"

Doc gave a slight nod.

Roland smiled. "Swell car. Wish I could afford one."

"It was a gift from my father," Doc said.

"Your old man must be pretty rich, huh?" He stuck a cigarette between his lips.

"He was a doctor and a scientist. But he always gave a substantial amount of his money to further the social causes he believed in," Doc said.

Roland lit the cigarette and began walking toward the hotel. "My old man gave to a lot of social causes too. Except they were collected down at the local tavern. Anyway, like I told you," he said, inhaling on the cigarette. "We got the boyfriend stashed in room thirteen twenty-seven. Sorta for safekeeping. The guys that broke in really did a number on him. Beat him up pretty good."

"Do you think it's strange they let him live?"

"Not really," Roland said with a shrug. "If their primary purpose was to grab the broad and hold her for ransom, then it was to their advantage to have him alive so he could tell us that she'd been snatched. If he hadn't been beat-up so bad, I woulda figured the dame faked the whole thing to get some money from her rich daddy."

"I assume you've interviewed him," Doc said. "Did he give you any pertinent information about the kidnapers?"

"The only thing he said was that there were four of 'em. All masked. They busted down the door and came right in and grabbed her, and commenced to beating the hell out of him." Roland paused as they approached the lobby doors. "I got two men in the lobby in plainclothes, two out back, and two more upstairs."

"Are they dependable men?"

"Are you kiddin'?" Roland said. "The guy I got in the room, Clancy, him and me go way back." He took one more drag on the cigarette then tossed it into the gutter. "Ahhh, I been needing that the whole damn way."

"Did Bloom say anything else about the abductors?" Doc asked as they pushed through the revolving glass doors.

"Only that he heard the guys saying something about taking the broad to someone named Casey."

"Casey?" Doc asked.

"Yeah, you know, like Casey at the bat," Roland said. He walked over to a chair in front of the desk and rattled the newspaper of a heavy-set man in a wrinkled brown suit. The man, who'd obviously been sleeping, snapped awake, looked around, then shot to his feet wearing an embarrassed look.

"Sorry, Sarge," the man said, "but it's been quieter than all get out around here. Pretty routine."

"Meyers," Roland said. "How many times do I have to tell you, there ain't nothing that's ever routine in police work. You gotta be alert at all times, expecting the worst, or you'll be going home in a box, you knucklehead."

"Sorry, Sarge."

"Where's the damn phone?" Roland asked the desk attendant. Then, after being handed a house phone, he said, "Meyers, meet Doc Atlas."

Meyers's jaw dropped as he saw the nattily clad, but immense figure standing behind Roland.

"Gosh," Meyers said. "I read all about you, but never thought I'd get a chance to meet you in person."

Doc just smiled and extended his hand. Roland spoke into the receiver that he and Doc were coming up.

"So get ready to let us in," he said before hanging up the phone. "It's all set."

They turned and began walking toward the elevator. Two men, both in dark pinstripe suits and wearing dark glasses, had just gotten on the open elevator. Its doors closed quickly. Another smaller man, hunched over and holding a handkerchief to his face, staggered drunkenly toward the only other standing elevator. His white Panama-style hat was pulled down over his face and his tan suit had sweaty patches under the arms. Doc and Roland had to come to a complete stop to avoid the stumbling figure. He bounded through the elevator door just ahead of them. The operator glanced at them collectively.

"What floors, gentlemen?" he asked.

"Thirteenth," Roland said. He looked at Doc. "I wonder who them two tough looking mugs were that got on the other elevator. You ever seen 'em before?"

Doc shook his head.

"I'll take ten," the small man said thickly. "No, nine." He blinked twice. "No, ten."

"Which is it?"

The man's face seemed to lengthen as he frowned. "Ten, please."

The operator nodded, gave a last quick check of the lobby, then closed the sliding door. The car rose quickly, then slowed as they passed the sixth floor. The number of each one was painted on the back of the respective set of elevator doors. The operator stopped the car as the large number ten became visible, and pulled the safety lever opening the doors.

"Ten, sir," the operator said. The drunk nodded a thank-you and began to amble off the car, then abruptly stopped.

"My good sir," the drunk said, using the doorframe for support. "I do believe that this is not the right floor."

"You said, ten, didn't you?"

"Ten?" the drunk said, as if asking himself. He wiggled his nose several times, like a sneezing rabbit then lurched unsteadily back into the car. "Perhaps you have the wrong floor," he said with exaggerated facial movement.

"Nope, this is ten," the elevator operator said. He was a young man in his early twenties with a red crew cut.

The drunk yawned copiously, then stared down the hallway.

"My good man, I do believe you are right," he said. "Could you possibly take me to the eleventh floor instead?"

"Yes, sir," the kid said, letting the doors slide closed.

He took it up one floor, and the drunk repeated his ritual of staring slowly out of the open doors. Then smiled and nodded.

"By, George, I think you've got it, this time," he said, and began to stagger out of the car, but stopped, standing half-in, half-out. Roland, his face split by a large grin, glanced at Doc. He was just about to offer a comment when the unmistakable sound of gunshots echoed from the floors above them. The drunken man stared at him dumbly. "My good man, may I trouble you for a–"

Roland shoved the drunk through the opening. "That sounds like a Tommy-gun," he said, his grin fading as he reached inside his jacket and withdrew his large thirty-eight revolver. "You got a gun?"

Doc shook his head.

"Then take this one, then," Roland said, shoving the thirty-eight toward Doc. He withdrew a forty-five automatic from the holster on his belt. "You," he growled at the operator, "move this thing up to thirteen and open the doors nice and slow. Got it."

The kid nodded, his face the color of broken chalk.

Cautiously he eased the car up to the thirteenth floor and Roland told him to open the doors just a crack. Silence permeated the level. The burly cop pushed down on the kid's hand, which was still on the lever. "Keep this car at this floor and don't open the doors for nobody but me." The kid nodded again, his eyes as wide as saucers. As the doors slowly opened all the way, Roland went out in a crouch, the big semi-automatic held out in front of him. Doc switched the thirty-eight to his left hand, surmising that room 1327 would be down the hall to their right, and having the gun in his left hand would allow him to flatten against the wall more effectively. His shooting hand mattered little, since he'd been trained from birth to be ambidextrous.

Roland was already at the corner, peeking his head down

the hallway. The door to the room was ajar, and a heavy smell of cordite hung in the air. Roland motioned for Doc to move up behind him.

"Cover me, Atlas. I'm goin' to the room," he said. Doc nodded and leveled the pistol down the hallway.

Roland moved with an uncharacteristic grace for a big man. In seconds he was at the door, his gun held at the ready. Then he whirled and kicked back the slightly open door. He disappeared from sight for about thirty seconds, then Doc heard him yell.

"Atlas, get in here!"

Doc ran swiftly to the door. On the floor inside the room lay three bodies. One, next to the door, had been shot in the face. Two others were slumped over a card table. They'd both been shot repeatedly. Blood leaked from both bodies and formed a crimson puddle on the carpeting.

"Check him," Roland said, his fingers on the neck of the body wearing the shoulder holster.

Doc stooped and felt the recumbent man's neck. No pulse.

"He's dead," Doc said.

"Clancy and Bloom too," Roland said, moving quickly toward Doc. He paused momentarily to kick a pair of dark glasses on the floor. "It had to be them tough looking mugs that beat us up in the other elevator." He stopped at the desk and grabbed the phone. When someone came on the line Roland yelled for the officers to seal the building. "Everybody's been killed up here," he screamed. "And watch it, one of them's got a machine gun." He hung up, then looked at Doc. "They gotta still be on this floor."

"Fire escape?" Doc asked, nodding toward the windows.

Roland shook his head. "Already checked it," he said.

"Come on." He stepped around the bodies and went back into the hall. Doc followed. They ran over to the elevators and Roland banged on the doors. They opened a crack.

"Anybody go down in the other cars?" he asked.

"Didn't hear nobody," the kid said. "But there's a freight elevator on the other side." He pointed off to the left hallway. Roland told him to keep the car there and close the doors again. Then he ran down the hall. At the end of the corridor a small section angled off toward what had to be the alley side of the building.

Roland reached forward and tried the doorknob. "Locked," he muttered and stepped back. He swung his leg forward and kicked the door just under the knob. It held and he kicked it again. This time the door flew back revealing a large janitorial room with an elongated set of horizontal doors at the far wall. The hum of a motor came from behind them.

Roland ran over to the freight elevator doors and tried to pry them apart, but they wouldn't budge. Doc grabbed a screwdriver from a nearby bench and jammed it into a circular hole high up on the door. Suddenly the doors split apart. Roland glanced down the shaft. The illumination from the room was enough to show the descending car, which was close to the bottom.

"Damn," Roland said. "We'll never catch them."

"Perhaps not," Doc said, sticking the revolver into his belt by his hip. He slipped his right arm out of the sleeve of his gray gabardine suit. "See if that flashlight works," he said to Roland.

The cop looked at the bench and saw the big, industrial-sized flashlight. He grabbed it and flipped the switch. A powerful beam shot out from the bulb. Doc took the flashlight and shone it into the shaft. The freight elevator was set up with hoist ropes encased in metal guides on each side. The oily cables rotated within their metallic frame.

"Meet me in back of the building," Doc said, suddenly leaping into the open elevator shaft. Roland did a double take, then saw that the golden giant had grabbed one of the metal guide-beams and held himself suspended against it. Doc's right hand held him in place as he placed the flashlight under his chin. Then he slipped his left arm out of his jacket and adjusted the coat so the material was between his hands and the metal. He clamped his legs around the guide-beam and adjusted the coat under his right hand. Suddenly he was gone. Roland looked into the darkness of the shaft and saw the diminishing luminescence of the flashlight descending at a rapid rate.

Doc used his feet as guides and controlled the rate of his descent with his powerful hands. The metal of the beams had begun to tear up his jacket, so halfway down he began squeezing his legs together, the soles of his shoes gripping the steel and slowing his descent. Beneath him he heard the whooshing of the car. It was perhaps fifty feet or so farther down the shaft than he. Certainly too far for a jump, especially in the dark confines of an elevator shaft. Then he heard the revolutions of the motor slow up slightly. They must be nearing the bottom. He quickened his descent. The motor wound down and the car beneath him slowed appreciably. Doc was only fifteen or twenty feet above it now. A sudden miscalculation caused him to speed up just as the elevator lurched to a sudden stop, and he landed heavily on top of the car, the flashlight bouncing from under his chin and making a clattering sound as it hit the metal.

"What the hell," a voice inside the freight elevator cried. Seconds later a spray of bullets perforated the roof of the cab. Doc rolled to one side and narrowly avoided being hit.

"There's somebody on top," the voice said.

"Come on," another voice yelled. "Let's get outta here."

"Not till I get 'em," the first voice said. More bullets sprang through the metal, dappling the interior of the shaft with light from inside the car. The shooter began circling the cab, his Thompson held perpendicular, shooting in concentric circles through the roof. Doc knew he had only seconds before being struck by one of the rounds, so he withdrew the revolver. He aimed carefully through the pattern of perforations, using a double-handed grip to minimize any recoil, and fired twice. The first bullet ripped through the metal and went wide. The second round, going through the same hole, struck the gunman right between the eyes. The thug sank back, his lolling head rolling over to reveal a gaping exit wound. Doc's eyes scanned the surface of the car, then he crept to the trap door at the opposite corner. Pulling it open cautiously, he peered down. The horizontal doors stood open revealing the semi-gloom of a storage area.

Opening the trap door fully, Doc swung to the floor of the cab and immediately went into a roll. Several bullets ricocheted around him and he scrambled forward, returning fire as he sought cover. A muzzle flashed in the darkness of the room about thirty feet away. Doc flattened out on the floor near a washing machine and squeezed off another round. By his count, his adversary should have one round left if his revolver had been fully loaded. The thug's gun flashed again, followed by an ominous click. Doc heard the sound of skittering feet on the wooden floor of the room. He rose and followed the sound. Another flash accompanied a clap of thunder. Somehow the hoodlum had managed to reload. Or he had two guns. Doc hit the floor, then seconds later a door opened, mid-day light spilling in from the alley. Several more shots sounded, and Doc was on his feet running. At the door he paused and glanced through the opening. Two bloody men lay sprawled motionless on the ground. One held a badge in his left hand. Kneeling beside the fallen men, Doc checked them for vital signs. Both were dead. He saw the gunman running toward the end of the alley. Within seconds Atlas was up and in pursuit. The hoodlum glanced furtively over his shoulder, and saw the huge figure bearing down on him. The thug paused and raised his gun. A burst of fire appeared and Doc felt a bullet whiz by his head, wide and to the left. Veering toward some nearby garbage cans, Doc scooped a heavy metal lid from one of them and stopped abruptly. He flipped the circular can lid toward the running figure. It struck the hoodlum's right leg and sent him tumbling down. Doc was upon him in seconds, just as the killer rolled over, his gun at the ready.

Doc's hand shot out in a golden blur, seizing the gangster's wrist and jerking him upward, the pistol discharging simultaneously. Doc's other hand snapped down on top of the gun, wrenching it from the thug's grasp. Doc swung his body around and whirled the hood into the wall. Recovering, the thug reached inside the pocket of his pinstriped suit and withdrew a switchblade knife. The long blade flicked open with a silver flash.

"You ain't takin' me alive," he snarled.

Doc stuck the thirty-eight into his belt again and calmly advanced toward the hoodlum. The man sprang from the wall toward the middle of the alley, holding the switchblade close to his chest, in the style of an experienced knife-fighter.

Before Doc could close the gap between them, a shot rang out and the hoodlum jerked. Blood bubbled out of his gaping mouth and a large crimson stain welled up just under the whiteness of his collar. He crumpled forward, a sad, almost perplexed look on his face.

Roland's silhouette was at the other end of the alley, lowering his pistol. He ran forward and asked Doc if he was all right.

"Yes," Doc said.

"Well, keep down," Roland said. "There's another one around here somewhere." His eyes scanned the alley.

"He's in the freight elevator," Doc said. "I had to tactically neutralize him. He was trying to kill me."

Roland relaxed slightly and his face twisted into a grim smile as he blew out a long breath. "Well, good job. Of course, you gotta come down to the precinct house to make a statement."

"Why did you shoot that man?" Doc demanded, pointing

to the body in the alley.

"Whadaya mean, why?" Roland said. "He had a knife. He was coming at ya."

"I'm aware of that," Doc said. "I wanted him alive."

"Well, so what? The SOB killed two cops upstairs." He glanced down the alley, said, "Oh, hell," then ran for the two prone bodies. Roland knelt beside each man, feeling for a pulse. Then he rose and slowly took his hat off his head and wiped his eyes.

"I checked them already," Doc said. "They were both dead when I reached them."

Roland's head nodded fractionally. "Make that four cops, and one of them was my good friend Clancy."

"I'm sorry," Doc said. He let the policeman have a moment of silence, then said, "I must tell you, getting back to the subject of that second hoodlum, if we could have captured him alive –"

"Let me tell you something," Roland snapped, his finger jerking in Doc's face. "Nobody who kills a copper in this town's gonna make it to the precinct house alive. Not if I have anything to say about it."

Doc felt sudden anger welling up inside and quickly took mental steps to calm himself. He'd been trained throughout his life not to show any emotion, nor let his feelings interfere with what he perceived as his clear duty. It disturbed him slightly that this man, Roland, had brought him so close to the precipice of antagonism.

"Have the bodies of the two thugs brought to my Manhattan office," Doc said. He handed Roland one of his cards. "I want to perform the autopsies myself. Perhaps some clues to this occurrence can still be salvaged."

Several other policemen, both uniformed and plainclothes, began filtering into the mouth of the alley. Roland's misty stare had turned harsh. When he spoke, his voice was a growl.

"Go to hell, Atlas."

Doc felt a sudden, uncharacteristic welling of anger, but he kept his voice even as he asked, "What did you say?"

"You heard me," Roland shot back. "We ain't taking these bodies out of Brooklyn, and if I have anything to say about it, you ain't never gonna be touching 'em."

He stepped forward, holstering the automatic in his belt, and stopped inches from Doc's chest.

"Gimme back my thirty-eight," he said.

Doc withdrew the revolver from his belt and handed it over, butt first.

"I can call the commissioner and supersede your authority," Doc said.

"Like I told you, Atlas, go to hell," Roland growled. "This is a New York City Police investigation, and you're just a civilian. I don't give a damn how many fancy titles you got, or how many friends you got in high places. As far as I'm concerned the only person authorized to examine 'em is somebody from the King County's Coroner's Office. So you got no jurisdiction. Go ahead and call anybody you damn well please, but now, get out of my way before I run you in."

Doc took a deep breath, then stepped back.

"Perhaps, when you've calmed down, Detective," he said, "this jurisdictional dispute can be resolved amicably."

"Sarge," Meyers, the heavy-set cop they'd seen in the lobby, called from the mouth of the alley. He was holding a little man in a tan suit and Panama hat. Meyers pushed the man toward the group. The little man did a stutter-step, but seemed to walk much better than he had only a few minutes ago, getting on the elevator.

"Look who I caught trying to sneak out the front," Meyers said. "This is Morrie the Mouse Moscowicz. He's a little bookie for the Burke mob. I arrested him a couple of years back when I was working bunco."

Roland collared the little man and pulled him close. "This little piece of crap got on the elevator just before us," Roland said. "Not so drunk now, are ya? What was your part in this?"

"I want to talk to my lawyer," Moscowicz said.

Roland slapped him across the face, bloodying the little man's lips and knocking off his white hat. "Run him in," Roland snarled. He shoved the small man toward the other cops, then turned back to Doc Atlas. "Now you see why it wouldn't have done any good to bring in that other guy? By the time we get down to the station there'll probably be some fancy would-be Perry Mason like Paul Milton waiting to get him out."

Doc stared at the other man intently for a moment, then said, "Obviously that disturbs you greatly."

"You're damn right it does," Roland said. "You're damn right." He took out a Chesterfield King and held it up in defiance as he began walking down the alley.

Michael A. Black

7

Of Martyrs, Men, and Bats

IT was one of the older churches that had been built in the Gothic style, long before utilitarian bleakness had replaced craft and flourish as the standard of architectural design. The dingy grayness of its mortar and the pockmarks on the outer walls and windows were evidence of the building's incremental decline. The neighborhood surrounding it had declined also, at a more rapid rate, and now the archdiocese saw little need to replace the missing shingles or the broken panes from the once magnificent stained glass windows. Instead they'd allowed the old structure to fall into a protracted state of disrepair, made more apparent by the long line of bedraggled humanity that extended out of the open side doors.

"Let's go in the front," Deagan said. "No sense trying to buck that chow line."

"Liable to get overpowered by the smell," Ace added.

Penny, who was disturbed more than the two men by the sight, withheld comment. While she felt a greater degree of compassion toward the unfortunates, the reality of the situation was that they were here to interview Father Antonio Gisseppi and little would be served by engaging in a debate about the plight of the lower social classes with Mad Dog and Ace. Assante was not as quick as Deagan in ascending the stone stairs and seemed slightly miffed when Mad Dog ostentatiously

87

held open the door with an expansive grin stretched over his face.

Despite the somewhat shabby exterior, the inside of the church was immaculate, except for the hanging flaps of peeling paint high up on the walls that could not be reached by probing brooms. The pews were made of heavy wood, once proudly varnished, but now worn bare in various spots by the fleeting presence of thousands of hands. The mid-day sun shone through the colored windows, showering the center portion of the aisle in a patchwork rainbow of color, but the symmetry of the prismatic radiance was interrupted by several intrusive beams, which filtered through the cracks and holes in the panes. Beyond the brass railing that surrounded the altar, an elderly nun sat near the front, her head bowed in prayer. Not wanting to disturb her they went along the side aisle toward the area where the offices were. After knocking lightly, Penny tried the door. It opened with a creak, and another nun, this one closer to middle age, smiled and asked if she could help them.

"I'm Penelope Cartier from the *Guardian* newspaper. I wonder if we might be able to speak with Father Gisseppi?"

"Father's working in the serving line," the nun said, "but if you want I can take you down there."

"That would be fine," Penny said.

The nun came out and led them past the right side of the altar to a doorway in back. If the praying nun was aware of them, she didn't show it. The door was solid wood, with ornate decorative lacing dividing its surface into a latticework of rectangles. It creaked open and the nun led them down to the basement. The stairway was made of heavy limestone, the edge of the stairs chipped away in spots. The dampness became more evident as they descended, as did the odor. An aromatically pungent wave stung their nostrils making it all too apparent the vast majority of the occupants of the immense room into which they'd just entered had not used soap or water for quite some time. Penny turned her head and wrinkled her nose.

"We'll have to make this a quick interview," she said softly.

Ace smiled in return. The basement had been transformed into a large cafeteria with plasterboard tables and metal folding chairs. Men as unkempt as those waiting in the line outside sat in rows silently eating, scraping their plates with thick bread crusts. The line seemed to originate near the south wall, which had another limestone staircase ascending to a large side door. Enormous metal pots sat on the sturdy wooden tables and various men and women in black clerical outfits stood behind each, with ladles. At the first station in the line, a large-boned priest dipped his ladle into the pot and deposited its contents on one of the plates.

"Please, Father, can't you gimme some more?" the old man holding the plate said.

"You know the rules, my friend," the priest said. "Not till everyone gets through the line."

The man proceeded to the next pot in silent dejection.

"That's Father Gisseppi," the nun said, indicating the first priest.

He was tall and darkly complexioned, his beard seeming to form a blue-black net over his cheeks. The sleeves of his jacket were stretched taut with the bulk of his arms, and his shoulders were wide. His eyes were piercing when he glanced over to give them a curious look. Strangely light colored eyes considering his olive complexion and dark hair. Penny let the nun approach first. The priest had to bend over so she could whisper in his ear. Straightening up, he motioned for one of the other priests to take over his position.

"And remember, no more than one piece of bread per person," the priest said. "Keep a tally for me."

The younger priest nodded, and Father Gisseppi slipped off his apron and stepped from around the table, passing through the chow line, as he approached them. When he drew closer they saw he was not as youthful as he appeared from a distance. While obviously in very good shape physically, he had a drawn look around his eyes. Penny estimated him to be in his late thirties or early forties.

"Sister Helen tells me you're from the newspapers," he said, holding out his hand to Penny.

"Yes," she said, shaking hands with the priest. "I wonder if we could speak to you for a few minutes?"

"I suppose," Gisseppi said. "But only if it doesn't take too long. This is our busy time."

"I promise it won't," Penny said, and tried to coax him with a smile. She wondered if he'd be immune. As the priest moved to one of the tables, he hesitated.

"Perhaps we'd better go upstairs to my office," he said. "It looks like we're going to be filled to capacity."

Penny shot a sideways glance of relief at Ace and Deagan as they walked to the staircase. Deagan grinned broadly.

The priest's office was sparsely furnished. A large mahogany desk stood in the corner near the windows. Beside it were three chairs, none of which looked very new. Heavily constructed bookcases, filled with well-worn volumes on religion and philosophy, lined the walls. Behind the desk hung several framed photographs. One was obviously of Father Gisseppi's parents, and another showed the priest as a young man, standing in a track outfit holding an Olympic-sized hammer. A third photo, of a group of men, was less distinct.

"Quite a varied selection of books, Father," Ace said, standing by one of the bookcases. "Chaucer, Upton Sinclair, John Dos Passos, George Orwell..."

"You'll find a copy of Norman Mailer's war novel in there, too," the priest said flashing a quick smile. "I spent some time as an army chaplain during the War."

"And you've been quoted numerous times by the press as being critical of the mayor, the police commissioner, and the governor," Penny said. "Quite a militant approach for a priest."

Father Gisseppi looked somewhat startled, but recovered quickly.

"I take it this is not going to be a typical interview about the parish's attempts to set up our food shelters," Gisseppi said.

"Well, I can say that I'll do my best to include something about your efforts in my article," Penny said. "However, I do have a very fastidious editor."

Gisseppi opened a drawer on the desk and took out a humidor. It contained four pipes. He removed a Bently and began packing it with a fine smelling tobacco.

"I hope you don't mind," he said. "It's one of the few vices I'm allowed."

"Nah, go ahead, Father," Deagan cut in. "Maybe it'll keep the smell from drifting up from downstairs."

"That smell, Mr. Deagan," Gisseppi said, pausing to light the pipe with a silver lighter, "serves as a reminder to me that the Lord's work is never done."

"Got ya," Deagan said with a grin. "Cleanliness is next to

Godliness, and all that, but who wouldn't rather eat than wash, right?" His eyes narrowed slightly. "Hey, nice lighter. You stationed with the first of the Eighty-second?"

"No, actually, this was given to me by a young man who was killed on Okinawa," Gisseppi said. "I carry it as another reminder of the Lord's work."

"Really?" Penny asked. "Isn't it rather hard to justify the Lord's work in the context of such violence as war?"

"Very much so," Gisseppi replied. "But violence has been around as long as mankind. Cain and Abel demonstrated that quite vividly."

"How about urban violence, Father?" Penny asked.

Gisseppi shrugged. "Unfortunately, at this point in our civilization, it seems to be an omnipresent by-product."

"Do you feel the police are effectively handling it?"

The priest removed the pipe from his mouth and blew out a puff of smoke. "Let's just say, I think more could be done to address the issue."

"And what about people who take the law into their own hands?" Penny asked. "How do you feel about them?"

"Why do you ask?" the priest said, his brows furrowing.

"Just my own curiosity," she answered. "You've gotten the reputation of a man who's fought the system on more than one occasion. Once you were touted as a shoe-in for Cardinal, weren't you?"

The priest blew out another cloud of smoke as he gripped the pipe with his long fingers.

"At one time, I suppose, it mattered more to me than it does now. Back then I saw the position of Cardinal as a way to effect positive changes within the church, and to address the pertinent issues." He leaned forward placing his large arms on the desk, his expression reminiscent of bygone days. "But that was a young priest's dream. Now, I'm content to do my humble best in my own way."

"I'm interested in your opinion of people who, in their own way, go against the system," Penny said. "People like yourself, who do things in a peaceful fashion, as opposed to those who are given to more violent methods."

His brow furrowed again. "I'm afraid I don't quite understand what it is you're getting at, Miss Cartier."

"Well," Penny said thoughtfully, putting her pencil to her lips like a schoolgirl. "Say a contrast in styles. You're obviously a man who's given up a great opportunity to advance in the church because you march to the beat of a different drummer, so to speak. And now, it seems you're fighting a losing battle."

Gisseppi removed the pipe again. It had gone out. "Sometimes it does seem that way." He reached for the lighter again and held the flame over the bowl, drawing and puffing on the stem as he spoke. "But each day I'm able to do something…I draw closer to my goal…. Our very presence here is a victory of sorts…because it stands out like a beacon before those who'd rather not see certain things."

"But didn't you stretch the rules, Father?" Penny persisted. "Didn't you step on the wrong toes with your militant stances of last year when you were quoted comparing that mysterious gunman, the Wraith, to Robin Hood?" She paged through her steno pad and then read: "Perhaps the old guard needs to be shaken up in the church just as this Wraith individual seems to be prodding law enforcement in this city to sit up and do its job." She looked at him, trying to effect an expression of inquisitive innocence. "So how do you feel about him dispensing all those deadly blessings?"

"Deadly blessings?" Gisseppi's head lolled back as he laughed heartily. "My dear girl," he said, regaining his composure and resetting the pipe stem between his teeth. He blew out a new cloud of grayish smoke. "That quote meant to be hyperbole, and was taken completely out of context. And, as you can guess, I'm still serving my penitence for it." He held up his hands to emphasize his surroundings. "When you're a celibate in New York, you unfortunately forget at times that you must be careful what you say. And to whom you say it." He leaned forward on the desk and blew copious amounts of smoke across at Penny. She responded by opening her handbag and removing her cigarette case. An awkward silence filled the space between them.

"Hey, is that you, Father?" Deagan asked, walking around the desk and pointing to the picture of the priest in his track uniform.

"Yes, in my younger days at Tolentine University," Gisseppi said.

"Looks like you was pretty good," Deagan said. "I see some kind of medal around your neck here."

"Yes," Gisseppi said. "At the time, I'd managed to set a new world's record with the hammer." He smiled briefly, then sighed. "It's since been broken many times. And I've had to sell off all my medals and trophies to make ends meet around here. I keep that picture as the sole reminder of my youthful triumphs."

"That's you in the picture with Randolph Grantman, isn't it?" Penny asked gesturing at another of the framed photographs on the wall.

"Yes," Gisseppi said somewhat harshly, turning slightly to

look at the picture. "Mr. Grantman was initially very generous in his contribution to the mission."

"You sound almost bitter," she said.

The priest inhaled deeply on the pipe.

"That was before I found out Randolph Grantman was merely acting out of guilt in giving us that donation," he said.

"Guilt? I don't understand."

He drew deeply on the pipe again, then blew twin clouds from his nose.

"I once thought quite highly of the man, " Gisseppi said. "Then I happened to find out that he owns interests in several construction companies that are involved in the Mid-Century Roadways."

Penny looked at him quizzically.

"The massive transportation project that is building freeways connecting the city with all the surrounding towns," Gisseppi said.

"I didn't figure you'd object to that, Father," Deagan said. "Look at all the jobs it makes."

"Yes, but at what price, Mr. Deagan?" the priest shot back. "Most of those downstairs once lived in the areas that are now being demolished in the name of progress. Displaced from their homes at a loss because of the government's eminent domain edict under the guise of the greater good." His disdain was obvious in the final words.

"Well," Deagan said, shrugging, "sometimes ya gotta break a few eggs to make an omelet,"

"Well put," Assante said sarcastically. "Father, why haven't you gone to the papers with this information?"

The priest laughed again. "You forget who owns the papers," he said bitterly. "No, to cause more of a public sensation at this time would only increase the suffering. But, as Seneca says, the wheel of fortune can spin many times in one's lifetime. Until it spins again, I keep that photograph as a reminder that sometimes you have to tweak the devil's tail to keep your own candles burning. But make no mistake," Gisseppi said, removing the pipe from his mouth and punctuating his words by pointing with the stem. "I fully expect that the Lord will ultimately enact divine judgment on those who have caused all this suffering." His light-colored eyes seemed to gleam through the haze of the smoke.

On the way out of the church Deagan and Ace each stuffed several bills into the poor box. As they descended the heavy stone steps they noticed that the line extending from around the side of the building seemed not to have shortened at all. In the car Mad Dog asked the others if they thought he was their man.

"I don't know," said Ace. "He certainly has the fire in his belly. But I have a hard time reconciling the image of a priest going around in a black costume killing people, even if they are hoodlums."

"And he seemed most passionately angry at Randolph, rather than the criminal element," Penny said.

"At least he looks like he could take care of himself," Deagan said. "You get a load of his arms? And the Wraith's supposed to dress in black, right? Well maybe the reason is 'cause priests already have black clothes."

"Once again your inscrutable logic never cease to amaze me," Ace said.

Deagan braked for a red light. He turned on the radio. Suddenly the LaSalle lurched forward jerkily as Mad Dog eased up on the clutch without depressing the gas pedal.

"Bromo Seltzer, Bromo Seltzer, Bromo Seltzer," Deagan chanted in unison with the radio commercial. "Fights headaches three ways."

"Isn't it bad enough we have to listen to those stupid commercials without you repeating them?" Ace said.

Deagan's grin was so wide his face crinkled.

"Ain't nothing wrong with commercials," he said. "In fact, I gotta make sure I listen to *The Shadow* tomorrow night. They're supposed to announce the winner of the Carey Salt contest."

"What?" Assante said.

"Oh sure, Ace," Penny said. "You send in a brief letter telling an unusual way you've used their salt product, and the winner gets a free watch."

"And not just any watch, either," added Deagan. "A hundred-and-seventeen jewel watch."

"You listen to *The Shadow*?'" Assante said to Penny, purposely ignoring Deagan.

"Sure I do," she said. "What way did you send in, Mad Dog?"

"Well," Deagan said, licking his lips in obvious relish that Penny had taken his side over Assante's. "I wrote 'em about when I was in the Army. And this is a sure winner. I used to soak my feet in my steel pot filled with salt water to toughen them up."

"Oh, there's no doubt that one's going to win," Ace said, his tone brimming with sarcasm. "In fact, I'll bet they got thousands of letters from service men saying the same thing."

"Oh yeah, well, that ain't all." Deagan's face crinkled again with a triumphant smirk. "I also wrote in there how when I was boxing, I used to soak my mitts and my face in the brine too,"

Ace roared with laughter. "Now I'm sure you'll never win."

"What? How come?" Deagan said.

"Because, they get one look at you, they'll be afraid they'll get sued for ruining your looks," Ace said.

Penny suppressed a laugh. Deagan frowned, then said, "Yeah, well I just thought of another one in case I don't win this week. I'll just tell them how I use a ton of their salt every week following this shyster lawyer around and taking a grain of it with everything he says."

Doc sat patiently in the police station squad room listening to the harsh bumps on the wall of the room next door where Hal Roland was interrogating the little man, Moscowicz. The sounds were muffled, but an occasional scream managed to filter through. Doc shook his head in disgust. The methods did not trouble him as much as the waste of time. Roland had steadfastly refused to allow Doc to even examine the bodies of the dead thugs. Doc was certain he could elicit the appropriate information from 'the Mouse' through hypnosis techniques. True, it was virtually impossible to hypnotize someone against his will, but Doc had perfected the procedure to an art. He also used a chemical injection to relax the subjects, if difficulties presented themselves.

He sighed and went back to his mental calculations. The overwhelming conclusion he reached time and time again was that there was not yet enough data. This business of the Wraith bothered him, too. He had been all set to immerse himself into the matter. The challenge beckoned to him like a quest for the holy grail, but the kidnapping of Bonnie Grantman had thrown the proverbial monkey wrench into his plan. Perhaps, he thought, Penny, Mad Dog, and Ace will gather some fruitful information.

He had been able to make arrangements to hypnotize Maria Hernandez, the girl who'd been abducted by the gang of hoodlums before being rescued by the Wraith. Maybe that would yield some information that might be useful in both cases, because as he sat there thinking, Doc somehow felt there was some common thread running through both cases. Something of which he was not yet fully cognizant. Something that he may have overlooked.

Another loud thump on the wall broke Doc's reverie. Then he heard loud voices and a door being slammed. Hal Roland suddenly appeared in the hallway shaking a Chesterfield out of his pack. His face was flushed and covered with sweat. He glanced at Doc and leaned against the doorframe.

"If you're done giving your statement, Atlas, you can leave," he said. "Sorry nobody told you sooner."

"That's all right, Sergeant," Doc said. "The sounds of your interrogation techniques have been most elucidating."

Roland looked at him for a moment, the cigarette loose between his parted lips, before snapping the wheel of his lighter. "I hope you don't mind," he said as he lighted the cigarette.

Doc's silence and lack of reaction seemed to bother him.

"Look, Atlas, we're dealing with scum here. I don't know what kind of circles you run in, but me, I grew up right here in Brooklyn."

"That's obvious from your accent," Doc said. "My

intention was not to be critical, but merely to point out that I might be able to elicit more information from the man, if I were given the opportunity."

Roland shook his head.

"I told you before, this is an official police investigation," he said. "That means no civilians. I don't care who you are or who you hobnob with." He drew deeply on the cigarette and exhaled a cloudy breath. "Anyway, I did want to thank you for plugging that one SOB in the freight elevator. The officers' widows'll rest easier knowing both of those killers are dead now."

Doc nodded an acknowledgment.

"Would it be possible to have someone drop me back at my car?" Doc asked.

Roland looked up at him, drew on the cigarette again, and nodded. "I'll see if I can find somebody."

"And I also wonder if I may use your phone to call my office," Doc said. "I have to notify my clerical staff to broadcast a special radio message, and they will be leaving work shortly."

Roland's brow furrowed as he drew some smoke through the Chesterfield and blew it out his nose. He nodded again and motioned for the golden giant to follow him.

The mansion sat on a large, heavily wooded estate a quarter hour's drive from the city. The sound of the chimes echoed deep within the walls, and presently a supercilious-looking butler dressed in a formal black suit and bow tie opened the heavily constructed oak door. The butler was tall, but a bit on the gaunt side, with one of those pencil-thin mustaches that were always just a tad out of style. He appeared to be in his late fifties, with heavily lacquered hair combed over his scalp in an unsuccessful attempt to conceal the absence of any hair on the top of his head.

"May I help you?" he asked, his eyes darting furtively from Penny to Deagan to Assante.

"We're here to see Mr. Morrison," Penny said. "I'm from the *New York Daily Guardian*." The butler admitted them to a large foyer and told them to wait. The room was tastefully decorated with lavish furniture, ceramic statues and vases, and numerous paintings. Deagan took out one of his enormous cigars and lighted it as he began pacing. His shoes made echoing sounds on the highly polished marble floor.

"Pretty fancy digs, huh?" he said.

"I'll say," Penny said. "Look at those vases. They must be Ming Dynasty."

Ace took out his own cigarette case and held it out toward Penny. As she was removing one of the cigarettes, the butler returned.

"I'm afraid Master Wayne says that there's apparently been some sort of mix-up," he said. "We'll be glad to schedule an appointment for a future date. In the meantime, I'll be happy to give you one of our standard information packets on the Morrison foundation."

"We're not here to do a story on the Morrison Foundation," Penny said. "It's more along the lines of a profile on the rich and famous of New York's social set."

The butler stared vacuously at her.

"If I can't speak to him directly," she continued, "I'm afraid I'll just have to recycle all the stale things that have already been printed."

"It'd really be better if we could see him, if only for a

minute," Ace said.

"And tell him we're friends of Doc Atlas," Deagan said puffing copiously on the cigar. "I'm sure he's heard of him."

"Well, Master Wayne is in the middle of one of his physical training sessions," the butler said.

One of the telephones on the mantle rang twice. The butler went over and picked it up, listened, hung up the phone, and then spoke crisply the group.

"Master Wayne will see you now. However, as I said you'll have to excuse his appearance. He has been training quite vigorously. I'm afraid you'll also have to extinguish all of your smoking materials at this time. Master Wayne does not allow tobacco use in his presence."

"We're used to that," Penny said, stubbing her barely smoked cigarette out.

"Damn waste of good Cuban tobacco," Deagan said, as he blew out a large cloud of smoke, then ceremoniously dropped his cigar into a nearby flowerpot with an accompanying hiss.

The butler cocked an eyebrow at this, but he said only, "Please follow me."

"Is that portrait of Mr. Morrison's parents?" Penny asked as they passed a life-sized oil painting that was hung above a huge fireplace.

"Yes," the butler said, pausing to gaze up at it. "They were wonderful people. Master Wayne painted that himself. He's incredibly talented, don't you think?"

"I'll say," Penny said. "I never knew he could paint so well. Does he have any exhibits planned?"

"Actually, no," the butler said. "His work of late has been somewhat...bizarre in nature. Amalgamations of men and bats. Human-like forms with large, leathery wings. He says it sort of a catharsis for him. Both his parents were murdered, you know."

Penny stole a glance at Deagan and Ace.

The butler led them down a long hallway. Numerous doors stood open giving glimpses of large rooms sumptuously filled with expensive furnishings. Outside one of the rooms stood a highly polished suit of armor, the metal fingers emptily clutching a long petard. The butler stopped and gestured for them to enter.

They heard a repetitive thumping sound, and Deagan smiled. "Hey, I know what that sound is."

The room expanded into a huge gymnasium, replete with more equipment than a well-stocked YMCA. One corner housed a full set of barbells, benches, and dumbbells. Next to those were parallel bars and a set of rings suspended from the ceiling. Two thick ropes descended next to the rings, and beyond them were several types of punching bags and a full-scale boxing ring. A dark-haired man worked one of the speed bags, maintaining it in a expert-like rhythm. He was tall and broad shouldered, with well-muscled arms and a thin waist.

"Hell, this is even bigger than Doc's gym," Deagan muttered.

As they drew closer, the man stopped punching the elliptical bag and turned toward them. The workout suit spanned his muscular chest and snugly extended over his abdomen and legs. He wore a pair of boxing trunks over gray tights, which made the powerful muscles of his legs look like those of a marble statue.

"I'm Wayne Morrison," the man said, stripping off his bag-glove and extending his taped right hand. His large square jaw and grayish eyes imbued his face with an incredibly rugged handsomeness.

"I'm Penelope Cartier from the *Guardian*," she said. "Thank you for seeing us on such short notice. I'm doing an article on–"

"I heard, Miss Cartier," Morrison said. "I have a listening device installed in the foyer for security reasons." He smiled. "It often comes in handy for eavesdropping, too."

Penny flushed slightly, then said, "So I take it you make a habit of listening in on your guests' conversations, then?"

"When they're uninvited, yes," he said. "If my parents had been as careful they might still be alive. Now, as Leonard informed you, we'll be glad to give you one of our standard information packets on the Morrison Foundation."

"But if you were listening in you also know that I was hoping to get something more substantial," Penny said with her most alluring smile. "You see, I have a very demanding editor."

"I'm sorry, I don't give interviews. Now, if you'll excuse me." He turned and began to walk back toward the set of bags, slipping the glove back on his right hand.

"Why did you agree to see us then?" Penny asked, the frustration sharpening her tone.

Morrison smiled again. "Your voice, Miss Cartier. It sounded very provocative. I wanted to see what its owner looked like up close."

Her lips drew together in a frown.

"Maybe this would be a good time to tell him you once sparred with Joe Louis," Ace said to Deagan.

Deagan glanced at Ace, then called out to Morrison. "Hey, fancy-pants."

Morrison stopped and turned.

"You got an extra set of gloves?" Mad Dog asked. "Thought we might go a couple."

"Perhaps another time," Morrison said.

"What's the matter?" Deagan said, cocking his head. "Is the only sparring you do against bags that don't hit back?"

A trace of a smile crossed the rich man's lips. "Leonard, will you get a pair of gloves for Mister...I'm sorry, I didn't catch your name."

"Deagan. Thomas M. But my friends call me Mad Dog." He grinned as he slipped off his jacket.

"I don't think this is such a good idea," Penny whispered nervously.

Deagan just shrugged and began stripping off his shirt. A thick crop of dark hair spilled over the top edge of his undershirt, and although his arms looked huge and powerful, the ridge of his gut crept over his belt in places.

"Penny's right," Ace said in a low voice. "This guy's got a few years on you."

"The day I can't whip some rich candy-ass," Deagan said, letting his voice trail off. "Gimme them gloves, Roscoe."

They watched him move forward rotating his muscular arms in windmill fashion. Morrison stood a full head taller than Deagan and was at least a dozen years younger. When the two men slipped on the gloves and stepped between the ropes the size disparity became more obvious. Deagan smacked his gloves together several times and watched as Leonard secured Morrison's with tape and placed a mouth guard in the bigger man's mouth.

Assante went to the corner and motioned for Deagan to come over.

"All right, look, I'm sorry for making that crack before

about you sparring with Joe Louis," he said in a low, worried tone. "There's no need to do this. You don't have to prove anything."

"He's right," Penny said. "You could get hurt."

"Ahh," Deagan said with a dismissive growl. "We wasn't getting nowhere the other way, and this'll be a good way to watch the guy's moves. The Wraith's supposed to be pretty fast with his fists."

"Are you ready, Mr. Deagan?" Leonard, the butler asked.

"Sure am, crows feet. Let 'er rip."

The butler's lips pursed and he rang the bell at the side of the ring. Both men walked forward. In the center Morrison extended his right glove and Deagan touched it with his. Then they began circling each other.

Morrison's left speared outward and caught Deagan in the face. The jab seemed to flick out at will, bouncing off the thick brow and nose of the shorter man. Each time Deagan moved in to try and catch Morrison, the taller man would step to the side, and deliver a stinging combination. The match soon became a repetitive dance, with Deagan plodding around the ring, his face reddening under the constant pummeling. Toward the end of the round, Morrison seemed to sense they were near the three-minute mark and accelerated his pace, ending with a blistering flurry. Deagan stumbled forward to his knees, catching himself on the ropes. Morrison checked his last punch as his opponent's knees touched the canvas.

The bell sounded and Morrison asked Deagan if he'd had enough.

"Not on your life," Deagan said. "I just needed to warm up."

Morrison shrugged and strode across the ring toward his corner. The butler was there to swab off the rich man's face and give him a sip of water. Assante helped Deagan to a stool and shot a quick glance across the ring.

"That guy's as good as a pro," he said. "It'd be stupid to go on."

"I'll be all right," Deagan said with a grunt. "I think I know what I did wrong."

"What you did wrong?" Ace said. "He's using your face for a damn punching bag."

Deagan took a couple of deep breaths.

"Thomas," Penny said, "please don't fight anymore. I'm afraid he'll hurt you."

"I'll get him this round," Deagan said. He got to his feet just as Leonard rang the bell for round two.

The second round was almost a repetition of the first. Deagan made more of an attempt to cut off the ring, but was out gunned and outmaneuvered by the quicker hands and feet of Morrison. Mad Dog was able to land some body shots, in the center of the ring, but they seemed to have little effect on the younger man's chiseled abdomen. At the round's end Morrison caught Deagan with an overhand right that split open his left eyebrow. Deagan backed against the ropes and covered up as Morrison tore into him with wicked body punches. Leonard rang the bell.

"I think you've had enough," Morrison said. "Want to quit?"

"Don't know the meaning of the word," Deagan grinned. His teeth were covered with blood. He staggered back toward his corner where Ace and Penny waited with the stool. Penny took out her handkerchief and dabbed at Mad Dog's torn face.

"Oh, my God, Tom, you're bleeding," she said.

"Yeah, I kinda figured it wasn't grape juice," Deagan said. "Guess I shoulda kept up with the Carey salt, huh?"

"What can we do?" Penny asked.

"Try to squeeze it shut," Deagan said. "To stem the bleeding."

Assante used his handkerchief to administer to Deagan's torn skin. "Look," Ace said, "I've already apologized for making fun of your army boxing. There's no need to do any more of this. You've got nothing to prove."

"Are you kidding?" Deagan said. "He's starting to get tired. I can feel it. He's punching himself out."

"Another round, Mr. Deagan?" Leonard called out across the ring.

"Let's get to it," Deagan yelled back. He stood, blood still streaming from his gaping eyebrow, and smacked his gloves together again.

"That's the only thing he's been able to hit," Assante said in a worried tone.

"Oh, Ace, can't you do something to stop him?" Penny

asked.

"You know Mad Dog," he replied.

The two combatants quickly made it to center ring, but instead of plodding after Morrison this time, Deagan stood in the center with his gloves elevated. Morrison, who'd been very effective dancing away from Deagan's previous advances, seemed momentarily confused. He shot out two quick jabs, both of which bounced off Deagan's bloody face, and danced away. But instead of following after the aggressor, Deagan stood in the center. Morrison moved in again, and this time Deagan was able to block both jabs and then cut to his right as Morrison danced away. Morrison threw two more series of jabs, but each time he retreated afterwards, Deagan moved laterally and cut off the ring.

Finally, the younger man felt his back against the ropes and Deagan stepped in like a fury, throwing every conceivable punch, the powerful body blows making a distinctive thwacking sound. Morrison instinctively lowered his arms to shield his sides. Deagan switched his punches upstairs and landed a vicious one-two to Morrison's head. Another left to the body and Morrison's knees sagged slightly. Sensing the kill, Deagan suddenly seemed to double his speed. His mouth was hanging open now, like a man sucking in air as he ran the low hurdles. Deagan smashed a looping right to Morrison's temple and watched him stiffen.

"Say good night, Gracie," Deagan said, as the other man toppled face first to the canvas.

Leonard crammed his linear body between the ropes with amazing agility and immediately ran across to the fallen rich man. The butler knelt down and checked Morrison's eyes, then he stood and stepped toward Deagan. His eyes narrowed as he stared at Mad Dog's face, then the butler said, "Mr. Deagan, I believe you are going to need stitches for the wound on your brow. Would you care for me to do that? We have an excellent medical room here at the manor."

Deagan wiped at his face and looked at the glove.

"Nah," he said. "Thanks, but Doc Atlas is the only person I'll let stitch me up."

"I assure you that Leonard is quite capable along those lines," Morrison said, rolling over on one elbow and glancing up at Deagan. "Good match, Mr. Deagan. You punch like a mule."

"He sparred with Joe Louis when he was in the service," said Assante, who'd stepped into the ring and began unlacing Deagan's gloves. "And I officially declare this match over with. That cut needs some attention."

"Oh, I'll be all right," Deagan said.

"At least allow me to apply a butterfly bandage to hold you on your drive back to the city, sir," Leonard said.

"Guys," Penny said, holding up Deagan's jacket. The pocket was emitting a periodic beeping signal.

"That's Doc's special miniature wireless receiver," Deagan said. "It's his way of contacting us if he wants us to call HQ right away. Can I use your phone?"

"Certainly," Morrison said. He was on his feet again, bouncing on his toes, and hardly looking any worse for the wear. "There's an extension in the other room. Leonard, would you show Mr. Deagan the phone."

"Perhaps I can get that butterfly bandage also, sir," Leonard said curtly. He handed Deagan his handkerchief and stepped through the ropes. Deagan followed. They walked across the gymnasium to the door, which Leonard opened. The room they entered was a study, containing several chairs and various large bookcases. The butler gave Deagan a moist towel and then pointed to a telephone on a massive desk. Deagan nodded and rolled the bloody handkerchief into a ball.

"If you'll excuse me, I'll obtain some antiseptic and the bandage," Leonard said. He went quickly out of the room. Deagan waited until the butler had gone, then picked up the receiver. He dialed the number for Doc's office. It rang three times before it was answered by a familiar female voice.

"Dr. Atlas's office, may I help you?"

"Hey, sweetie," Deagan said, recognizing Polly's voice immediately. "It's me. I got the signal. What's up?"

"Doc called from the police station," she said, as if reciting a message by rote. "He said he's tied up there right now, but he wants you guys to come back for a briefing, then go pick up the girl who was kidnapped by that gang of thugs last night and rescued by the Wraith."

"Doc called from where?" Deagan asked, interrupting her.

"Some police station in Brooklyn," she said, somewhat annoyed. "Now don't interrupt me before I finish."

"Sorry," Deagan said. "I been hearing some bells ringing."

"What? I don't hear them."

"Never mind," Deagan said. "What's her address and what time we supposed to get her?"

Polly dispatched the rest of the information in her nasal tone. "Doc said he'll give it to you when you get back to HQ. He also wants you to call some of your military contacts to check on the service records of the people on the list, but he says you can do it all after dinner."

"Yeah, okay," Deagan said. "Anything else?"

"Yeah. Are we still going to the show tonight?" she added. "There's a Danny Kaye movie at the Empire."

"Well, we'll have see," Deagan said, dabbing the towel to his face and checking the amount of blood on it. "If there aren't any bad guys to catch." He checked the crimson spots on the towel again. "I'll see you later, baby."

"Okay, sweetie," Polly said. "Bye."

Deagan lowered the receiver, then quickly brought it back up to his ear in time to hear a distinct click. He lowered the phone to its cradle and turned in time to see Leonard return holding a bottle of astringent, a gauze pad, and some bandages. The butler paused in the face of Deagan's stare.

"Is everything all right, sir?" Leonard asked.

You oughta know, pal, he thought. "Yeah. Perfect," Deagan replied. "Just perfect."

8

Beautiful Dreamer

DEAGAN looked at his reflection in the rear-vision mirror when they came to a stop light on the edge of the city. The afternoon traffic was reasonably heavy, and the sun had begun to cast a lingering glow through the western skyline. He smirked and pointed his big index finger at the butterfly bandage Leonard had expertly taped in place.

"That butler did a pretty good job, don't you think?" he said.

"Considering what he had to work with," Assante said.

He glanced at the traffic light, then back to his reflection. "No, I mean this set-up looks as good as something I woulda got when I was fighting."

"I was referring to your mug," Ace said, grinning. "It was probably like trying to bandage a sow's ear to make it look like a silk purse."

"Ace, will you stop?" Penny was seated between them again, and had no desire to be in the middle of another one of their good-natured arguments. Turning to Deagan she asked, "How you feeling, Mad Dog?"

"As if my mug's been through a meat grinder," Deagan quipped. "Like I said before, guess I shoulda kept up with the Carey Salt treatments."

"What you should have done was not make a fool of

yourself by getting involved in that ridiculous boxing match in the first place," Ace said caustically.

"Well, it was worth it, wasn't it?" Deagan shot back. "We know for sure that that guy ain't the Wraith."

"How so?" Penny asked.

"Well I knocked him out with one good one." Deagan smiled as if re-living the final punch sequence in his mind. "I mean, I'm pretty powerful, but I still wonder if the real Wraith would've caved in so easily. The guy's no push-over."

"Oh, I don't know," Ace said, grinning. "I got the impression that Morrison let you win."

"Whaddaya mean?" Deagan's jaw jutted outward. "That guy's a pansy."

"Well," Ace shot back, "that pansy obviously felt sorry for you that he allowed you to knock him down so you could save face."

"You're full of crap," Deagan said, then added, "Sorry, Penny."

"Oh, I agree with you," she said. "Ace, Mad Dog cleaned that guy's clock all right." She gave Assante's left leg a surreptitious little kick.

"Well, you also have to take into account that Wayne Morrison is no Joe Louis," Ace said, his tone lilting with sarcasm. "Although at times in the ring today, I thought he was making you look like Tony Two-Ton Galento."

Deagan snorted as he took the LaSalle through the gear sequence. Then he said, "Still, there's something fishy about that guy."

"You're right about that," Ace said. "That listening device in his foyer. What normal person would have something like that?"

"Well," Penny said, "playing the devil's advocate, you also should remember that his parents were viciously murdered."

"True." Ace smoothed his mustache. "That has to affect someone, especially if it occurs at such a young age."

"That Leonard's a weird one, too, ain't he?" Deagan said. "How many butlers know how to be corner cut men and could stitch a guy up, or put on a butterfly bandage?"

"Perhaps he was just being nice to you, hoping you'd return for a re-match so he can get more practice," Ace said with a grin, throwing a couple of mock jabs at the windshield. "Probably save wear and tear on his punching bags."

"You oughta be on the Fred Allen Show," Deagan said. "Then I could shut you off." Ace frowned. "Anyway, I'm sure that butler was listening in on an extension when I called the office, too."

"Well, all things considered," Penny said, "I'm not so sure we can scratch him from our list. Any ideas on the guys we've checked so far?"

Assante sighed. "I'd say we can eliminate Frasier Clark and the priest for sure."

"I don't know about Gisseppi," Deagan said. "And what about Casper, Vernon, and Milton? As far as I'm concerned, it could be any one of them guys."

"Hardly," Ace said. "They're all officers of the court. They all have too much respect for the law to circumvent it."

"Yeah, well remember that Shakespeare quote." Deagan's face cracked into a grin, and the expression made him wince.

"Poetic justice," Ace said, noticing the reaction. He smiled slightly.

"Oh, you think it's funny, huh?" Deagan said. His tone was becoming more and more belligerent.

"Guys, please," Penny said, crossing her arms.

"So you still sticking to your theory that it's Morrison then?" Deagan asked.

"I keep an open mind until I examine all the evidence."

"Well I'd be willing to bet my next pension check that it ain't him."

"Maybe you should wait till all the bells in your head have stopped ringing before you make a statement like that," Ace said with understated derision.

"Guys, please," Penny said. "Let's just ride the rest of the way in peace, okay? My head's starting to ring from all this arguing. If I didn't know better, I'd swear that you two fellows weren't friends."

"Friends!" Deagan said. "Us?"

"Ha!" Ace snorted.

But both of them had wide grins on their faces.

As soon as Doc spotted Deagan's cut eyebrow he strode forward and examined the wound. He removed a small, but powerful flashlight from his pocket and shone it over Mad Dog's face.

"This bandage looks expertly applied, but you are going to need some stitches," Doc said. "How did this happen, Thomas?"

"It's kind of a long story, Doc."

"We were trying to gather some intelligence on Wayne Morrison and Mad Dog decided to try and use his head," Ace said. "To knock on a few doors."

Doc showed no reaction to the quip. He spoke to Assante and Penny over his shoulder. "Why don't you two go in the dining room while I stitch this up. Thomas, we need to do that immediately before it spreads anymore."

"Yeah, but I gotta take a shower and change, too," Deagan said. "I promised to take Polly to the movies tonight."

"Good idea." Ace said with a grin. "About the shower, I mean."

"Why is it you always try to get the last word?" Deagan said over his shoulder as Doc led him into the infirmary, which was adjacent to the foyer by the elevators.

Ace and Penny walked down the hall toward the dining room area. Penny laid her steno pad on the table and went to the window. Assante followed and took out his cigarette case. After offering her one and lighting it, he stuck one in his own mouth and stared out the window at the skyline.

"So what's your intuition tell you about this?" he asked.

"It's too early to tell, but I do know one thing," she said, as the smoke trailed upward from her slightly parted lips. "It's going to make one hell of a story."

"Maybe you'll get another Pulitzer." Ace silently admired her fine profile as she exhaled another cloudy breath. A fleeting glimpse of the times they'd shared danced through his memory. Had it meant something to her? Or had he just been a lark to get closer to Doc? She had one arm crossed under her full breasts, the other drooping down, holding the smoldering cigarette.

"So why did you ask me before how I'd been?" he said suddenly.

She turned toward him, her blue eyes staring into his. She looked about to answer when Polly came barging in. Her head turned as she surveyed the room.

"Okay, I give up," she said. "Where is he?"

"He's in the infirmary getting stitched up," Ace said. "He

sustained a slight cut on his eyebrow during a heroic venture."

"Goodness," Polly said, the space between her eyebrows furrowing slightly. "Is he all right?"

"Mad Dog's the toughest man I know," Ace said, smiling. "No need to worry about him, but I'm sure he'd like to know you were worried."

Polly's mouth drew into a tight line and she turned abruptly and left. Ace turned back to Penny and was about to speak when she reached out and touched his hand.

"Please..." she said softly, "don't ask."

"What did you learn today in the interviews?" Doc asked, leaning back with his after-dinner cup of coffee.

Penny flipped open her steno pad and read a summary of all their meetings that day. Assante and Deagan shaded the accounts with their opinions. Polly, whom Doc had invited to dine with them, seemed to hang on Deagan's every word. When Penny came to the part about the impromptu boxing match between Mad Dog and Morrison, Doc frowned slightly.

"I've already heard about that one," he said.

"But this time, would you like to hear the real story?" Ace said with a grin.

Mad Dog flushed a deep crimson, but said nothing. Doc had put a bandage over the expanse of stitches, which, along with the incremental swelling, gave Deagan's face a brutish look.

"So by my account," Penny said, closing her pad, "the only person on the list we haven't had a chance to talk to yet, is Detective Sergeant Hal Roland."

"You needn't bother with him just yet," Doc said. "I met him today."

"Think he's our man, Doc?" Deagan asked.

"It's hard to say at this point," Doc said. "I've been devoting most of my mental energy to thinking about the Grantman kidnapping. But I do have this inexplicable feeling that the two cases are somehow related, that there's some common thread we're missing."

"Roland does have the reputation of being one tough cop," Ace said.

"And he does his best to live up to it," Doc said. "Regardless, the man's an exceptional shot with a pistol, and harbors a great antipathy toward the criminal element, both of which correlate with our profile of the Wraith."

"Pistol shot?" Penny asked curiously. "Exactly what were the circumstances of this meeting?"

Doc briefly recounted the events in the hotel beginning with the assassination of Ira Bloom and ending with the subsequent shootings.

"Roland was most adamant about not letting me examine the bodies of the hoodlums," Doc said. "Something I want you to work on tomorrow, Ace."

"I'll get on it first thing," Assante said.

"And I'd better go call this stuff in," Penny said, scribbling frantically on her pad. "That story about the hotel shootout is dynamite."

"As soon as you finish," Doc said, "I would appreciate it if you went with Vincent and Thomas to pick up the Hernandez girl. I'd like to interview her without further delay."

Maria Hernandez lived in a three-flat brownstone on the fringes of Spanish Harlem. The area was composed largely of Puerto Ricans, Mexicans, and various other immigrants who all shared Spanish as their primary language. The bank in which Maria worked was one of the smaller branch affiliates that had sprung up in response to the massive repopulation of the city. Now that all the men were coming back from the War, and desiring veterans' loans to buy houses, small banks were popping up everywhere. It was still a long bus-ride away from the area where she lived. After Maria's ordeal during and after the robbery, Penny wondered if the poor girl would feel safe working there again, much less riding public transportation to and from work.

"Do you think Doc will be able to help her?" Penny asked as Deagan pulled the LaSalle to a stop in front of the building.

"I've seen him do some amazing things," Ace said. "Mad Dog, why don't you wait in the car. Penny and I will go up alone." He opened the door and slid out, holding it open for Penny. "I mean, the poor girl's been through enough. There's no sense scaring her with your mug, especially in its most recent incarnation."

He slammed the door and grinned, but they'd only gone a few steps when Deagan called to them.

Penny and Ace turned to see Deagan leaning out of the rolled down passenger side window.

"This is for him, Penny," Deagan said. He stuck out his tongue and emitted a loud Bronx cheer.

"My," Ace said, walking away. "You are trying to expand your limited vocabulary, aren't you?"

"You don't fool me for a minute," Penny said as they were walking up the steps. "You two guys really love each other."

"Oh, *please*," Ace said with exaggerated emphasis. He pulled open the outside door and scanned the listings. After pressing the appropriate bell, they were buzzed in, and walked up to the second floor. The steps were covered with a worn, green carpeting that was threadbare in many places. Ace raised his hand to knock on the door, but it swung open suddenly and a heavy-set woman stared at them with dark, questioning eyes.

"Hello," Penny said. "I'm Penelope Cartier and this is Mr. Assante. We've come to speak with Maria."

The woman continued to stare at them, then furrowed her brows slightly. "You come see Maria?" she asked in halting English. "Son policias?"

"Senora," Assante said. He smiled and began talking to the woman in flawless Spanish, explaining who they were, and what their intentions were. The woman seemed to relax slightly at the explanation in her native tongue. She asked what appeared to Penny to be a serious question.

"*Claro, senora*," Ace said. "*La aseguro, a usted.*"

The woman smiled and nodded. She disappeared from the doorway and Penny said, "I'm impressed. I didn't know you spoke Spanish."

"Actually I majored in romance languages before I went into law," Ace said. "I kept up with my Spanish in case I was ever shot down over German lines, I could claim to be related to General Franco."

"So what was that last comment?" Penny asked.

"She's obviously worried about her daughter's safety," he said, "but I told her to trust me."

Penny smiled and was about to say that many a mother had probably heard that line before, when the woman brought Maria to the door. They were both struck by her beauty, but also at how vulnerable she appeared. Her face had a tired and drawn look, and her eyes, like those of a frightened bird, flashed to each of their faces.

"Hello," Penny said, extending her hand. "We spoke earlier about taking you to see Doc Atlas."

"Yes," Maria said. "I'm ready." She did not look at Assante after the initial introduction, and once, when his hand accidentally brushed her arm as they went down the stairs, he felt her shudder.

Doc's got his work cut out for him with this one, Ace thought.

"Perhaps, Miss Hernandez, you would care for a glass of wine?" Doc said as they walked into his lavishly furnished waiting room. The girl nodded and Doc asked Assante to pour her a glass. "If you'll excuse me for a moment, I will prepare the other room."

He left as Ace got three glasses and handed one to Penny and another to Maria. He noticed she wouldn't meet his gaze as he poured some of the rich red wine into her glass. He poured a glass for himself and sat next to Penny on the sofa. An awkward silence descended upon the room. Deagan stood in the corner silently puffing on one of his huge cigars. A few minutes later Doc, now wearing his white doctor-style shirt, stepped back into the waiting room.

"If you'll step this way, please, Miss Hernandez," he said, holding the door to his infirmary open. Maria rose rather hesitantly and walked over to him.

"Would you feel more comfortable with Miss Cartier with you?" Doc asked.

She nodded and Penny stood and walked over to Maria. They went inside the room and Doc had Maria sit in a comfortable chair near the door. He pulled a regular wooden chair close in front of her.

"I know this has been difficult for you, Miss Hernandez, but, if I may, I would like to question you about the incident concerning your abduction."

"Do I have to?" Maria asked, turning her face downward. "I've already told the police everything I can remember."

"Sometimes," Doc said gently, "we can recall more through a recounting of the episode while under hypnosis. I know this is very hard for you, but often the process is very beneficial."

"Are you saying you could make me remember more?" Her head turned away. "All I want to do is forget."

"Then let me try to help you," Doc said. "Lean back and relax, and concentrate on this beam." He removed a small flashlight and shined it in front of Maria's face. "Follow the beam with your eyes." His voice was steady and mesmerizing.

Maria's dark eyes traced the movement of the light until it became only a sight oscillation. Doc continued talking to her until finally he told her that she was getting very tired. So tired that she was falling asleep. "Begin counting to ten," he said. "By the time you reach five, you will be asleep, but you'll still be able to hear my voice when I speak to you."

At three her head lolled back against the cushion. Folding his hands, Doc studied her momentarily, then, satisfied Maria was completely under, he rose silently and opened the door to the waiting room. Deagan and Assante quietly entered and stood next to Penny.

"Pay particular attention to the details she gives us about the Wraith," Doc said to them. "It may give us a valuable clue. Let's see what information she can provide us." He turned back to the slumbering girl. Her breathing was coming evenly and heavily.

"Maria," Doc said. "Can you hear me?"

"Yes." Her voice sounded slightly disjointed.

"Good, I want you to recount everything, step by step, about your abduction this morning, starting when you first saw the men enter the bank. The scene is unfolding before you like a movie. You'll describe everything you see and hear."

In a steady voice she described the crime: the three men came in with dark handkerchiefs tied over their faces. They pointed their guns at the tellers and demanded money. While two of them filled up their large canvas bag, the other one ordered all the women to step out from behind the counter. After looking at everyone, the man told Maria to step forward. "He says that the boss will be pleased," she said dreamily.

"The boss?" Doc asked. "Are those the exact words he used?"

"Yes," she answered.

The rest of the robbery was quick and brutal. One of the tellers was pistol whipped for not getting into the vault fast enough. When the bank guard tried to protest, the man with the crinkled-looking skin around the eyes shot him.

"That would be Calson," Doc said to the others. "His face was severely scarred by burns. Now, Maria, while you were being transported to the warehouse, do you recall any names?"

She took a deep breath before answering.

"One is called Weasel," she said. "They also call him Rodney to make him angry."

"Any other names?"

"Yes. They keep mentioning someone named Casey."

Doc's eyes narrowed.

Maria went on. "One asks if they should take me to Casey's first. Before they split up the money."

"And what was the reply?"

"The one with the deep voice, the big man, he said not yet."

Methodically Maria recounted the rest of it. Her brutal manhandling by the thugs immediately prior to the attempted rape, the mention of body parts, the song, and the rescue.

"The song?" Doc asked. "What song?"

"The song he whistled," she said. "The man who rescued me."

"Do you know this song?"

"It's…" her voice trailed off and she took another deep breath. "I know the song, but I can't remember the name of it."

"Can you reproduce it for me?" Doc asked. "Sing it, or hum it?"

Maria swallowed and then began humming the melody. It

was familiar sounding to each of them.

"Hum it again, Maria."

She did, and the melody became clearer.

"Isn't that…'Beautiful Dreamer?'" Penny whispered. Doc glanced at her and nodded.

"Maria, I want you to look at the man who was whistling the song," Doc said. "You see him very clearly now. Describe what he looks like."

"He's big, and dressed all in black. He's wearing something over his face. It looks like a mask, but you can see through it. Like a veil. Under it, his face is dark and terribly twisted."

"What else does the man do?" Doc asked.

"He picks up my crucifix and gives it to me," she said. "At first I think he's going to hurt me, but he doesn't. He hands me my clothes and takes me to another room. Then he tells me to stay there, and to call the police. There's a phone, and I call them."

"Maria," Doc said. "You're going to begin counting to ten. When you reach five you will be wide awake. But first you'll take all the bad memories of what happened today and put them in a special drawer in your mind. You'll file this special drawer away and not be able to remember any of those bad things unless I specifically ask you. Nothing that happened to you during the abduction will frighten you anymore, and you'll awake feeling refreshed and happy. Do you understand?"

"Yes," she said.

"Good. Now begin counting."

When Maria came to, she blinked several times, then sat up, looking around the room, at each of their faces. Then a perplexed expression crossed her face.

"Was I of any help?" she asked, smiling. "I seem to have dozed off and can't remember anything. But I feel so...wonderful."

"You were a great help," Doc said. "My associates will take you home now." He smiled benevolently.

Deagan and Ace rose simultaneously. Penny got up and grabbed Maria by the arm.

"We'll be with you in a minute, boys," she said. "Come on, let's go powder our noses first."

The men watched them go. Doc got up and moved to the desk and began scribbling notes about the session. He seemed deep in thought. Deagan stared at him for a moment, then nudged Assante, indicating for him to move back into the waiting room. When they were alone, Mad Dog said in a hushed voice, "What's your thinking on this?"

"What do you mean?"

"You know," Deagan's big face twisted into a pensive frown, "I hate to say it, but after listening to what she told us, I ain't so sure that this Wraith guy didn't do anything that I wouldn't have done."

Ace nodded grimly. "Me either."

MELODY OF VENGEANCE

9

The Question Mark

THE elevator doors closed and the car began its stomach-wrenching express ride back to Doc's personal floor. Penny lit a cigarette and stuck the lighter back in her purse, a little unsure as to exactly why she was feeling so angry. It had started when the three of them left to take Maria home. Deagan had used his special key to stop the express elevator at Doc's office section, one floor below, so he could pick up Polly. She'd already closed the office and had been finishing up some special assignments that Doc had asked her to complete. When the doors opened she was there, and in her usual boisterous manner had blurted about going to the movies.

Ace, who'd been chatting in Spanish with Maria, said something and the girl replied, "Oh, I just love Danny Kaye." That was enough for loudmouth Polly to invite her and Ace to join them.

Penny blew out twin clouds of smoke through her nose, and thought cynically of the way Maria pronounced it: "Dahny Key." That little Mexican tart. And Ace fawning up to her like that. They'd probably end up in bed together before the intermission. But then, she thought suddenly, why should it matter to her, anyway? He was entitled, wasn't he?

She stared at the envelope Clyde O'Bannion, the head doorman, had asked her to give to Doc. Just a plain white one without any postage. A ruler had obviously been used as a border to print out the block letters TO DOC ATLAS on the front. She shrugged, and took a few more quick puffs on her cigarette before the elevator got to the top. At least, she thought, tonight I'll be alone with Doc. For a while. She took one more drag on the cigarette and stubbed it out in the elevator's ashtray.

When the doors opened she walked into the foyer and rang the buzzer. Presently Doc came to the door, raising his eyebrows at her presence.

"That was a rather quick trip," he said, standing aside so she could enter his office area. "Where are the others?"

"They decided to double-date." Penny noticed Doc's gaze on the envelope in her hand. She held it toward him. "Here, the doorman said someone dropped this off for you."

Doc took the envelope, handling it carefully. He held it to the light, trying to read through the opaqueness of the paper. Unable to do so, he went to his desk and extracted a letter opener. The edge had been honed to razor-sharpness, and Doc slid the point under the lip of the flap. He cautiously cut it open, still handling the envelope rather gingerly. Then, he

dumped the contents out on the desktop.

A three-by-five white index card fluttered out, landing face down. Doc used the point of the letter opener to flip over the card. His eyes widened slightly as he read the message, which was printed in the same, block-style writing as the envelope.

Penny, who'd been staring from the other side of the desk, looked from the card to his face.

"Oh, my God," she said. "Do you think it's from him?"

"I'm not sure," he said. "Come on. Let's go talk to O'Bannion."

Clyde O'Bannion had been the captain of the doormen for at least a dozen years. He was a big, barrel-chested Irishman who took pride in his job, and did his utmost to maintain the security of the building. He constantly walked the huge, five-story lobby.

"Well, Dr. Atlas, I was just getting ready to lock the doors and let the night shift take over," he said. "I wouldn't have even been here this time a night, but that damn Pinkerton called in late on me. I'm going to have to do something about that fella. Too undependable. You'd think that he could manage to hold a simple job like sweeping up inside the building, wouldn't you?"

Doc frowned slightly. He'd viewed Pinkerton as one of his successful rehabilitations from his upstate clinic. But even before the operation, the man had an intellect so retarded that any progress toward normalcy seemed impressive.

"Could you describe the man who gave you the envelope addressed to me?" Doc asked.

"Well," O'Bannion said, scratching his chin. "Let me see. I thought he was a bit on the strange side, being all dressed up in a long overcoat and wide-brimmed hat, the weather being as warm as it's been. Dark glasses on too, even though the sun's been down a good long time."

"Did he have any other distinguishing features?"

O'Bannion ran his tongue over his teeth.

"He had himself a great black beard and mustache," O'Bannion raised a bushy eyebrow, "but I had a suspicion that the hair wasn't really his."

"How big a man was he?" Doc asked. "And how old?"

"He was a good-sized man. Nowhere near as big as yourself, of course," O'Bannion said with a quick smile. "A bit taller than me. Now, seeing as how he was all bundled up, I couldn't really tell how old a man he was."

"Could you tell anything about his voice? Did he sound like a New Yorker?"

Again O'Bannion smiled.

"Well, seeing as how I don't sound much like your typical New Yorker, either," he said with a grin. "But, no, he had a rather gruff-sounding voice. Just said, 'Could you please see that Doc Atlas gets this?' Polite, he was. Then he shoved the envelope and a dollar bill in my hand, and turned and walked off. A whole dollar just to deliver a letter when he could've let the postal service do it for three pennies."

"How about his hands?" Doc asked. "Anything distinguishing? Rings? Scars?"

"That was another strange thing," O'Bannion said, the space between his eyebrows wrinkling. "The man was wearing a pair of tight leather gloves"

Doc's expression showed no change. "Through which doors did he exit?"

O'Bannion pursed his lips and stared up at the immense metallic mosaic that depicted the Empire State Building. "That I do remember. It was over there. The one underneath the electricity emblem." He pointed across the capacious lobby toward the gold plate set into the fine-grained marble wall above the exit way. "Say, Doc, I didn't do anything wrong by accepting that letter, did I?"

"Of course not, Clyde," Doc said, giving the doorman's shoulder a friendly squeeze. "If you see him around here again, give me a call on the phone, all right?"

"I sure will, Doc," he said, then leaning close, whispered, "My relief's here now, but do you want I should stay on here a while longer in case the man comes back?"

"No." Do's gaze drifted toward the glass doors and the nighttime street beyond. "I don't think he'll be back. At least not tonight. Go home and spend some time with your family."

On the way back up in the elevator Penny looked up at him, his chiseled profile deep in concentration, his lips drawn into a thin line.

"Do you think it was him?" she asked.

"It fits his profile," Doc said. "And obviously, we've stirred something up. But the Wraith isn't usually this obtrusive."

Upon arriving at his floor, Doc went inside his apartment and picked up the telephone. He dialed a number and listened. After a moment Penny heard him say, "May I speak to Detective Roland, please."

"He ain't in," the voice on the other end of the line said. "This is Detective Belson. Anything I can help you with?"

"This is Doctor Michael Atlas. I was with Roland this afternoon. He told me to call him back."

"The Doc Atlas?" Belson asked incredulously. "Well, sir, Hal took off for the night."

"May I ask how long has he been gone? I was certain he told me to call him at the precinct this evening."

"Jeez, he left outta here at least an hour ago," Belson said.

133

"I could try him at home if it's real important. Otherwise, he'll be back in the morning."

"I see," Doc said. "Could I just leave a message to have him get in touch with me tomorrow?" He read off the standard phone number for his headquarters.

"Not in, eh?" Penny asked as Doc hung up the phone.

He shook his head.

"So, the message…. You think it was Roland who left it?" Her eyes flashed with excitement. "Is he the Wraith?"

"It's hard to say at this point," Doc answered. He motioned for her to follow him toward the lab section. "It could be just a coincidence that the message was delivered after he left work. But whoever delivered it took elaborate means not to be recognized. This suggests several possibilities, among them that it was someone with whom we've made previous contact. Roland's certainly been gone long enough from his precinct to don a disguise and make a quick trip over here. I suspect that if we looked, we'd find the disguise in some alley trash container close to this building."

"Careful guy," Penny said. "But I know you'll get him."

"Eventually," Doc said. He opened the door to the lab and stepped back so she could enter first.

Inside Doc went to a long table and set up a special glass case inside a fuming hood. He took the envelope and card and, using tweezers, placed them both on a wire holder assembly inside the glass. After securing them in place, Doc slipped on a pair of rubber gloves and safety glasses and mixed up a solution of ninhydrin and ether. He placed the mixture in a specially designed canister and set it inside the glass case. After attaching a long, cylindrical tube to the rubber nipple on top of the canister, Doc closed the lid, allowing the end of the long tube to protrude through a specially designed opening. He took a deep breath then blew steadily into the tube. Wisps of steam-like tendrils swirled from the canister and began to bring out the delicate ridges of the fingerprints on the envelope. One set of whirls was noticeably smaller than the other.

"Those are, in all probably, yours," Doc said to Penny. "The larger ones most likely belong to O'Bannion."

She stared at the rapidly delineating lines in amazement. "I've never seen that done before."

Doc smiled slightly.

"The vapors adhere to the residual oils left by the fingertips," he said, looking carefully at the card. It remained clear. "Unfortunately, it looks like the only prints that are present were on the envelope. And, as I said, those are probably yours and O'Bannion's."

"Darn," Penny said.

"I expected as much. But in any case–" The abrupt ringing of the telephone interrupted. He stripped off the gloves, went to a nearby table, and picked up one of the many extensions. "Good evening," he said.

"Atlas?" a frantic voice said. "Is that you?"

"Yes. Who is this?"

"It's Randolph Grantman. That madman just called."

Grantman's tone was abrupt and desperate sounding.

"One moment, please," Doc said. He reached down and twisted a lever on the base of the instrument then plugged in the wire to a small speaker device next to the telephone. He set the receiver back in the cradle and Grantman's next words came over the speaker.

"What did you say?" the voice boomed.

"Go on with what you were saying, Mr. Grantman," Doc

said calmly.

"That fiend, the Wraith. He's got my daughter." The man's voice sounded a mere decibel away from a scream.

"Sir, calm down," Doc said. He waited a few seconds, then added, "Now, tell me what exactly did he say?"

"Here, I've got the whole damn thing on this blasted wire recorder." They heard noises interspersed with Grantman's heavy breathing. It became more sonorous as he evidently fiddled with the knobs of the machine. "Okay, here it is. Listen."

After a few seconds of static, they heard the ringing of a telephone, after which Grantman could be heard saying hello. He said hello again, and then an eerie voice, obviously disguised, came over the receiver. "Grantman, I have your daughter."

"What? Who is this? What do you want?"

"What do I want?" the voice said. A heavy, humorless chuckle sounded, then, "I will tell you in due time."

"Look, I demand to know who I'm speaking to," Grantman said. "How do I know this isn't some crackpot?"

The questions were met with momentary silence, then the voice spoke again.

"I have her, Grantman, and if you don't want to receive her back in the mail, piece-by-piece, you'd better do exactly what I tell you. Do you understand?"

"Good lord, yes, but–"

"Shut up and listen. I will be contacting you soon with further instructions. Be ready."

"Wait. Who is this?"

"This is the Wraith," the voice said gruffly, then the line went dead. Grantman came back on.

"Did you hear?" he asked.

"Yes," Doc said. "Have you contacted Special Agent Efrem?"

"He's on the way," Grantman said. "What should I do, Atlas? Do you think he means to harm Bonnie?"

"Presumptions at this point can only be counterproductive," Doc said. "As difficult as it seems, the best thing to do now is to wait. Agent Efrem will know what to do, and I assure you, I'm working on a few things from this end, as well. But we must remain calm."

It took Doc a few more minutes to reassure the man before terminating the conversation. After he'd hung up Penny looked at him and said, "Wow. Now what?"

Doc lips compressed into a thin line once more as he obviously contemplated his answer very carefully. "I'm not sure. Something's been bothering me about this case," he said. "Dancing on the edge of memory. I'm not sure what it is, but I'm certain there's something I've overlooked, especially now that the two cases have seemingly overlapped."

"I'm sure you'll think of it," she said, softly running her fingers over his forearm. "You probably just need to…relax a little."

He glanced down at her caress, his features showing no change or emotion.

"Why don't you wait for me in the living room," he said. "I'm going to put these items away and properly dispose of these chemicals."

After Penny had left, Doc removed the card and envelope from the glass case and placed them in manila envelopes. He went to a cabinet and removed a paper bag, which contained the remnants of his ruined jacket and sorted through them.

Using tweezers, he retrieved K.C. Edgar's business card from the outside right pocket. Doc quickly placed the card inside the glass case and watched as the patterns of an index finger and thumb appeared on opposite sides of the card. After removing the card, Doc used special clear tape to preserve the prints. He spent a moment classifying each one according to the standard designations, then drafted a brief note to Polly requesting she run the classifications through the FBI tomorrow for an identification check. He then took the ninhydrin-ether solution and carefully poured it in a special waste container. After stowing the protective clothing and gloves, the final thing he did was to wash his hands very thoroughly. When he went into the living room he saw Penny standing by the picture window, staring out over the buildings below, a cigarette smoldering between her fingers. Doc stopped by the liquor cabinet and withdrew a glass and some fine brandy. After pouring some into the glass he moved silently to her side.

"I thought you might like some of this," he said, handing her the snifter.

"Thank you," she said, taking a sip. She extinguished her cigarette in an ashtray, looking up at him with a guilty expression. Then, her gaze returned to the window. "This is so beautiful. You can see all the way to the Hudson from up here."

He nodded.

"The water looks so pretty at night, doesn't it?" she said, touching the glass to her lips again. "All those reflected points of light. It's almost as if the stars had magically settled down on the city."

"That's very poetic," he said. "I've never quite thought of it that way."

"Oh, look what I found," Penny said, still holding the snifter, she grabbed his hand and led him over to the baby-grand piano on the other side of the room. "I found the sheet music in the bench." She sat at the piano and placed the glass on the top of the instrument. After adjusting the sheet music, she began playing "Beautiful Dreamer."

"It says here that this was the last song written by Stephen Foster before his death in eighteen sixty-four," she said, continuing to play. "Written only hours before he died."

Doc listened as the notes ascended the scale and coalesced into the familiar melody.

"Actually, it's believed that the song was really penned in eighteen sixty-two," he said. "That rather maudlin epigram was promulgated by his publishers to capitalize on his demise."

"How did he die?"

"His last years were troubled by alcoholism and poverty," Doc said. "He was penniless and being treated at Bellevue Hospital here in New York. He died of a severe laceration to the neck."

"Oh, my god," Penny said, her fingers still moving over the keys. "That sounds as though he killed himself."

"It's a distinct possibility. He was alone in his hotel room in the Bowery when they found him."

"If you listen to the lyrics, the song almost sounds like a death elegy, doesn't it?" she said. "Why do you think the Wraith was whistling it?"

"When we find that out," Doc said, "we'll have a pretty good idea who he actually is."

She finished the notes of the last stanza and then let her hand drift upward to close over his. The half-empty snifter stood on the top of the piano between them. Standing, Penny stepped around the end of the keyboard and kissed him softly. "Alone at last," she whispered.

The moonlight streamed through the partially open Venetian blinds, and Penny's thoughts lingered on how long it had been since they'd been together like this. *Too long.* Suddenly, nothing else in the world mattered more than being with him at this moment. She glanced down at Doc, his face partially covered by slats of darkness. As she looked at him, her breathing quickened, and she quickly leaned forward, placing her mouth on his, her tongue darting. A rush of air blew in through the open windows, stirring the blinds and the accompanying shadows. Penny got a quick glimpse of the amber-colored eyes as they fluttered open with a sudden start, accompanied by an involuntary tremor in his neck. As she looked into them she sensed a distance, an odd detachment, something almost clinical, in his gaze. All at once she wondered, even though their bodies were together, if he was thinking of her, or was his mind off somewhere pursuing an elusive wraith?

1o

Whistling in the Dark

Ⓣ𝐇𝐄 lighted, sequined globe above the bar twisted like a spinning top, sending a myriad of stunning colors over the stripper's body. Leo Burke paused on his way upstairs to watch her for a moment. She was one of the new girls, and even through the haze of cigarette smoke Leo could see she was well endowed. Very well endowed, indeed, and she'd just begun the slow undulations of her shoulders that started the tassels on her pasties swinging.

Nice touch, Leo thought. He'd have to check them out a little bit later. Right now, he had more important business to attend to. And it had to do with money. The beady eyes in his heavy face narrowed as he studied the crowd and then motioned for Moose LeDoux to come over to the stairway.

Moose, who had once been a fairly respectable professional boxer, lumbered over, wearing his garish plaid sport coat. The material looked strained as it tightly covered his massive upper body. Moose was six foot eight, the same height as Buddy Baer, and had once fought on the undercard at one of Joe Louis's matches. Unfortunately, his boxing career evaporated because of his unbreakable tendency to hit his opponents below the belt and when they were down, thus leading to Moose's repeated disqualifications. After a time, it became impossible for any manager to book him on fight cards.

141

It was then that Moose began to devote all his attention to his muscling activities for the mob. Now he was Leo Burke's right hand man.

"Yeah, boss," LeDoux said, moving over to the stairway. Burke moved up a step so he'd be taller than Moose, and leaned forward causing his protuberant belly to loll over the handrail.

"Go around with Blackie and collect from the tables," Burke said. "And then bring it upstairs so I can put it in the safe."

Moose nodded and moved off into the crowd. Leo glanced over the club again and grinned. Business was picking up, despite the sluggish economy. Even with all the strikes, and a lot of men out of work, people always seemed to find time and money for the essential vices: broads and gambling. And it's my job to supply them, Leo thought. He pondered this as he climbed the stairs and walked down the dimly lighted corridor to his office. After opening the door, he flicked on the lights and went to his desk. As he removed one of his fine Cuban cigars from the glass humidor, he felt the breeze from the open window behind him.

Leo held a match to the end of the cigar. *Funny, I don't remember leaving the window open.*

The curtains blew forward like silken tendrils. He turned and went to close the window, but stopped suddenly. At the same moment he saw the circular hole that had been cut in the glass above the locking mechanism, he heard the low whistling. It was coming from behind him. He turned slowly.

The whistling stopped and a harsh sounding voice said, "Don't close the window just yet, Leo. I had a hell of a time getting it open."

Burke let the cigar smoke drift from his mouth and

feigned a smile. He stared at the shadows in the corner near his filing cabinets and then saw the dark figure standing next to the wall. The long dark coat was open and the gloved hands hung loosely at his sides. Burke debated his chances of going for the gun in his top drawer and decided against it just yet.

"So whadda ya want?" Leo asked, trying to sound nonchalant. He puffed on the cigar in an effort to appear insouciant.

The Wraith moved forward and, with a deft gesture, plucked the cigar from Burke's mouth.

"Hey," Burke said as the gloved fingers stubbed the ash-covered end onto the finely polished wooden surface on the desk.

"It's been a while, Leo," the dark man said. "Do you remember the last time I came for a little visit?"

"Yeah, yeah, I remember." The memory made him shiver. Feigning as much bravado as he could muster, Leo said, "Now,

whadda ya want?"

The Wraith's hand shot out and grabbed Burke's corpulent neck. The gangster's tongue curled out of his mouth. When the hoodlum's gurgling breathing became labored, the gloved fingers relaxed slightly. The shadowy face moved closer.

"I want answers, Leo. Who's behind this Grantman kidnapping and the murder of her boyfriend?"

"I don't know," Burke gasped. "I swear I don't know nothing."

"Wrong answer, Leo," the Wraith snarled. His fingers tightened again, forcing Burke down on his knees. "Your little man, Morrie the Mouse, was arrested at the hotel today where the boyfriend was murdered. And everybody knows that the Cole gang was on your payroll." The fingers pressed deeper into the fleshy surface. Just as it seemed that Burke was going to lose consciousness, the Wraith released him and smacked the back of his hand across the kneeling man's face.

"Do you want to talk to me, Leo, or do you want to take a little dive out of the window? Head first."

Burke's breathing was still ragged. He eyed the desktop drawer, which was now only inches away from his face.

"Okay, okay," he said. "Whadda ya want to know?"

"Start with the kidnapping of the girl from the bank." The Wraith leaned down close to Leo's ear and spoke in a heavy whisper. "Why did they take her when they hit the place?"

Burke drew a few deep breaths in his open mouth before struggling to speak.

"They got the okay," he paused and tried to swallow, "to do the bank job on the condition that they grab a broad teller and bring her along."

"Why?" the growling whisper asked.

"It was something Frank wanted. He called and told me that he wanted a broad for something special," Burke said. "Some broad nobody'd miss. I guess they figured she'd do."

The Frank he referred to was Big Frank Costello, the head of organized crime in New York. He was a powerful man who manipulated politicians as easily as he controlled lower echelon mobsters like Leo Burke.

"What about the Grantman girl? And the shootout this afternoon at the hotel?"

"I dunno what's going on," Burke said. The gloved hand tightened over his windpipe again and he gasped. "I swear it's the truth. Frank just called again and told me to set up the hit, so I sent some of my boys over there. He told us there was cops guarding the kike, and we was supposed to get them before Roland and that Atlas guy got there. They had to wait till Roland called up to the room to find out exactly which one they was in."

The leather-encased fingers tightened around Burke's neck slightly. "And?"

"And the Mouse was supposed to delay them, so the torpedoes could nail 'em all in the room."

"You've told me all the things I already know," the Wraith snarled. "Now tell me the reason for all this." He punctuated his request with a short chopping slap to Burke's left eye. The kneeling gangster recoiled like he'd been bitten by a snake.

His words came spilling out, so the spittle shot forth from his lips. "It was Frank that set it up. He don't tell me what's going on. He just calls and says do this or do that. You know how he is." The Wraith eased his grip on the fat neck. Burke took several breaths. "Alls I know is it's something big they been planning. Something big. Real big."

Before the Wraith could ask another question there was a scratching sound at the door, accompanied by voices. The tone was jocular. Two men talking and laughing. The distraction was enough for Leo to make a move for the drawer. He pulled it open and shoved his hand inside, searching for the small caliber semi-automatic pistol he kept there. The Wraith slammed the side of his body against the drawer, trapping Burke's hand between the drawer and the desktop. Before Leo could cry out in pain, a gloved fist smacked against his temple sending him into oblivion.

The door swung open and Moose LeDoux came in, carrying a large, heavily laden cloth sack. Behind him was a smaller, wiry man with jet black hair and a closely cropped mustache. The smaller man, known as Blackie the Pearl because of his toughness and unctuous looks, held a large-frame revolver in his right hand.

"Boss?" Moose said as he stepped inside. Blackie followed.

As soon as they'd stepped fully into the room, the door swung shut behind them. A dark hand shot out and grabbed the Pearl's right wrist, slamming him into a nearby coat-rack. The pistol discharged, sending a loud echo through the room, the round piercing the wall near the floorboard. Moose dropped the sack of money and tried to whirl, but a sudden impact cracked him just above the left ear. The big man felt the sting, and seconds later a cascade of blood down his neck. His big arms raised instinctively, but the sap swung in a looping fashion and once again collided with his head. Moose sank to his knees, dazed and bleeding.

"What the hell?" he managed to say.

A fist smacked into the point of his jaw as his arms drooped.

"You're dead," Blackie snarled as he tried to level the gun on the black phantom before him. But the Wraith's left leg snapped out from his side, catching Blackie in the solar plexus and knocking him against the wall. Before he could attempt to steady the gun, it was snatched from his hand, then the butt of it was rammed against his temple. The Wraith straightened up and jumped to the door, clicking on the locking mechanism. Blackie rolled over onto his hands and knees and started to get up. The fingers of his right hand probed inside the pocket of his sport coat and pulled out a switchblade. The blade snapped open with a silvery flash and Blackie rose to a crouch.

"I'm gonna cut you up good." His voice was low and guttural.

The Wraith circled the hood slowly, his hands extended. The blade swung outward, slashing at the dark man's arm. Outside, the sound of feet running down the corridor could be heard. Blackie lurched forward with the knife again, but this time the dark figure sidestepped and grabbed the other man's wrist. The Wraith brought his left foot up and smacked against Blackie's nose, stifling any cry. Then, with twisting motion, the dark figure drew Blackie's arm behind him and twisted the knife from his grasp. Grabbing the collar of the hoodlum's sport coat, the Wraith drove the smaller man forward, smashing his head into the hard plaster of the wall area beside the door, leaving a smashed in half-moon on the striped wallpaper. Blackie slumped down in a heap just as someone began pounding on the door from outside in the hallway.

"Boss, you all right?" the voice asked. "We thought we heard a shot."

Leo Burke opened his eyes and, saw the barrel of a forty-five staring him in the face. It took a moment to orient himself, and he heard the harsh whisper in his ear.

"Get rid of them or you'll be dead before they can break

down the door," the Wraith whispered. He shoved the barrel in front of Leo's right eye.

"Boss, you okay?" the voice called again. The doorknob twisted against the lock.

"Yeah," Leo said weakly. "Blackie was just playing around with his rod and accidentally fired one off. Get back downstairs."

He heard a snorting laugh and the sound of retreating footsteps, then Leo felt the cold steel of the pistol barrel against his cheekbone once more.

"That was very nice, Leo. Very nice. Now, get up and sit in your chair like a good little boy."

Burke complied. The Wraith held the forty-five on him while he ripped loose the telephone and then wound the cord around Burke's body. He used some heavy tape to secure Leo's wrists to the arms of the chair. After retrieving the small pistol from the desk drawer, the dark man went around and picked up the bag of cash near the still unconscious Moose.

"This will be forfeit because you weren't forthcoming with me," the Wraith said.

"Aww, come on." Burke's voice was a plaintive whine. "Big Frank'll kill me."

"That's your problem," the Wraith said. He stooped and picked up Blackie's revolver and dropped it into the sack with the money. Then he moved back to Leo and shoved the chair toward the open window. Burke suddenly felt the chair being lifted up, forcing his upper body against the sill, his head outside hanging over the edge of the building affording him the view of the alleyway below. It was only one story, but from this viewpoint, it looked like the top of the Empire State Building. Burke felt his bladder release and the warm wetness seize his crotch.

"Please…No."

"Last chance, Leo," the Wraith whispered softly. "Tell me what I want to know, or you'll be down there kissing your rodent brethren."

Moose's eyes rolled around in his head and he snorted several times getting to his feet. For a split second he could hear the roar of the crowd urging him onward. He smiled a crooked smile. He must be in the ring again. At least the fans were pulling for him.

"Moose! Moose!" they cried.

He blinked twice more and staggered into his fighting crouch, his blurry vision scanning the area before him for his opponent or the referee. He pawed at his head, and his hand came away red.

The roar continued: "Moose! Moose, you stupid punch-drunk pug!"

He looked around again, and his eyes began to focus. He wasn't in the ring after all. He was in a room, and someone was sitting right in front of him.

It was Leo, trussed up in his big leather easy chair.

Moose gazed at his boss with a perplexed expression as the fat man's words became clearer and clearer,

"Boss, what you doing over there?"

"Untie me, you dumb idiot." Burke's face was twisted in pain. "And go get me a damn doctor. I think he broke my damn hand."

11

Sex, Lies, Videos, and Tapes

AS Doc's enormous arm muscles raised his suspended body for the hundred-and-first time, he pondered the events of the previous night. His lower legs, which were looped around an eighty-pound dumbbell, were curled back at an angle so that with each repetition he lowered himself between the parallel bars, the dumbbell came just inches short of touching the floor. Last night's experience with Penny had been pleasant, up until the point where she became angry and abruptly told him to stop. Her behavior was inexplicable. He had made his best attempt to be tender, asking her what was wrong, only to see her begin to cry. His corresponding ambivalence caused him to withdraw, which seemed to make an already inscrutable situation that much more perplexing. Finally, she turned her back to him and told him she was leaving. She had even refused his offer to drive her to her apartment, electing instead to take a taxi. The vision of the moonlight illuminating her bare back lingered in his mind's eye for a moment more. As brilliant as he was, Doc realized the mysteries of the feminine mind still required much more study, if he was ever going to figure out the intricacies of the fairer sex.

He did realize, however, that he had been taking her for granted recently. Without meaning to, he'd let this current case involving the pursuit of the Wraith and the Grantman kidnapping preoccupy much of his thinking. Perhaps too much so, and at the wrong times. Even when they were involved in the intimacies of romance, he'd had trouble relaxing his mental calculations. Thinking about a case while doing other things had never been a problem for him, but relationships were. Had she sensed his distraction?

Doc's father has raised him according to a strict code that allowed for little else in his life except for the preparation of the conquest of evil. But now, as he felt himself reaching the pinnacle of his success, at times he longed for more mundane things. The serenity of spending time with Penny pleased him in ways he'd never thought possible. He'd never previously considered the possibility of settling down, never thought there would be a time when it might not be feasible to jump into one of his cars or airplanes and travel to the far reaches of the earth to investigate some strange, sinister phenomenon. This was his life–the life he'd trained for since his childhood. Would the type of existence he had to offer really be fair to anyone? To someone like Penny? And what of the countless evildoers who might try to get at him through his loved ones? Deagan and Ace could take care of themselves, but Penny…. That was why he went to such extreme lengths to keep his private life out of the public eye. He had never lied to Penny about his intentions, about the role he had taken on, the duty to which he subscribed. And she had never once asked him to give it all up.

Doc smiled. He was certain of one thing. She loved him. And it seemed to be an unconditional love. The reflection caused him to momentarily wonder at the absence of conditions, restrictions. She asked for nothing, demanded little. Her company pleased him, but was it what he ultimately sought?

The buzzer on the south wall of the gym sounded, indicating someone was ascending in the express elevator. Doc pressed out a few more repetitions, bringing his total up to one hundred and twenty-five, before dropping the dumbbell and lowering himself to the floor. He went to the series of video monitors and switched them on. Adjusting the channels he found the camera inside the elevator and saw Polly busily digging in her handbag. He watched as she removed her compact and quickly checked her reflection, adding a few pats of makeup before putting it away and using her special key to stop the elevator at the office floor. He allowed himself another slight smile. Frailty, thou art is women, he thought. As Doc watched her leave the elevator, he grabbed a towel and wiped some of the perspiration that had begun to run down his forehead. He switched the channel to the office camera then switched on the intercom.

"Good morning, Polly," he said.

The video screen registered her startled jump, then a wry smile.

"Doc, you know I always hate it when you surprise me like that," she said, her hand on her chest.

"My apologies," he said into the intercom. Five bowling pins were lined up on the same table as the video monitor. Doc picked up three of the pins and began juggling as he spoke into the voice box. "I took the liberty of leaving you an envelope with some specific assignments for this morning. I'd like you to attend to them right away."

"Right away, Doc?" she asked. She was self-conscious in her movements, obviously knowing that he was watching her, but she couldn't see him. "I still have a ton of work to do updating those new files for your computer." Her voice was a plaintive.

"You'll have to leave Diana in charge of that," he said. The three bowling pins danced in the air in front of him as he moved his hands so quickly they were a blur. "I also left two fingerprint classifications in the envelope. I want an immediate identification check on them. These assignments are of the utmost urgency in the cases we're working on."

"Oh yeah, which one? The kidnapping or the Wraith?" she asked.

"I forgot that you haven't been fully briefed," he said. "The two have seemingly intertwined. A person identifying himself as the Wraith called Grantman last night, and claimed to have his daughter. He received another call this morning from the same individual making a ransom demand."

"Golly, a ransom. How much?"

"I'm not sure," he said, grabbing a fourth bowling pin and rotating it into the series. "I heard this latest information third-hand. I plan to go out there shortly and listen to both tapes, which is why I need you to go research the items listed, first thing this morning." He watched her progress as she walked through the office toward her desk.

Polly picked up the envelope and asked if this was it. Doc shot a quick glance at the monitor and replied in the affirmative. He then quickly snatched the fifth bowling pin and began to toss them higher and faster. He saw Polly open the envelope and begin reading the list of instructions.

"Gosh, I'll have to go all the way down to city hall for a Photostat of this," Polly said. "And I don't even know where this Fowser Music Room is."

"It's in the public library," Doc said. As the bowling pins descended, he set them one-by-one back on the table. "Have you seen Thomas and Ace?"

"Well," she said with an embarrassed shrug, "to tell you the truth, we all sort of had a late night last evening. I imagine they'll be along in a little while."

"Very well," he said. "If they don't get here before I leave, be sure to remind Thomas that I need him to check on the military backgrounds of our list of subjects as soon as possible. And I want Ace to work on overturning Roland's refusal to let me examine the bodies from yesterday. Additionally, I want him to look into the feasibility of obtaining some old court transcripts." He walked to the edge of a strip of red tape on the floor which indicated a demarcation line. Two long, parallel lines about three feet apart ran the length of the floor, ending at some gymnastic equipment. Pausing in front of the starting line, Doc glanced at his wristwatch, then said to Polly, via the intercom, "Also, I wonder if you could do something else for me. Call the flower shop and have two dozen red roses sent to the *Guardian* for Penelope."

"Oh, Doc, you're so romantic," Polly said. "Did you two have a good time after we left?" He watched her look up at the camera and smile. "I was thinking about asking you both to come along with us, but figured you'd rather spend some time alone together. Was I right?"

In typical fashion, Doc ignored the question. "I'll check back with you later," he said, and switched off the video and the intercom. Monitoring his watch again, he waited for the minute hand to sweep around the face to the twelve o'clock position. Then he shot down the taped corridor to the first apparatus, a horse. Doc leaped forward, gripping the two rungs and spun his legs overhead. The extra lift from his powerful arms and shoulders allowed him to land near two suspended rings about fifteen feet away. Quickly snatching one in each hand, Doc first raised himself into a handstand, then lowered his body to an iron cross. Holding steady for a few seconds, he

 then began to swing his legs, gathering momentum. He swung back and forth three times before he attempted the next jump. Two heavy ropes, set a good ten feet apart, had been suspended from an I-beam in the high ceiling, allowing for a twenty-five foot climb. Doc released the rings at the peak of his swing and seized the rope closest to him. Using his hands only, he climbed quickly to the top, then went hand-over-hand along the I-beam. He reached the second rope and quickly descended. As soon as he'd landed, he briskly ran toward to a high-jump bar set at six feet. Despite his considerable size, Doc's powerful leg muscles allowed him to jump amazingly high. This time, however, his foot hit the bar and knocked it off. It banged heavily to the floor a second before he did.

Landing on his side on the mat, Doc rolled to his feet and checked his watch. He was ten seconds off his standard time, with a missed high jump to boot. Was it the result of his amorous encounter with Penelope last night? He'd never really done any clinical examination of how sex the evening before

might affect his athletic ability. Or was it the result of the heavier body weight he was now carrying due to his recently increased weightlifting? Allowing himself another rare grin, Doc decided the former hypothesis might just merit some further examination. Perhaps, after this case was over with, extensive experimentation with Penelope on some remote Caribbean island would be in order. He grabbed his towel and walked toward the shower room. Of course, they'd have to take proper precautions against the equatorial sun.

Doc watched as Randolph Grantman twisted the knobs of the recording box after winding the spool of wire through the various slots and crevices. To his immediate right stood FBI Agent Steve Efrem, District Attorney Hamilton Vernon, and Detective Hal Roland. K.C. Edgar and his bodyguard, Khan sat on an adjacent sofa. Edgar sipped daintily at a cup of lemon-flavored herbal tea. Across from them, looking much more subdued than the last time he'd been present, sat Warren Grantman, the short sleeves of his pink shirt, exposing a pair of sickly looking arms. He held a large glass full of an amber-colored liquid in his right hand.

Grantman twisted the knob and the hissing static of the second recorded tape came through the speakers. The single ring was followed by Grantman's voice. "Hello," he said. "Hello," he said again. Then the eerie voice of the person claiming to be the Wraith came on.

"Grantman, this is the Wraith. Listen carefully to this, so you get it right. I won't repeat it. Have your driver bring one-hundred-and fifty thousand in small bills in a suitcase to the China Gate restaurant in Chinatown tonight at seven sharp. There'll be a table reserved for a Mr. Greer." The voice paused for a heavy chuckle. "Have him sit at that table and he'll be contacted. No cops."

"Wait. My daughter. Is she all right?"

"No cops," the voice repeated. The connection went dead.

Grantman abruptly reached down and switched off the recorder.

"Dammit all, man," he said, his face becoming a bit more florid. "How many more times are you going to listen to those blasted things? You've already heard them again and again…"

"Actually," Doc said slowly, "this would have been the fourth time for the first recording, counting your phone call to me last night, which will suffice."

Grantman glared at Atlas, but said nothing. He whirled toward Efrem, an ugly snarl twisting over his face, his finger pointing at the FBI man. "I want you to know that I'm holding you totally responsible for this." His hand shot down and grabbed the newspaper, the headline shouting:

GRANTMAN GIRL KIDNAPPED.
WRAITH SOUGHT.

"*The Daily News*, too, no less," Grantman said, crumpling the page. "Scooped by our biggest competitor."

"Mr. Grantman," Efrem said nervously, "I assure you no one from the Bureau said anything to the press. We were as surprised as you were, sir."

"Then how the hell do you explain it?" Grantman shot back.

"Well, sometimes it can't be helped when you have so many other, unofficial people involved in an investigation."

"Meaning who?"

Efrem's gaze traveled to Doc and then K. C. Edgar, but he remained silent.

Grantman's face shook in disgust. "And what's the damn Bureau done for me? For my daughter?"

K.C. Edgar set his cup and saucer down on an end table and rose. He walked quickly over to Grantman's side and placed a hand on the newspaper tycoon's left shoulder. The hulking Khan rose and followed along silently.

"There, there, Randolph. This whole episode has taken a terrible toll on you, and that's perfectly understandable," Edgar said soothingly. "But just remember everything I've prophesied thus far has come to pass. And I am just as certain that Bonnie will be found unharmed and returned safely to us."

Grantman reached up and patted Edgar's hand. He seemed slightly reassured by the other man's words. "Thanks, K.C.," he said.

"I'm sure everyone will understand if you weren't able to deliver the commencement address at the fund raiser tonight, Randolph," Vernon said.

"Oh *come* now," Warren Grantman said, rising from his chair and walking unsteadily to the wet bar on the other side of the room. His words were slightly slurred, and a cruel expression canted his features. "You can't expect *him* to give up his life's main, driving passion now, *can* you?" He picked up a bottle of scotch with drunken gesticulation, and poured a considerable amount into the empty glass. "It's my father's life's blood, more important to him than me, or Bonnie, or Mother, or all his of mistresses and their rosebuds. It has to do with the only thing that *really* matters…. Power." As an afterthought, he splashed in a small bit of seltzer before ambling toward the hall.

They all watched the man's sullen retreat.

"I would hope that you would excuse my son, gentlemen," said Grantman, straightening slightly. He looked at the floor. "I'm afraid this whole ordeal has been…" Edgar squeezed the rich man's shoulder once more and gave an comforting little nod. "Of course you're right, Hamilton. Even though I'm the one who's hosting the dinner, I can't possibly leave the house without knowing what's happened to Bonnie. Anyway, you heard that madman. I wonder why he wants Stephan, my driver, to deliver the money?"

"Perhaps he knows what the man looks like and plans to follow him before calling you back with further instructions," Doc offered.

Roland slanted his eyes to Doc. The cop smirked as he took out his pack of Chesterfields and shook one out, holding it up toward Doc.

"I'm going outside for a smoke," Roland said. "Anybody wanta join me?" He didn't wait for a reply and started walking.

Vernon watched the heavyset cop edge toward the doorway, then looked back to Grantman.

"Mr. Edgar's right, Randolph," he said. "Now that we know for sure that the Wraith is involved, it's just a matter of time before we track this maniac down. We will get her back."

"You can be certain of that, sir," Special Agent Efrem added. "We've mobilized every available man to stake out that Chinese restaurant tonight. You just have to persevere and keep recording those calls."

"What the hell do you think I've been doing?" Grantman said savagely. Then, seconds later, after his shoulder was again squeezed by Edgar, he said, "I'm…sorry. This whole ordeal…."

The phone rang again, just as Doc was glancing at his wristwatch. His amber eyes stared at the ringing telephone as Grantman quickly picked it up, his hand ready on the start-knob of the recording machine.

"Yes, Randolph Grantman here," his thick fingers twisted the knob on as he spoke, then, twisted it back to the off position. His entire face seemed to collapse in stages. "Yes, he's here." He held the phone toward Doc and sank into a nearby chair. "It's for you. Your secretary."

Doc nodded and took the phone, pleased at the way his instructions had been carried out. He'd instructed Polly's assistant, Diana, to call him precisely fifteen minutes after he called her at the office from Grantman's residence. "Have Misters Deagan and Assante arrived yet?" he said into the phone.

"Yeah, they're here, both looking like something the cat dragged in," Diana said.

"If you could instruct Ace that I need him to look into that legal matter as soon as possible, to allow me to examine those bodies from the shootout at the Lexington yesterday," Doc said. He murmured a thank you and handed the phone back to Grantman.

"I hope you don't mind," Doc said. "I told my staff they could reach me here."

"Not at all," Grantman said.

"Some legal problem, Dr. Atlas?" Vernon asked. "Is there any way I could help?"

Briefly Doc explained his desire to perform autopsies on the dead thugs from yesterday, in order to gain any possible clues that the examining doctor may have missed.

"That doesn't seem too hard to arrange," Vernon said,

scratching his chin. "Perhaps I could have you appointed special assistant to the coroner, or something. After all, you are very well-known in the medical profession."

Grantman stood up. "Anything you can do to expedite my daughter's safe return will be appreciated, Hamilton." His face seemed to tighten and become more resolute as he spoke. "And it won't go unnoticed, either."

"Does that mean I'll get to make the speech tonight, instead of Ward?" Vernon asked with a quick smile.

Grantman's eyes narrowed slightly, and his lips pursed, as if he were going to blurt something out. Instead, he swallowed noticeably and said, "You know that we decided on Ward weeks ago. You were thoroughly briefed on our reasoning, and I certainly don't appreciate you bringing it up at his time."

"Sorry," Vernon said. His face reddened as he turned to Doc. "Just have Ace Assante give me a call. I'm headed back to the office now, anyway. I'll see what I can do."

"Thank you." Doc turned to Grantman. "I have to be going also."

Both men walked toward the foyer after saying their good-byes. As they waited for the butler to open the front door, Doc looked at Vernon.

"What speech were you referring to?"

"Oh, it's for the Democratic fund raiser tonight," Vernon said with a smile. "Ward Casper is being groomed as the next fair-haired-boy by the kingmakers."

"He isn't happy as a judge?"

"Let's face it, the way Truman looks in the polls, Dewey might just beat him next year. That opens up all kinds of possibilities." Vernon grinned. "Ward is fully aware of them, and with the sympathy vote for the poor widower, who the hell could run against him?"

As they went outside, they saw Roland leaning against the fender of Doc's LaSalle. His arms were crossed and a cigarette dangled from his lips.

"Like I told you," Vernon said, shaking Doc's hand, "have Ace give me a call. The sooner the better."

"I'll certainly do that," Doc told him. Vernon got into his vehicle and started it up. Doc strolled over to Roland.

"No sports car today?" Roland asked, nodding toward the sedan.

Doc shook his head.

"The Transcendental Prophet get any more hot flashes?"

Doc shook his head again. "What about that man, Moscowicz? Did he implicate anyone else?"

"Are you kidding?" Roland said, choking off a laugh. "He just clammed up and called his mouthpiece. Paul Milton showed up yesterday with a writ, so we had to let the little crook walk."

Doc considered this. "What type of man is Milton?"

Roland shrugged. "He's the best, him and your buddy Assante. But they're still no damn good, as far as I'm concerned." He drew on the Chesterfield causing the ash to glow brightly. "Me and Milton go back a ways, too. Back before the War, he used to work for the D.A.'s office. He was a pretty good Joe in those days. But, I guess he decided to go for the big money when he got back. As far as I'm concerned, he sold out." His breath was smoky as he talked. He stopped and stared up at Doc.

"So are you still mad at me, Atlas?" Roland asked, taking the cigarette out of his mouth. "About yesterday, I mean?"

"I understand your point of view." He studied the heavyset

cop a moment. "However, I find it diametrically opposed to the pursuit of an expedient resolution to this case."

Roland blew out a breath. "Say that again, so I can understand it. And speak English this time."

Doc spoke slowly. "My point was that it would be more expeditious if we worked together to solve this."

"Look, Atlas." Roland took one more drag on the cigarette and tossed it away. "I was just doing my damn job, and I got people jumping all over me for it, like I broke wind in the presence of the Pope, or something. All of us cops ain't imbeciles, you know, so don't go acting like we are. Every time I work one of these cases where some civilian hot shots try to take over...."

He took out another cigarette.

Doc had been watching him carefully. After a moment he spoke. "Perhaps it might be advantageous for us to share information at some point, Detective. For instance, your disparagement of Mr. Edgar was not lost on me. In fact, I think his involvement is more than just peripheral."

Roland was placing the cigarette between his lips, but stopped midway. "Whadda ya mean?"

"I am no more a believer of Edgar's psychic abilities than you are," Doc said. "The man is a charlatan, so I was immediately suspicious when he so conveniently predicted that the Wraith was involved in the kidnapping."

"You too, huh?" He took out his silver lighter.

"And this subsequent telephone call from the individual claiming to be the Wraith is much too pat," Doc continued. "It shocked me that they would try such a sloppy ploy in a plan seemingly so sophisticated. But yet, they probably weren't aware of the vital piece of information they let slip."

"Yeah?" Roland said slowly. He held the flame to the end of the cigarette, snapped the lid closed, and put his lighter back in his pocket. "And what vital piece are you referring to?"

"Do you recall our conversation immediately prior to our entrance into the Lexington Hotel yesterday?" Doc asked. Without waiting for Roland to answer, Doc continued. "You told me that Ira Bloom had remembered one of the hoods who had kidnapped Bonnie mentioning the name of Casey." Roland nodded. "When I hypnotized Maria Hernandez last night, she, too, recalled hearing that name being spoken by her abductors. She also mentioned something about being cut into pieces, which this Wraith-caller said to Grantman on the first recorded conversation."

Roland's eyes narrowed as he blew smoke through his nostrils. Suddenly, he grinned broadly. "Are you saying what I think you're saying?"

"It's my contention that the 'Casey' they were talking about is K.C. Edgar," Doc said, enunciating each of the initials carefully. "And this caller on the tape—"

"Ain't really the Wraith," Roland finished. "Hell, I coulda told you that all along. It ain't his style, snatching some rich broad." He paused to contemplate, and removed the cigarette from his mouth. "So you think Edgar's really the one behind all this, then?"

Doc considered this for a moment. "He's involved, but I doubt he's the mastermind. I sense this whole thing is vastly more complex than we've been led to believe. It's far too elaborate for a simple kidnapping."

Roland stuck the cigarette between his lips and drew on it. "Maybe I should go bring old K.C. down to the station house for a little friendly conversation."

"That wouldn't be wise," Doc said. "As I said, Edgar's little more than a bit player in this. His schemes have always reeked of churlishness and a lack of sophistication. This case seems to have many variant layers. Perhaps it would be elucidating to let this little drama play itself out."

"Yeah, you're right," Roland said. "I'd better go back to HQ and run this by the boss. Maybe, if we can spare 'em, I'll have a couple of guys start shadowing the Transcendental Prophet." He grinned.

Doc allowed himself to smile back, although he didn't mention to his new ally the most significant suspicion he had after his visit to the Grantman estate. That would have to wait till the proper time.

12

Probability Equations

"Oℏℏℏℏℏ…" Deagan said, holding his head between his big palms as the mid-day sun peeked through the high windows of the library section of Doc's quarters. "I think I'm gonna need another Bromo."

"I'm going to need another one too, if you don't pipe down so I can finish this research," Ace said, looking up from the massive volume he had spread open before him. His fingers grasped a pencil and several long sheets of paper were strewn across the top of the fine, cherry wood table. "Unlike your assignment, mine takes real brainpower."

"So what are you saying, then?" Deagan asked, forcing a smile. "That you need me to help ya?"

"Hardly," Ace said, burying his nose in the book again. They were both seated in high-backed chairs on opposite sides of the large table. Several thick legal tomes were stacked in front of Ace. A telephone had been pushed off to Mad Dog's far right.

"Aww, what's the matter with you today, anyhow?" Deagan said. "You strike out last night with that Maria dame, or something?"

"Not that it's any of your business," Ace said, "but she doesn't happen to be that kind of girl."

Deagan snorted. "That ain't never stopped you before, has

it?"

A slight smile crept over Ace's lips and he said, "Actually, the whole time we were out, I kept having recollections of her beetle-browed mother glaring at me when we picked her up. It was all I could do to muster enough courage to walk the poor girl to her door." He paused, looked up, and smiled wistfully. "She's been through a lot as it was."

Deagan was about to utter another salacious comment when the side door opened and Penny came through into the room. She held up a newspaper in her right hand and smiled at them.

"*The News* really blew this story about the kidnapping wide open," she said. "You guys read it yet?"

"No, we both been trying to do as little as possible," Deagan said. "Only Ace is acting like he's accomplished at it."

"Speak for yourself," Ace said. His body stiffened slightly as he looked at Penny.

"I always do," Deagan answered, obviously relishing what he thought was his one-upmanship of Assante.

Penny sat down next to Deagan and took out her cigarette case. He didn't move, so she snapped open her lighter and lit the smoke herself, staring out of the corner of her eye at Ace.

"So you feeling bad they scooped you?" Deagan asked. He buried his head between his massive hands again.

"Nah," she said, spreading the newspaper out of the tabletop. "My editor put the kibosh on it because of old man Grantman owning the paper, but I'll get the exclusive once it's all over, like I always do."

"You ain't gonna write another one of them pulp magazine stories about this case, are you?" Deagan asked. "The ones where I always act dumb and look like the monkey's uncle."

"Of course she is.," Ace said, still poring over the law volume. "She's a reporter. She's got to stick to the facts."

"Hey, I've netted some pretty good money for those, even if I do have to use a masculine pseudonym," she smiled. "Bought me lots of nice clothes." She held out the short sleeve of her yellow dress. "You see this new outfit?"

"Yeah, but I always sound like such a dope," Deagan said.

"As I said, she has to stick to the real-life facts," Ace said. He paused to scribble another note on the paper in front of him, then sighed. "But I must admit my character isn't much better. A supercilious and haughty lawyer who insults everyone."

"Just like the original shyster we've all known for years," Deagan said spreading his sausage-sized fingers far enough away from his face to be heard. "The only one that's depicted favorably is Doc."

"Oh, you guys are just jealous," she said. She blew out a cloud of smoke and pretended to be engrossed in the paper. Suddenly the alarm bell rang, signaling the elevator's rise, and Deagan slowly looked over at the video monitor. Doc Atlas's picture appeared on the screen. Penny stood, went to the ashtray, and took one more long drag on her cigarette. As she stubbed it out, she pointed to the fans on the walls. Deagan groaned, but got up and flipped the switch to activate them.

"Now you owe me," he said as he sat back down and cradled his face in his hands once more.

A few moments later Doc strode into the room. His nostrils flared almost imperceptibly and he glanced at Penny.

He unbuttoned his brown sport jacket, folded it neatly, and placed it over a chair.

"Did you get the flowers?" he asked.

"Yes," she said. "Thank you. They were lovely."

Doc nodded and turned to Deagan.

"Thomas," he said. "Did you make those phone calls I requested?"

"Yeah, Doc, I'm waiting on a call back now. They gotta find the records and look 'em up."

"I see you're busy too, Ace," Doc said. "I ran into Hamilton Vernon this morning out at the Grantman estate. After I explained our dilemma, he said for you to call him and perhaps he could expedite the matter."

Assante grinned "That's the best news I've heard all morning."

"Hey, Doc," Deagan said. "You and Penny shoulda come with us last night. That Danny Kaye movie was real good. *The Secret Life of Walter Mitty*. It was about this real milksop-kinda guy, who daydreams he's a hero all the time. Had that same song as last night in it, too. You know, 'Beautiful Dreamer.' Him and Virginia Mayo were whistling it. Man, is she a sweetie. But that movie had me laughing like a hyena."

"Careful," Ace said, closing the law book. "If the Bronx Zoo hears it, they might come after you."

Deagan glanced at him and frowned. "I wonder where they come up with the ideas for them movies?"

"That particular movie was based on the short story by James Thurber," Ace said, still paging through the legal volume. "You might have known that if you'd read a good magazine sometime, instead of all that pulp crap."

Penny looked at him, but said nothing.

"I ain't laughed so hard since *The Kid From Brooklyn*," Deagan chuckled. "Danny Kaye was in that one, too. He played this milkman that they turned into a boxer. Ya see, he knew how to duck a punch, and the middleweight champ takes a swing at him, see, and–"

"Oh, please," Ace said. "Spare us. My tolerance for mediocrity and melodramatics is at an end."

Penny's eyes flashed from Ace to Deagan, then back to Ace.

"What the hell is eating you, anyway?" Deagan said, his broad face turning a shade darker. "You been egging me on the whole damn morning. If I didn't know better, I'd say you're–"

Suddenly two bells sounded simultaneously. One was the telephone, which Deagan fumbled with before finally getting the receiver next to his ear. The other was the elevator alarm again. Doc glanced at the monitor.

"Looks like Polly's back," he said, glancing at his wristwatch. "Why don't we re-convene here after we have lunch and we can go over the information we've gathered, thus far."

Doc had a large blackboard set up in the library when they finished eating. The meal had consisted of five of the plates that Doc's Aunt Nana had prepared and then frozen for quick defrosting and consumption after Doc heated them in his specially designed toaster oven. It ran on the principle of microwaves, which heated the food incredibly fast. Aunt Nana, Doc's father's only sister, had been preparing his special food since he was a toddler, and he still kept her on his payroll as a cook and housekeeper.

"I've written several points on the blackboard," Doc said as they assembled in the chairs around the large table. "The first, is that the two cases have undeniable ties. You see I have the Wraith here," he pointed to the upper left corner, "and the Grantman kidnapping here." He indicated the right corner.

"Strangely," he continued, "a person claiming to be the Wraith has called Grantman twice. The first time to state he was holding Bonnie Grantman, and then this morning to demand a one-hundred-fifty thousand dollar ransom be taken to a Chinatown restaurant tonight at seven."

Deagan gave a low whistle. "A hundred and fifty Gs."

"But why would the Wraith ask for money from Grantman when he left the cash stolen by the Cole gang when he rescued Maria?" Assante asked.

"That's precisely the question I had," Doc said. "It leads me to believe the caller is not the actual Wraith, but a clever imposter. There seems to be an undeniable mob element here that needs to be factored into this. Thomas, what did you find out about the military backgrounds on our list of subjects?"

Deagan licked his lips and began paging through his stack of papers.

"Pretty much what we expected, Doc," he said. "No military records for Frasier Clark, Wayne Morrison, or Paul Milton. Judge Casper and Hamilton Vernon were both assigned to the European Theater. Casper was part of the A/B

Ranger's Battalion. Specialized in advanced recon. He went up to staff sergeant, but somehow managed to end up an officer by the time he was discharged. A butter bean lieutenant. Vernon was a first-looie. An operations officer in the 503rd MP Battalion, and then was assigned to the Adjutant General's Office right after Germany fell, and during the occupation. Obviously because of his legal background." He flipped to a second page. "Father Gisseppi was assigned in the Pacific as a chaplain. Hal Roland was in the Third Marine Division and was also in the Pacific Theater. He separated as a gunnery sergeant. Lots of blood-stripes."

"Can you check on another subject for me as soon as possible?" Doc said. "Warren Grantman."

Deagan's brow furrowed. "That name sounds like it should be familiar, don't it?"

"Warren Grantman is Randolph Grantman's son," Doc said. He gave Deagan the man's birth date and full name.

"Sure thing," Deagan said, reaching for the telephone. "I'll put in another call now." As he was dialing, Penny looked at Doc quizzically

"You certainly don't think Mr. Grantman's own son is involved, do you?" she asked.

"There are too many independent variables for any clear hypothesis to be postulated at this time," Doc said. "However, there is certainly more at work here than is readily discernible. For instance," he held up a black-and-white Photostat. "This is the copy of Alexander P. Casper's birth certificate."

"Ward Casper's son?" Penny asked. "The one who died with his mother in the explosion?"

Doc nodded as he handed the document to Assante.

"The space for the father's name," Ace said. "It's blank."

"Not exactly blank, Ace," Doc said. "If you'll look closely you'll see that a name was started there, but then scratched out."

Assante's brow furrowed and he handed the document to Penny.

"The birth certificate is usually filled out by the mother after delivery," she said. "Why would she leave Ward Casper's name off?"

"Maybe he wasn't the kid's real daddy," Deagan said, hanging up the phone. He grinned, obviously feeling triumphant he'd been able to follow the room conversation while on the phone. "They're gonna call back when they find the Colonel."

Doc was at the phonograph placing a record on the spinning turntable. A stunning instrumental version of 'Beautiful Dreamer' came on.

"This is one of Ellen Casper's recordings," Doc said. He paused to let the melody continue.

"She played beautifully," Penny said. "Much better than the one I did on Doc's piano last night."

Assante looked at her, then turned his gaze to the windows.

"Polly found three other recordings at the library that she made," Doc said. "Each contained a version of this particular song."

"Hmph, I guess she musta really liked it," Deagan said. "But, Doc, I'm getting so confused now, I don't know what in the hell to think. How does all this stuff fit together?"

Doc moved back to the chalkboard. "I'm assuming this song somehow ties Ellen Casper to the Wraith," he said, gesturing with the chalk. "Remember, the first two of his known victims were gangsters Webber and Boggs, the men accused of killing Ellen and her son. Now, someone claiming to be the Wraith has taken credit for kidnapping Bonnie Grantman, but it is dubious that it's the real Wraith. Yet somehow, the actual Wraith is running a parallel course to our investigation. When we find out who he is, we may find out why. There's also a high probability the kidnappers have at least one confederate in the Grantman household."

"Oh, so that's why you want me to check on the kid," Deagan said.

"Warren Grantman appears to be a disturbed young man," Doc said. "He obviously dislikes his father to the point of hatred, but whether he would try to get back at him by kidnapping his own sister is unknown. I have no evidence to suggest what type of relationship they had. However, until we've positively ruled them out, we can't afford to discard any variables."

"So who's the inside man at the Grantman place?" Penny asked.

"K.C. Edgar for one," Doc said. "The man was far too accurate with his predictions to suit me. And he's obviously a substance abuser. I was able to obtain an identification check on his fingerprints. His real name is Edgar Casey Foxgrover. He was originally from California, where he served five years for drug smuggling." He set the chalk down on the ledge and placed both his hands behind his back. "That was over ten years ago. Now he seems to have assumed this new identity as the Transcendental Prophet, and entered into a similar illicit operation on this coast. His background and association with his huge Indian companion suggests the possibility of drug trafficking from India. Certainly his mail-order book business would be conducive to smuggling of that type, and it's alleged he has a large following in Bombay. That's why I wanted to do the autopsies on those thugs who attacked me yesterday at the Lexington Hotel. From their sensitivity to light and imperviousness to pain, I'm certain they were also under the influence of some sort of opiate intoxicant."

"And that might ultimately tie them to Edgar," Ace said. "I'll keep working on that, Doc."

The phone rang and Doc answered it.

"Yes, he's here now," he said, glancing at Ace. "We were just discussing that. Fine, I'll let you speak to him." He handed the receiver to Assante and said, "It's the District Attorney."

"Ham," Ace said, cradling the phone on his shoulder and leaning back with an air of complete relaxation. "We were just discussing your kind offer to help us expedite our little problem." He looked at Doc and Penny and winked.

Doc turned and addressed Polly in a hushed tone. "I need you to do another important assignment." He handed her a slip of paper. "Go to the hall of records and check on the real estate holdings of these two individuals."

Polly unfolded the paper with a sigh. She seemed about to speak when Assante hung up the phone and let out a triumphant laugh. They turned toward him.

"Hamilton told me Judge Casper is willing to sign a temporary order authorizing you to examine the bodies," he said, grinning. "They can be brought here shortly. All we have to do is go pick it up."

"Excellent," Doc said. "The sooner we have established the credibility of the unproven variables, the sooner the whole equation will become solvable. Ace, why don't you take the La Salle? It's in the parking garage."

"Great," Polly said. "You can drop me off on the way. It'll save me taxi fare."

"You know," Deagan said, getting up and stretching. "I wouldn't mind a little outing to get some fresh air myself."

"I'll go, too," Penny said. "If I'm going to have to chronicle all this, I'd better try to get a handle on it from the ground level. Unless there's something I can do here." She let her voice trail off and gave Doc a quick sidelong glance to see if he would make some indication that he wanted her to stay with him.

Doc merely nodded, his mind obviously racing over the questionable elements he had yet to discuss.

"Very well," he said. "I'll remain here and wait for the bodies. Perhaps I need to run all the variables through the computer to collate them into a probability pattern."

"Sounds like something you'll enjoy," Penny said, her voice straining a bit to sound cordial.

Doc remained silent and impassive as he watched all of them exit the room.

13

The Music Box

DEAGAN eased the LaSalle out of first gear as they turned onto Eighty-sixth Street. The comfortable pressure of Polly's leg pressing against his felt nice, but he couldn't help wondering what was bothering Penny. She'd jumped in the back seat as he'd opened the driver's door, and hadn't said a word. Then he watched as she silently lit a cigarette and seemed to blow a steady stream of smoke at the back of Assante's head. Ace, who was sitting next to Polly up front, seemed not to notice.

"Maybe next year I'll talk Doc into buying a car with one of them new hydroglides," Deagan said, trying to make small talk. He brought the shift lever up to second. "You know, an automatic transmission. You don't have to shift it. You just put it into gear and it does all the work for you." He was also thinking about how much trouble driving a standard transmission was for Ace, with his bad knee. "Or maybe another LaSalle with a clutchless transmission." When no one commented, he added, "That sure was a good movie last night, wasn't it?"

"Sure was," Polly said. She pushed her leg against his as she turned her head around toward the back seat. "Penny, did you get those flowers Doc sent to you at the *Guardian* okay?"

Penny just murmured an affirmative, "*Mmm-huh,*" and continued to smoke. She blew another stream of smoke at Ace.

Polly began to cough.

"Would you mind opening the window some more?" she said. "Your cigarette's really giving me a headache."

"Sorry," Penny said, and stubbed out her cigarette in the rear-door ashtray. "I forgot you don't smoke."

"Oh that's okay," Polly said. "I gotta get out up the street here, anyways." She pointed to the Hall of Records. "Just drop me off up there, sweetie."

Deagan blushed as he pulled over to the curb and shifted to neutral. He checked the mirror, ready to open his door. Before he could move, Ace was already outside, had the passenger door open, and Polly was sliding out. She stopped, slid back across the seat, and gave Deagan a quick peck on the cheek. "I'll see you later, sweetie." She slid across the seat again, and smoothed her skirt out as she stood. Assante stood there offering his hand to assist her at the curb.

"Thanks, Ace," she said. "I'll see you later."

Assante got back in and slammed the door. As Deagan pulled away from the curb he waved at Polly who was waiting to cross the street, then glanced in the rear-vision mirror to watch her cross. He half expected Assante was going to make some smart-aleck remark about Polly saying 'sweetie,' but he just sat there looking solemn. Like he was brooding about something.

Maybe he's going sweet on that Maria dame, Deagan thought. Looks like a case of woman trouble for sure.

He glanced in the rear-vision mirror again and saw Penny had already lighted another cigarette and was blowing more smoke in Ace's direction.

* * *

Remarkably, a car was pulling out from a space directly in

front of the King County Criminal Courts Building. Deagan, seeing the space, immediately pulled into it and parked. He grinned broadly.

"Can't ask for better than this," he said. "Maybe our luck's changing."

"Swell," Penny said sullenly. "I need a change of luck."

"Me, too," Ace said.

Deagan looked at each of them as he backed up, letting the wheel spin back to its standard position.

I wonder what's eating them? he thought.

As they left the LaSalle, Assante tapped Deagan slightly on the arm and nodded his head toward the doors. Paul Milton was entering the building rather quickly.

"Hey, Paul," Ace called.

Paul Milton stopped, looked, and smiled in recognition. "Ace, how you doing?"

"You look like a man in a hurry."

"I have a last minute motion that needs to be filed," Milton said in his clipped British accent. "I'm certain you know how it is, old boy."

"Certainly," Ace said. "Good luck."

Milton nodded and walked away, his black leather briefcase tucked under his arm.

"Ta-ta," Deagan said in a disparaging tone as they all watched Milton disappear into the crowded hall. In a voice loud enough for the departing lawyer to overhear, he added, "You sure that guy ain't lavender?"

Penny raised her eyebrows at the remark.

"Now was that a nice thing to say?" Ace asked.

"Hell," Deagan said. "I'm sick and tired of being nice. We're going nowhere on this case, and I want some action. A guy like me craves action. It's when I function at my best."

"What does that have to do with being rude to my friend?" Ace asked.

"Some friend," Deagan said. "All of us overseas fighting in the War, and he wasn't even in the service. Probably back here dating all the girls and getting rich. I got no respect for a man like that."

"Maybe he had an excuse like your blowhard buddy, Frasier Clark," Ace shot back.

"He ain't no buddy of mine."

"Guys, please," Penny said. "Don't we have some reason for being here besides squabbling?"

Deagan's big lips puckered, but instead of speaking, he pointed to Assante and emitted a loud Bronx Cheer.

"There you go trying to increase your vocabulary again," Ace said. He held up the agreement deputizing Doc as a temporary assistant to the King County Coroner. "Come on, I want to get up to Hamilton's office so I can get this signed. If you're through with the monkey shines, that is."

Deagan grinned. "Come on, shyster. Like I said, I was built for action."

They went through the doorway to District Attorney's Office, only to be told that Mr. Vernon was up in Judge Casper's chambers working some sort of special document.

"Probably the same thing that I've already taken the liberty of drawing up," Ace said. "Come on, let's go up there. It'll save us time and trouble."

"I'm all for that," Deagan said.

"Ditto," Penny added.

The three of them took the rear stairway up one flight. Ace, who obviously knew the inner recesses of the building well, led them through the back hallways to the judge's chambers.

"Jeez." Deagan's head rotated like a pivot on a tree trunk. "This place is like a labyrinth back here, ain't it?"

"There're all kinds of secret passages if you know the building," Ace said. "Why, there's even special tunnel section that goes under the street from one building to the next."

"Swell," Penny said. "And here we are without any breadcrumbs."

Assante stared at her briefly, but said nothing. They went down a deserted corridor with only a few dimly lit bulbs to show the way. Ace stopped at a solid door, concentrated for a moment, and knocked softly with his knuckles. After few moments he pushed the door open and beyond them lay Judge Casper's chambers. The judge was sitting behind his desk studying some papers. Hamilton Vernon sat in front of the desk. He rose when everyone came in. The judge leaned back in his chair and smiled slyly. Penny suddenly got that creepy feeling she got whenever she noticed a guy trying to look down her blouse.

"Ace," he said. "That was quick. I just called Doc Atlas a little while ago."

"We're working hard trying to get this Grantman kidnapping cleared up," Ace said. "If you recall, we're in need of a temporarily order assigning Doc to the coroner's office, thereby granting him the authority to examine the bodies of those dead hoods."

"Yeah," Vernon said, "this morning, out at the Grantman's place, he mentioned the jurisdictional problem that jerk Roland's been giving him. I think, with help of the Judge here, we've got it almost straightened out."

Penny felt Casper's x-ray gaze as he smiled at her. "How's your investigation going?" he asked. "Catch any bad guys yet?"

"No, but we're getting close," Deagan said. "Real close."

"Is that a fact?" the Judge answered.

"Ace, I've got a preliminary order drafted," Vernon said. "If you want to step down to my office, you can take a quick look at it, and then the judge can sign it."

"Well," Ace said with a grin, "I've already drafted one of my own." He handed the order he'd prepared to Vernon. "Want to flip a coin?"

"Swell," Vernon said, grinning. "Encouraging a person endowed with the public's trust to gamble openly in court. Come on, we can take our choice when we get down to my office, and I'll have my secretary notarize the one we choose."

"Fine," Assante said.

Casper rose from his chair and beamed down at Penny.

"And how are you today, Miss Cartier?" he asked.

"I'm fine," she said, feeling a bit uncomfortable. "But I do need to go powder my nose. Is there a ladies' room around here somewhere?"

"Please," the judge said, walking around the desk and grabbing her elbow in a vise-like grip and steering her around the desk to the opposite wall. "Feel free to make use of my private facilities." He opened a heavy oak door slightly, displaying a water closet. "We won't be gone long." He turned to Mad Dog. "And Mr. Deagan, won't you accompany these fine counselors and me? Hamilton has something quite amusing, in a masculine sort of way, that a man of your extensive military background will find very interesting." He grinned rakishly.

Deagan nodded with a knowing grin and headed out the door. Casper turned his head and spoke to Penny over his shoulder as he was leaving. "You can wait in here, Miss Cartier, but don't wander too far. Things are very labyrinthine back here. I wouldn't want you to get lost."

"I should have brought my string," she said to the back of his retreating black robe.

Masher, she thought. His touch made her skin crawl, but she felt a bit more at ease once the four men had left the room.

Penny slammed the door to the water closet. After finishing, she adjusted her hair and make-up, then went back into the judge's room and took a seat in front of the large desk. The condescending attitude of Casper infuriated her. Who was he to suggest that she was some schoolgirl, not intelligent enough to wander in the back corridors of the court building without getting lost? Sometimes men tended not to take her seriously, but she was as good as they were, and she knew it. Blowing out a long breath, her thoughts drifted to Doc's seeming indifference to her of late. Didn't he realize how much she contributed to their investigations? How much she contributed to his life? She reached in her purse and took out a cigarette, angry with the judge and Ace and Deagan, and all men who acted as if she wasn't their equal. All men–but especially Doc.

I'll show him, she thought. I'll solve this damn case before he does.

She wasn't sure quite how she would, but she was determined, and damn well knew she could if she set her mind to it.

Her lighter produced only a spark as the wheel rubbed against the flint. She shook it and realized the fluid had run out. Replacing the lighter in her purse, she surveyed the Judge's desk for some matches. The area was immaculate, with papers all arranged in precise stacks. A stapler sat on one side of a blotter next to a ring of keys. On the front section was a gold-plated pen-and-pencil set. Next to it sat small wooden box that Penny took to be a matchbook holder. She flipped up the top of it and a miniature piano with a painted figurine of a woman in a black evening gown sprang up. The small piano began to rotate on a plate, and a melody sprang from beneath it. The tune was startlingly familiar. It was the same one she'd heard only a little while ago. The same one she'd played on Doc's piano last evening: "Beautiful Dreamer."

The miniature damsel continued to whirl as the prongs methodically plucked out the song. Putting the unlit cigarette back in her pack and placing it in her purse, Penny moved slowly around the desk and walked to the heavy closet door. After a moment's hesitation, she tried the knob. It was locked. Casting a furtive glance at the closed door of the chambers, she went back to the desk and seized the ring of keys, and began trying them in the lock. After a few wrong tries, one of the keys twisted with an oiled precision, and the door opened. Several black judicial robes hung consecutively on a round-wooden rack. The pins of the music box continued to ping out the melody. Penny reached along the rack and pulled the hanging robes toward her. Another set of black garments hung all the way against the back wall of the closet. They were made of coarser material than the silken robes. A heavy shirt and a pair of black pants. As she spread open the folds of the shirt she saw several more items: an Australian bush hat and a dark mask.

"That was my late wife's favorite song," A voice said suddenly, from right behind her.

Penny half-turned, but found herself caught in the same

viselike grip as before. The piercing eyes stared down at her from either side of the aquiline nose.

"You! You're the Wraith," she managed to say before he crammed a medicinal-smelling rag over her nose and mouth, its pungent sweetness assailing her senses, making her dizzy. Seconds later, on the edge of a blurry darkness, she recognized the smell: chloroform. As the last vestiges of her consciousness slipped away, Penny could hear the heavy, grating laugh of Judge Ward Casper.

MELODY OF VENGEANCE

14

Under Siege

Doc placed the photostat of Alexander P. Casper's birth certificate under the bulb of the opaque projector and adjusted the focus of the image against the screen. He studied the whorls, loops, and other characteristics of Ellen Taylor Casper's writing on the rest of the form. He rapidly shuffled mentally through the alternatives as he continued to study the projection. After a few more seconds of close study, the answer suddenly appeared to him. Then the telephone rang and Doc picked it up.

"Hello, I'm trying to reach Mad Dog Deagan," the voice at the other end of the line said.

Doc recognized it immediately as Colonel 'Happy Jack' Harding, the former commanding officer of both Deagan and himself when they were stationed in Italy together.

"Colonel Harding, this is Michael Atlas. Thomas is out, but he contacted you at my behest."

"Atlas, huh? Well, it's General Harding now," the voice said. "So, what can I do for you, son?"

"I'm working on an investigation and have a special request," Doc said. "It may take some time, but I assure you that it's of the utmost importance."

"Ain't it always, when somebody wants a favor?"

Doc assumed the man was trying to make an ineffectual

joke, but the humor of it eluded him. He felt silence was the best reply. When he didn't speak after a few long seconds, the general did.

"But anyway," Harding continued, "since I'm here at the Pentagon, trying to placate these damn politicians, time is money, even though there's no war to run right now."

"I'm sure if there's another one, General, our country will be well served by men such as yourself," Doc said.

"Dammit, Atlas, quit trying to butter me up and say what's on your mind." After a moment more, the general added, "And it's not 'if there's another war.' It's only a question of when. The Reds are breathing down our necks in Germany. Is this about them? Some kind of Communist plot? Like that Nazi spy ring you guys uncovered that time when you were on leave?"

"Something far different, sir," Doc said, "but almost as sinister." Slightly amused that 'Happy Jack' seemed as irascible as ever, he briefly told the general what he needed.

Harding's voice exploded through the phone-line: "Hell's bells, son. You know what I'd have to go through to get a look at a file like that?"

"I realize that all too well, General," Doc said. "But I can only tell you that lives are hanging in the balance and may depend on your help."

Doc could hear sonorous breathing on the other end of the line. Then Harding said, "I'll call you back in half an hour." The connection was broken. Doc softly set the phone back in its cradle.

Exactly twenty-nine minutes and thirty-six seconds later the phone rang again and Doc once again answered it.

"All right, Atlas," Harding said. "I made a few discreet

inquiries." His sigh was audible. "But I have to have your assurance that what I tell you will remain in the strictest confidence. The integrity of the military depends on it."

"General, as I stated previously, I am trying to save a young woman's life, and for that reason, I have had to delve into this rather sordid pool. Moving in that pool has stirred up some sediment. It is regrettable, and also unfortunate to a certain degree. However, I will do my utmost not to use this information gratuitously. You have my word on it."

"Hellfire and damnation, you sure haven't changed from the time you were under my command," Harding muttered gruffly. "And I still don't understand half of what you say when you talk. But I'm an old soldier, and I know enough to go on gut instinct. Plus I know what kind of man you are…. One of the best I ever met…. So I'll tell you." His voice paused, and Doc could hear him take a breath. "It was during the occupation. Not too long after you had the showdown in that castle with that Von Strohm guy." Doc heard the man take another deep breath. This was obviously not a pleasant story. "A young German boy, eleven years old, was…assaulted. It was messy. Very messy. The accused soldier was naturally court-martialed."

Harding's voice grew almost tremulous as he continued. "The soldier's father…was a very rich and influential man back in this country." He paused to sigh once more. "So naturally, he had contacts in Europe and in the military as well. An excellent legal defense was prepared, and the soldier was acquitted after an unfortunate event."

"What type of event?"

"The victim and his family were," Harding paused momentarily, "killed in an accident prior to the case coming to full trial."

"Was that the basis for the acquittal?"

"More or less," Harding said. "It was difficult to proceed without any complaining witnesses. No victim, either. But they'd already made statements, which the prosecutor was trying to get admitted so he could proceed. Then some key evidence…disappeared."

"What type of accident was it?" Doc asked.

"It's my understanding that it was some type of automobile accident." Harding paused. "But those were common over there after the War. Look at what happened to poor old Georgie Patton."

"Do you have any details?"

"Damn few. Basically, just what I already told you." Harding paused again and Doc heard him clearing his throat. Obviously, the general was ready to take his leave. "Well, anyway, the charges had to be dropped, but the defending counsel demanded trial, to prevent any future prosecution. You can't try a man twice for the same crime, no matter what it is, if he's been acquitted."

"It sounds as though Warren Grantman was well represented," Doc said. "Can you give me the names of the officers who prosecuted and defended the case?"

"I suppose it won't do any harm at this point," Harding's voice gained in strength and authority as he continued. "But I want to re-emphasize that I'd like this entire matter to be placed in the proper perspective. Grantman's father was good to the army. He donated a lot of money to the USO, and was always someone we could count on when the chips were down. Plus, he was instrumental in setting up that Luciano-assistance for the landings in 'forty-three in Sicily."

"Grantman has ties to organized crime then?" Doc asked.

"Now, I never said that." Harding sounded flustered. "He apparently knew Luciano. How, I don't know, but he approached the man at our request. Those landings were rough. A lot more GIs would've died if that gangster hadn't used his Italian contacts."

"And he called in a favor to save his son at eleventh hour." Doc meant it more as a comment than a question, but its rhetorical nature was lost on General Harding.

"It was war, man," the general said, "and even the aftermath of war can be hell."

"As we both well know, sir."

Harding read off the names of the two military tribunal attorneys, but Doc had already surmised their identities. He thanked the general and assured him again that everything possible would be done to safeguard the integrity of the army. After hanging up, Doc considered the possibilities of the current situation for a moment, then went to his radio. He set the special frequency that would activate the miniature wireless receiver in Deagan's pocket. It was a long established procedure that upon receiving such a signal, Deagan, or any member of Doc's crew, would call back to headquarters as soon as possible. When the telephone rang several minutes later, Doc was expecting Deagan when he answered it.

"Dr. Atlas, Clyde O'Bannion here," the doorman said. "I've got some men from the coroner's office down here and they wish to speak with you on a matter they say is of utmost importance."

"Very well," Doc said. "I'll speak to one of them." After a muffled transfer, a strange voice came on the line.

"Dr. Atlas. I'm from the coroner's office. I got two stiffs,

I mean bodies, to drop off to you."

"I'll have my special elevator sent down for them," Doc said. "Just place them inside the car and step back. I'll unload them from here."

"No, sir," the man said nervously. "I need a signature from you, personally, taking responsibility for the bodies. You see, we ain't never taken them from the morgue and dropped them off in Manhattan before. Will you be coming down, or should we come up, sir?"

"I'm expecting an important call and have to remain up here," Doc considered the situation. "I'll send my elevator down for you and your cargo."

"Okay, sir. We'll be bringing them right up, then."

Doc went to the foyer, leaving the door to his quarters open so he could hear the phone, in case Deagan called. He used his passkey to send the elevator down to the first floor. Planning to have the attendants carry the stretchers into the main receiving room, he could direct them into the adjacent laboratory. From there he could place the bodies in his large freezer compartment until such time as he could withdraw the tissue samples for examination. He automatically flipped on the video monitor to watch the progress of the men in the large elevator.

Five men, in white uniforms with starched white caps, got on. Four of them were carrying two stretchers covered by heavily woven white sheets. The fifth, holding a clipboard, seemed to be the supervisor. Presumably, he was the one Doc had spoken to on the phone. This supervisor was a small dark-complexioned man with a thin mustache. The left side of his face appeared swollen and discolored. The attendant standing next to him was a much bigger man, so tall that his face was almost at eye-level with the camera. His rugged features resembled those of a prizefighter, and were strangely familiar. Doc tried to recall where he'd seen them before. Or did the man's looks merely remind him of Deagan's own crooked features?

The elevator doors slid open and the group emerged. Doc stood in the open doorway and motioned the men forward.

"If you'll be so kind as to bring them in here, gentlemen," he started to say. But before he could finish, the alarm bell rang suddenly, as the attendants stepped forward and passed through the electronic sensor system in the foyer.

Doc quickly dived under his desk as the two 'corpses' abruptly sat up on their stretchers and began spraying the room with Thompson submachine guns. The big man called a halt to the firing and dropped his end of the stretcher. He tore open his jacket and pulled up a double-barreled, sawed-off shotgun that had been suspended from his shoulder by a sling. With surprising lightness for such a huge man, he barreled through the still open door into Doc's office.

"Blackie," the big man said, motioning with one hand. "Cover me."

Blackie Pearl, the man who had been acting as the supervisor, withdrew a large, forty-five caliber Colt Government Model 1911 semiautomatic pistol from the waistband of his trousers and sprang next to the doorjamb.

"Gotcha, Moose."

Moose LeDoux kept the shotgun perpendicular to his side as he entered the office area. The Thompsons had chewed large holes in the desk and walls of the room. Moose ran his tongue over his lips and, with a quick movement, leapt around the desk.

"Damn," he muttered. "He ain't here, but we musta winged him." His big index finger pointed to the crimson splashes on the floor behind the battered desk.

"The blood trail goes that way," Blackie said, motioning for the other men to enter the office. He went to the door of the laboratory and pushed it gently with the barrel of his gun. Moose moved to the other side and muttered, "Otto. Tracy." A jerk of his huge head indicated that he wanted the two men with the Thompsons to step up to the doorway. Positioning themselves in front of the door, they leveled the machine guns at waist-height and nodded. Moose reared back and gave the door a tremendous kick, sending it hurdling back into the adjacent room.

Tracy and Otto stepped in and immediately opened up with the Tommy guns. The room, which contained several heavy wooden desks cluttered with a multitude of beakers and test tubes, was Doc's laboratory. Each desk had a faucet and sink, along with Bunsen burners and elaborate sets of titration equipment. Glass shattered as they peppered the room, spraying each desk heavily. When the deafening roars came to a stop, both Otto and Tracy stepped to the outside aisles.

Moose was set to move in behind them when he saw a golden blur. Doc reared up from behind one of the heavy desks and hurled a capped glass beaker toward the closest man, as hard as Ty Cobb gunning down a runner trying to steal second base. As it collided with Otto's face, the beaker exploded, spewing its contents. Otto recoiled with a scream of pain as sulfuric acid seared his facial membranes. His automatic reaction was to begin firing blindly. Moose ducked as the volley exploded around the room. When it became apparent that Otto was out of control, Moose pointed the sawed-off at him and fired. The blast knocked Otto back against a wall. He slid to the floor, where he lay crumpled and twisted.

"What'd ya shoot him for?" an incredulous Tracy asked, his own Tommy gun lowered toward the floor.

"Because he was a stupid idiot," Moose said, looking at him. "Come on, dammit. Move up. Atlas is only one guy, and if he'd had a gun he woulda shot it at us already."

Suddenly Doc popped up again, this time with a scalpel held like a throwing knife. Moose pulled the second trigger, but the blast went high. Still, it was good enough to offset Doc's aim, and the scalpel stuck in the wooden trim around the door. Streaking through the next doorway, Doc twisted off the end of an electrical extension cord, exposing the copper wires, and dropped them on the floor. He had already ripped open the lower portion of the lab desk and pulled loose one of the water pipes to the sink.

Moose and Blackie hugged the far wall as they went toward the door. "There he goes," Blackie yelled. "Get him!"

Tracy ran forward and had just reached the doorway when the expanding puddle from the ruptured pipe met the bare wires. A horrific boom and a flash of light accompanied Tracy's spasming body as it slammed into the wall about three feet away.

"What the hell was that?" said Blackie.

"He put an extension cord into some water, that's all," Moose said. "Come on. He's bleedin' bad. He's gotta be desperate."

Blackie stayed put and let the others continue toward the door. If it was one thing he hated, it was electricity. Moose pulled the end of the plug from the socket and tossed it aside. Then he sidled up to the door, stared at the long pattern of bloody dots on the white tile floor, and wondered what was holding this guy Atlas up. Cautiously, he pushed open the door to the next room. It was in semi-darkness, but some light was coming in through the high windows allowing a kind of limited visibility. Moose was about to go in when he remembered he had to reload, and he broke open the shotgun with a violent, snapping motion, ejected the spent shells, and jammed two more into the double breech.

Inside the gym Doc scrambled over to the table where the bowling pins were. Grabbing two of them, he ran down to the far end of the large room and paused. The pain in his left side, where the bullet had struck him, was nauseating. Still, he knew if he were to survive this siege, he would have to ignore the pain and keep functioning. Quickly stripping the laces out of his boots, he knotted the strings together and secured the narrow neck of a bowling pin with each end. Looping the line over his shoulder so the pins hung against his right chest and back, he quickly climbed up the rope to the I-beam. Once at the top he continued hand-over-hand along the beam, snaring the thick rope between his legs as he went, and drawing it along with him until it was fully extended. Then he stopped, hanging suspended about thirty feet above the floor, and waited.

The door from the lab opened cautiously and the first of the five remaining hoods came in. Doc decided to take the one carrying the Thompson out first, since his weapon obviously was the greatest threat. The others, with the exception of the shotgun toting big man, had handguns. Doc drew his legs up and fastened his feet securely around the end of the rope, keeping his legs in an L-shape. Then, he released his grip on the beam with his right hand, and dangled by only his left. Withdrawing the connected bowling pins from around his neck, Doc began spinning them, holding the laces in the middle. He released the whirling pins and, at the same instant, let go of the beam and snatched the rope with both hands. The pins sailed, in bolo-fashion, toward the hoodlum with the machine gun. He made a gurgling sound and dropped the Thompson as the heavy laces, propelled by the centrifugal force of the spinning pins, wound tightly around his neck.

Doc's body on the swinging rope smashed into a second man, knocking him into the wall with a thudding impact. Landing on his feet, Doc whirled and delivered a side kick to Moose, whose shotgun discharged into the floor. The third man pointed his pistol at Doc, but the golden giant pivoted again, knocking the revolver from the hoodlum's grasp with a perfectly executed spinning kick. Before the would-be killer could recover, Doc grabbed the man's arm, twisted under him, and raised up suddenly. Rotating the hood's hyper-extended elbow, Doc snapped the arm downward against his own shoulder. The echoing crack sent the hoodlum into a spasm of pain as he collapsed into a moaning heap on the floor. Upon seeing this, Blackie Pearl quickly backtracked through the doorway into the lab.

This guy Atlas ain't human, he thought.

Doc sought to follow him, but whirled when he heard a stirring sound behind him.

"A tough guy, huh?" Moose said, getting to his feet and balling up his fists. "Come on, Atlas, let's see what you got." He shucked off the heavy white coat to reveal his hulking chest and powerful shoulders.

Doc raised his hands and stepped forward. Moose

assumed a crouching position, but even in this crouch, he was taller than Doc. The big man shot out a surprisingly quick jab, which snapped against Doc's left temple. Doc stepped forward with a jab of his own, but the big man merely rolled his head and shoulders, slipping the punch.

"Come on," Moose sneered. "You don't look so tough to me." A grin twisted over his ring-scarred features.

Doc stepped forward gingerly, conscious of the burning pain in his left side. His white shirt had a large crimson stain

on it, and a cascade of tiny red droplets splashed onto the wooden floor. Moose feinted, then slammed a left hook into Doc's body. The ham-sized fist was smeared with Doc's blood as Moose withdrew his hand. Doc knew he had ruptured more tissue and vessels as the pain seemed to explode inside of him. The big man's strategy became ruthlessly apparent: keep hitting and moving and wait for Doc's blood-loss to substantially weaken him. The big man had time on his side.

Doc stepped toward his larger opponent, conscious that he had to end this quickly or risk either bleeding out or being beaten to death. With every sudden movement, however, the pain seared more sharply and the crimson stain expanded. Trying to concentrate on Deagan's long hours of instruction in the boxing gym, Doc moved in closer and threw a darting jab. The blow snapped Moose's head back, but the bigger man merely skipped away. Without any ropes to contain him, the experienced ring technician could keep weaving backwards with impunity. The knowledge that his confederate was still at large with a weapon also troubled Doc. The man could appear at any moment and fire his weapon. Doc knew he couldn't dodge a well-placed bullet.

Glancing around, Doc dropped his hands and stared at Moose momentarily, then turned his head toward the weapons on the floor. He feinted a half turn toward the guns, which brought Moose lurching forward. Doc was able to lash out with a carefully placed roundhouse kick to the side of LeDoux's left thigh. Moose stopped and threw an ineffective looping hook, which Doc blocked and countered with a straight right. Moose's eyes glazed over and Doc knew the man must being seeing the swarm of black dots beginning to coalesce in front of his eyes. Moose immediately began throwing a plethora of wild punches, but this time it was Doc's turn to sidestep. A well-placed blow to the solar plexus seemed to weaken the big man. Doc smashed another kick to the left thigh area, and as Moose attempted to back-up, Doc grabbed the bigger man's shirt.

Moose, the veteran of many street-fights as well as ring-wars, lashed out with his hand at Doc's face, attempting to gouge an eye-socket. But Doc swerved his head out of the way so that the clawing hands only scratched his forehead. He slammed his instep into the back of Moose's knees. The giant fell heavily to the wooden floor. As he struggled to get up as

Doc clipped a short right to the man's temple.

"Dirty son-of-a…" snarled Moose. "Why the hell don't ya fight fair?"

Amused by Moose's admonishment, Doc brought the edge of his hand across the big man's throat in a quick chopping blow. Gurgling and gasping, the huge Moose sagged onto his hands and knees. Doc watched as the ex-pug tried futilely to rise. Stepping forward he delivered a powerful uppercut that sent the big man careening over backwards. Moose's legs jerked spasmodically for a few moments, then he lay totally still.

Doc's hands went immediately to his left side. He tore open his shirt and checked the wound site. The bullet had entered the external oblique muscle area. As his fingers probed the wound, Doc could still feel the rounded dome of the projectile inside. It would have to be extracted as soon as possible. Hopefully it had not damaged his large intestine, but he still had one more hoodlum to subdue before he could check into that. Prior to checking the fallen Moose, Doc strode to the other fallen thugs and retrieved the weapons. The Thompson was almost empty, but the second man's revolver had not been fired. The hoodlum who had been snared by the bowling pins was asphyxiated, his eyes bulging, his teeth set into his distended tongue. And the one Doc had swung into via the rope, had evidently been struck a little too hard, sustaining a broken neck. Moose and the man with the shattered arm were both still alive, albeit unconscious.

Feeling that Moose was still dangerous, Doc took a few moments to secure the big man's hands behind him with some extra strong tape from one of the nearby foot lockers. He wrapped several lengths around the man's knees and ankles as well. He repeated this on the man with the shattered arm, although Doc doubted that hoodlum had any fight left in him. Doc then quickly stowed their weapons, except for the hoodlum's unfired revolver, in another footlocker and moved to the door going into the lab. The hood who'd stepped on the electrified puddle was dead also, apparently from cardiac failure.

Not uncommon in cases of severe electrical shock, Doc thought. He also reflected on the reports of electrocutions he'd read, and how they never failed to mention that it was purportedly a painless death.

The sixth hoodlum, the one called Otto, had apparently been killed instantly when he was hit with the load of buckshot the big man had fired. A large crimson stain, the size of a dinner plate, covered the front of the man's chest. Doc stepped over him, raising his gun, as he proceeded back into the remnants of his shattered office.

Six down, and one to go, he thought.

Blackie Pearl had only one thought uppermost in his mind, and that was to get the holy hell out of there. The amazing reflexes and fighting ability of this wounded man had suddenly convinced him that Atlas was something akin to Superman. Blackie had quickly crept back through the lab and the office area to get back to the foyer where they'd come in. It was only then that he realized the elevator's doors were closed. The indicator above them indicated it wasn't even on this floor anymore. Plus, he suddenly remembered, it could only be summoned by some sort of special key. Atlas had the key. There wasn't even a button for him to push.

Stairs, Blackie thought. There's gotta be a set of stairs.

With Moose and the rest of them keeping Atlas busy, maybe, just maybe, he could reach the bottom before the cops got here. To hell with Moose and the others. If they got outta here, he'd deal with them later.

Swearing frantically as he searched for some way out, he suddenly heard what sounded like a godsend: the hyper-accelerated hum of the elevator motors. He held his large pistol outstretched, so that he could shoot at Atlas if he came through the office door, and then positioned himself to the left of the elevator doors.

Maybe I'll get outta this yet. Blackie allowed himself a rueful smile.

Doc's ultra-sensitive hearing picked up the sound of the elevator motors, too. He hurried to the laboratory video monitor, which had somehow miraculously escaped the hail of bullets. Switching it on, he adjusted the channel to see if the remaining hoodlum had somehow gotten the elevator to work. But to his horror, he saw the lift was ascending, and standing alone in it, oblivious to all that had happened up here, was Polly. Doc flipped to the other channel to scan the foyer, and saw Blackie's flattened body next to the wall. He quickly rushed out of the laboratory and through the office door just as the elevator opened and Polly stepped through the aperture.

Blackie, catching a glimpse of Doc, lunged forward and fired a shot at him, the spent casing flipping off from the side of the big forty-five. The bullet went wide, striking the wall near Doc's head. Doc brought the revolver up, but before he could return fire, Blackie grabbed Polly. She attempted to twist away from him, but with strength borne from desperation, he managed to lock his left arm securely around her neck. The elevator doors whooshed closed behind the struggling couple. Doc stepped into the room as Blackie, still holding Polly, stuck his revolver against the bright auburn hair of her right temple.

"Hold it, Atlas," Blackie said. "You take another step and I'll kill her. I swear I will."

Doc raised his pistol and aimed it at Blackie, who cocked back the hammer of his own weapon. "Release her immediately."

The hood's head shook. "Huh-un. Shoot me and my reflexes will still pull this trigger," he snarled. "It'll splatter her brains all over this floor here. Is that what you want, big man?"

"Let her go, or face neutralization," Doc said, still keeping his gun trained on Blackie. Polly's face contorted in terror, but she said nothing, her breath coming in faint gasps.

"I know all about you, Atlas," Blackie said. "I know you don't like to kill people. Even a hood, like me." His lips curled back over crooked teeth. "But me, I got nothing to lose, see, so I want the damn key to that elevator right now, or I blow the dame's red head off."

Doc seemed to consider this for a moment.

"You can have the key, but let the girl go first," he said.

"You think I'm stupid, or something," Blackie said, his upper lip curling back over his teeth again. "Huh-un. Me and her are taking a little ride together. I let her go when I get to where I'm going."

Doc reached into his pocket with his left hand, still holding the revolver straight out in front of him with his right, he withdrew the passkey and held it up.

"All right," he said. "Here it is."

He made a looping underhand toss, and scrutinized the

movement of Blackie's eyes as they zeroed in on the arcing key. Anticipating the exact location of the particular cervical nerves he needed to sever, Doc adjusted his sight-picture and squeezed off one shot from the revolver. The bullet struck Blackie's neck, just under the chin, plowing through the soft tissues exactly as Doc had anticipated and cleaving the spinal cord. The hoodlum's mouth sagged open spewing blood. The gun dropped from suddenly lax fingers, and his eyes showed that split-second realization of life's sudden end.

Doc rushed forward as Polly collapsed. He knelt down beside her and checked her pulse. It was rapid, but shallow. She had fainted from the shock. Doc grabbed the large Colt forty-five Blackie had dropped and snapped the safety on. Then, placing both guns to the side, he gently picked Polly up off the floor and carried her into his infirmary.

15

On the Wings of Hermes

As if she were waking from a bad dream, Polly's eyes opened with a sudden snap. After a moment of disorientation, Doc Atlas's shirtless torso came into focus. She blinked twice, having never seen Doc without his shirt and watched, fascinated as the muscles rippled under his tawny skin. Polly tried to swallow, but her mouth was too dry. When she did manage to speak, her voice seemed to creak.

"Doc, you're bleeding."

He stood a few feet away, injecting his side with a long syringe.

"How are you feeling?" he asked. He removed the syringe and re-inserted the needle in another section of the wound site.

"What happened?" Polly asked. She started to sit up then suddenly realized she was naked from the waist up, except for her brassiere, and was covered by a white sheet. "What happened to my blouse?"

"I took the liberty of cleaning some of that hoodlum's blood from your face and neck with an alcohol swab," Doc said. "I also thought it prudent to check you for injuries. You have none, but I'm afraid that your blouse was badly stained. I put one of my lab shirts there for you to wear. There's also a glass of sherry on the table."

He set the syringe down and waited while the Novocain

took effect. Several bottles of antiseptic, a fishhook needle, and a pair of tongs were on the table next to him. Doc went to one of the cabinets along the wall and removed a spool of delicate looking thread, two more syringes, and two small vials of clear liquid.

Polly sat up, holding the sheet around her with one hand and picked up the lab shirt with the other. When Doc saw her doing this, he turned his back, allowing her a modicum of privacy.

"Oh, Doc," she said, "you're such a gentleman."

"If you wouldn't mind hurrying," he said, still facing the other direction, "I need you to monitor the phones while I put in these sutures." He held one of the vials up to eye level and stuck the syringe needle into the rubberized top.

Polly slipped into the shirt, which was very large on her. She had to roll the sleeves several times on each arm, and the neck and shoulders were so big it kept falling off on one side or the other. She slid off the bed and went to the mirror on the wall.

"Do you know where my purse is?" she asked, fluffing out her hair with her fingers.

"I believe it's in the sitting room," Doc said, injecting his left shoulder with the contents of one of the syringes: a massive dose of penicillin. He set that one down and picked up the second. "If Ace or Thomas calls, tell him there is imminent danger and to report back here immediately," he added. "I sent out a signal approximately twenty-five minutes ago and have not yet received any response. Please send out another."

He turned and glanced at her in the overly large shirt.

"Perhaps I can find something more suitable for you after I get this taken care of," he said, pointing to the wound. He selected another injection site on his shoulder and stuck in the second syringe, this one containing tetanus vaccine.

"What happened?" she asked, lifting the glass of sherry to her lips and taking a dainty sip. She felt slightly better as the warmth rushed through her. "Who was that guy?"

Doc didn't reply. He'd already gripped the tongs and had the pointed end inserted into the wound. His fingers of his left hand probed the outside portion of his side. Then with a slight grimace, he withdrew the tongs and dropped a bloody half-moon shaped slug onto table. He quickly poured antiseptic on the large cotton swabs and used them to cauterize the raw looking hole.

"Oh, my God," Polly said. "Is that a bullet?"

"Yes." Doc picked up the fishhook needle and looped some of the fine thread through it. "Luckily it missed any vital organs and lodged in the muscle tissue. Hopefully, these sutures will hold until I can get it properly attended to."

"Doc, you need to go to the hospital." Polly brought the glass to her mouth again and, this time, took a larger sip.

"No time for that now, Polly. The penultimate act of this little drama has already been set into motion. We'll have to move quickly, or all may be lost." He pinched the ragged tissue together and inserted the end of the fishhook through his skin, drawing the dark thread after it.

Polly looked away.

"I think I'll wait in the other room, okay?" she said.

Without looking up, Doc nodded.

After he had tied off the all of the sutures, Doc went to the closet in his bedroom and selected some new garments. He chose one of the standard tan chambray shirts, with various pockets sewn on both the outside and the inside. He took out a new pair of boots, and got out his utility belt and sidearm. He didn't normally like to carry a weapon, but with Penny, Thomas, and Ace in danger, he felt he could hardly afford not to. He sat on the bed and gingerly slipped on the boots, taking care not to rupture the delicate stitching. After lacing the boots, he started to put on the shirt. Hesitating, he returned to the closet, and removed his specially woven bulletproof vest. It was made of incredibly strong synthetic fibers that Doc had refined in his laboratory. The vest would stop a round from most standard pistols and was relatively light. It was also surprisingly thin, so it could be worn unobtrusively underneath a regular garment. Doc laced it in place around his large upper body, then slipped on his shirt. Once the shirt had been buttoned, he checked himself in the mirror. The vest was virtually undetectable.

He strode into the sitting room and looked expectantly at Polly. She was sitting at his long walnut table trying to scrub the crimson stains in her blouse. A cup of water and a discolored handkerchief sat in front of her. She'd spread a newspaper out to protect the fine wood.

"I'll be glad to pay for a new one, Polly."

"That's okay, Doc" She looked up at him with a worried expression. "I feel better doing something, you know?"

Doc nodded. "Any word from Thomas yet?"

She shook her head, then asked in a timid voice, "Are they in very much danger?"

"At this point, that's impossible to know." His lips compressed into a thin line. "But, I'm afraid it doesn't bode well that they haven't called. You did broadcast the second signal?"

Polly nodded.

Doc went to the radio and adjusted the frequency. "I'm activating the emergency tracking signal," he said. A part of the miniature transmitter Deagan carried with him would act as a foil, reflecting certain radio waves back to the source. It was a fail-safe device that Doc had installed for emergencies, such as this one, where he might have to locate his aides. He then went to his telephone and dialed a number. When a voice on the other end answered, he spoke into the receiver, "This is Doctor Michael Atlas. I'd like to speak to Detective Hal Roland, please."

He heard the sound of the phone being set down, and a disinterested voice say, "Hey, Roland. It's for you."

More than just a few moments later, a voice said, "Roland. Can I help you?"

"Detective Roland, this is Doc Atlas. I wonder if you might clear something up for me."

"What's that?" Doc heard the quick snap of a lighter over the line and knew the man had lighted one of his Chesterfields.

"Do you remember Webber and Boggs, the two hoodlums who were killed a few years ago?" Doc asked.

"The two mutts that were suspects in the Casper bombing?" Roland said. "Yeah, what about 'em?"

"They were out on bond at the time they were killed, correct?"

"Yeah," Roland said. "Ain't our legal system a wonderful thing?"

Doc ignored the man's sarcasm. "And their attorney was Paul Milton?"

"Right again, Atlas." Doc heard a sigh. "Look, is this going anywhere, 'cause if it ain't, I'm a little busy to be playing twenty questions with you."

"If you could just bear with me a moment more, I'd like your opinion on something," Doc said. "Do you think Milton could have conspired with Casper to have them released on a lowered bond? I mean it's customary to hold murder suspects without bond, is it not?"

"Yeah, but as I remember it, the case was pretty flimsy. All circumstantial stuff," Roland said. "No witnesses, and everybody knew that an attorney like Milton would make mince meat out of the D.A.'s case when it came to trial. He claimed they were just fall guys."

"Was Judge Casper involved in the process at all?"

"Nah, that woulda been seen as a conflict of interest." Doc could hear his loud exhalation. "Besides, Milton and Casper didn't get along too good."

"Why was that?"

"Beats me," Roland said. "But who can tell about judges and lawyers. If you ask me—"

"I have just one more question," Doc said, cutting him off. "Earlier today you mentioned you and Milton knew each other before the War, correct?"

"Yeah, that's right."

"Then you said something that I found confusing," Doc continued. "I believe you alluded to Milton's leaving the District Attorney's Office before the War began."

"Yeah, he went back to England, or something. Then they bombed Pearl Harbor, and I was so pissed off about Pearl and what the damn Japs did that I enlisted. But so what? So did a lot of guys."

"I thought it strange, since there is no record of Milton ever being in the military," Doc said.

There was a pause, then Roland said, "Nah, he was in. He's half-Brit, so he enlisted in some limey-commando outfit right after Pearl Harbor. SAS or something. I bumped into him once over in Australia. Why?"

"Some dissonant cognition," Doc said.

"Huh?"

"Never mind, Detective. By the way, some gangsters invaded my headquarters and tried to assassinate me a little while ago."

"What?" Roland said. "Anybody hurt?"

"Yes," Doc said, "and unfortunately I had to dispatch several of them," Doc said

"Dispatch," Roland repeated slowly. "You mean...you killed them?"

"Precisely," Doc answered.

"How many?"

"There are seven total," Doc said. "Two are injured, but still alive. If I can prevail upon you to notify the proper police authorities in Manhattan, I have some pressing business and must leave immediately."

"Hey, wait a minute, Atlas," Roland said quickly. "You mean you ain't called nobody about it yet? And there's a bunch of dead guys there?"

"As I said, two are still alive." Doc glanced at his watch. "But that's essentially correct."

"Hold on just one second, buster," Roland said. Doc could hear the mouthpiece on the other end being covered. Approximately ten seconds later he came back on the line.

"So tell me what happened, Doc," Roland said, his tone becoming almost amiable. "I know you're a crack shot and can take care of yourself in a fight. You proved that in the alley the other day."

"Detective, I already told you that I have pressing business elsewhere. I'll be available to give a full statement later, but for now, I must go. I'll leave my secretary Polly here at my headquarters to admit the proper authorities."

"Wait a minute, Atlas," Roland said, his voice raising a few decibels. "You gotta stay there. You can't leave. It's a crime scene."

"Regrettably, I must," Doc said. He heard Roland yelling something about issuing a lawful order to remain there, and if not an APB would be put out. Doc hung up and turned to Polly. "I must go now to see if I can find the others. The police are on their way. When they get here give them every courtesy and cooperation."

"But I still don't know what happened, Doc," Polly pleaded.

He placed his hand on her shoulder.

"Polly, I can't think of a more capable person to brief them," he said. "Now, did you check on those names at the tax office?"

"Yeah, I did," she said. She reached for her purse and took out two long sheets of paper. "I backtracked on both of their holdings like you said. Everything's listed under various company names and dummy corporations. Edgar's got a large estate west of the city he uses as some sort of sanatorium or religious retreat." She held up one of the papers. "This is where it's listed."

Doc looked at the address, then went to a section of large maps in his library. Polly followed along behind him. As he scanned the maps, he said, "I can't delay any longer. The police will most likely be looking for me, so I'm going to use the Hermes."

Polly nodded.

"But how will you get over to the waterfront?" she asked. "They'll be watching for the Auburn, and the LaSalle's not back yet."

"I'll have to find a less conspicuous way," he said. He turned to leave and felt her hand on his arm.

"Doc," Polly said, moving forward to embrace him. "I haven't even thanked you for saving my life. That guy was going to kill me, wasn't he?" She leaned the side of her face against his massive chest.

A slight smile traced over his lips, and he kissed her forehead gently. "That was something I was not going to allow to happen."

"So...." Her voice was tentative, uncertain. "Do you think my Tommy will be okay?"

Doc searched for some comforting phrase to reassure her, but couldn't think of anything to say, except, "I'll do my best to find him."

Doc took the special elevator down to the first floor. Instead of going through the lobby, he turned and slipped through the door leading to the rear loading dock. He walked quickly out of the building and began a fast trot down the alleyway but slowed suddenly, being somewhat weakened by the loss of blood and the pulling sensation in his side. The stitches were starting to rupture slightly. At the corner he heard the wail of several police sirens. They would be here momentarily.

Doc knew he had to get to the large waterfront building where he stored many of his cars, boats, and planes. But he also knew he would be exceptionally conspicuous on a trek of several blocks. He needed a way to get there that would not attract undue attention from the police force that was undoubtedly alerted to be on the lookout for him. Perhaps he could flag down a cab, although that might seem particularly obvious. As he neared the mouth of the alley, Doc saw a large bus idling by the curb. He ran to the folding doors and knocked on them. A heavy-set man with blond hair was sitting behind the wheel eating a well-stuffed sandwich and reading a Captain Marvel comic book. He glanced at Doc and shook his head before turning back to the comic.

Doc knocked again, a little more insistently this time. The man turned again, and his eyes narrowed as he stared through the glass. The doors folded open with a hiss.

"I'm sorry, mister, but I'm not in service," the driver said. Suddenly his eyes widened as he realized who was standing at the curbside. "Say, ain't you Doc Atlas?"

Doc nodded.

The driver put down his sandwich and the comic as he stepped over to the door extending his palm.

"I'm Pat Cunningham," he said with a fawning grin. "I gotta tell you, I'm your biggest fan. I read all about you in the papers all the time. And in the pulps too, even though they use a different name for you."

Doc shook the man's hand and placed his foot on the first step.

"Patrick, I need your help," he said. "It's imperative I get to the waterfront immediately, and without being seen. Can you help me?"

"Well, I guess so. My route starts in fifteen minutes, but if it's important…."

"It's quite literally a matter of life and death," Doc said.

Pat jumped back behind the wheel and pressed the starter button. As the big diesel engine rumbled to life, he raised up slightly and adjusted the legend on the front of the bus to read CHARTER. As he drove, he kept talking about how he followed Doc's adventures and how much of a pleasure it was to meet him face-to-face.

"You got time to sign an autograph, Doc?" Pat asked. "It's not for me, it's for my kid."

"Certainly," Doc said, as the silhouette of the waterfront came into view just beyond Thirty-fourth and West.

Doc unlocked the hangar-like doors of the warehouse and went inside. He strode quickly to the light panel and flipped the switch. The inside of the building was suddenly illuminated by numerous hanging sodium vapor lights. To the right were several sections that housed Doc's other cars. He had various automobiles that were painted to resemble police and fire vehicles, as well as government sedans and taxis. But the situation was such that he couldn't afford wasting time driving to his destination. Nor could he take the chance he would be spotted by a roving patrol car that most certainly had received a broadcast to detain him if spotted. He moved past these partitions to the hangar area.

Doc stored his regular airplanes at a small airport outside the city, but he did keep the Hermes at this location. It was a special prototype motorized glider Doc had built along the lines of the CG4A Glider that had been used so successfully during the war. Doc had cast the Hermes out of extra-strength tubular steel and fashioned wings from a specially treated cloth. The small craft could be disassembled and carried in the back of a regular truck, if necessary. When bolted together, the wingspan was only thirty feet, its length only seventeen. Two seats, side-by-side, were mounted in front of a light, but powerful engine, which operated the overhead propeller system.

Doc did a pre-flight safety check of all the cables, gauges, equipment, and the fuel level. Slipping on his goggles and wrist altimeter, he pushed the Hermes so it faced a large sliding door on the river side of the building. Before getting in the pilot's seat, he went to one of the large cabinets standing against the wall and removed a small, battery-operated radio-wave receiving device. Turning it on, he watched the flickering needle vibrate hesitantly. He ran briskly to the large door and, after unlocking it, pressed the electronic-opening switch, then set the timer to automatically close the door after one minute. After getting into the pilot seat, he watched the door slide upward along its tracks to expose the dark, roiling surface of the Hudson.

The engine roared to life and Doc taxied toward the open door. Outside, the cement strip adjacent to the warehouse was over two hundred feet long, which was more than adequate to effect a take-off. Doc angled the Hermes into the wind and glanced back at the open doorway. The door was beginning its automated descent. He concentrated on achieving the proper lift-off, and felt the Hermes' wheels leave the ground. As he gained speed Doc rolled the craft to his right, zooming out over the water. He banked left and pulled back on the stick to gather as much altitude as he could before heading west. He felt a silent thrill as the tall skyline shrank beneath him as the small, lightweight aircraft lifted him farther and farther into the sky. The sun hung like a gigantic orange globe over the western horizon and Doc estimated he had maybe forty minutes of daylight left. Forty minutes to find Penny, Thomas, and Ace. He checked the altimeter and glanced at the radio-wave receiver. The needle still hovered only slightly above zero. In his mind's eye, Doc reviewed the maps that he'd studied before he'd left. He had a general idea where K.C. Edgar's rural estate was located, but finding it from the air could be a bit tricky. Fuel was always an important factor whenever flying, but it was critical in the Hermes. He didn't have the luxury to waste even a drop. Hopefully the miniature receiver would help him find their location quickly, before darkness fell, because, besides the fuel factor, landing the Hermes at night on unfamiliar rough ground was a task he wasn't anxious to attempt. It was something akin to suicide. He glanced at the quickly fading light, compressed his lips, and considered a grim thought.

What other choice did he have?

16

Theater of Death

DEAGAN suddenly became aware that he was conscious, but his extensive military training kept him from moving. Instead he lay still and tried to collect his thoughts, and listened. The last thing he remembered, he was in the court building on his way through the back corridors when somebody'd laid a sap just above his right ear. The tight, unnatural position in which he was lying, and the numbness creeping through his arms and legs, told him he was bound hand and foot. He cautiously peered out through his lashes and saw the bound bodies of Penny and Ace next to him. They appeared to be in some sort of room with large, hanging curtains. Like a movie theater. The floor, made of hard wooden planks, seemed elevated, like some kind of stage or platform. Beyond the curtains were rows and rows of finely cushioned chairs. It was a theater of some kind, and they were on the stage. Then he heard the voices. One was Hamilton Vernon's. The other sounded strangely familiar, but he wasn't sure why. A moment later it came to him.

"Look, K.C., this whole thing's gotten out-of-hand. We can't afford to dally. Let's just kill them and make it look like the Wraith did it."

"Patience, Hamilton, patience," Edgar said. The man's voice had a patronizing lilt to it. He was dressed in a dirty looking tan robe, which had probably been white once upon a time. "The boss wants us to find out just how much they know so we can better formulate our planned explanation. Remember, there's still the last phase of our operation to complete tonight."

"The longer we delay, the greater the chances that Atlas will find us," Vernon said. "You don't know the guy. He's not human."

"Will you relax? I told you, Atlas is being dealt with as we speak." Edgar laughed. "Leo sent Moose and six of the boys to deal with him. The good doctor has probably gone the way of all heroic legends by now."

Doc ambushed? Deagan thought. No way. They bit off more than they could chew with doing that. But the uncertainty danced through his mind like a winding flame.

"Atlas is a lot tougher than you think," Vernon said. "He probably took care of your clowns, and now he's going to know I set him up."

Edgar laughed, "Were you this nervous when you and Ward took care of that little matter in Germany? The way I heard it, that little traffic crash you set up was artistry. Pure artistry."

"That was different," Vernon said. "They were just some dumb krauts. They were the enemy. It was war-time, for the love of Pete."

"But remember, the key ingredients are still the same," Edgar said. "As long as we're the ones ultimately controlling the investigation we'll be all right." He took out what appeared to be a hand rolled cigarette and lit it. "That's why we have to find out what Atlas and his group know. Or rather, what they knew." He held the smoke in for an unusually long time, then exhaled. Deagan recognized the sweetish smell of the burning substance from the times he'd been in Mexico. It was marijuana.

Edgar chuckled softly. "Now, I've instructed Khan to procure the proper equipment for our interrogation. I suggest that we do the woman first, in front of the two men. They'll break faster that way." He walked over toward the bound figures on the floor and took another long drag on the cigarette. "A pity to have to disfigure such a beautiful woman," he said. "But I'm sure you'll find Khan's technique very instructive. It's known as the death of a thousand cuts."

"You're sick," Vernon said.

"Such squeamishness." Edgar laughed. He took one more long inhalation and raised his foot, tapping the cinder out on the sole of his thick sandal. "After all you've been involved in? But don't fret. We'll tie this one up just as neatly as we did the little error with dear Ellen." He touched the burned end of the cigarette a few times, then dumped it into the pocket of his robe.

Crummy slob, thought Deagan. He had to figure a way to get out of these damn bonds. Otherwise, they were goners. Ace and he knew what they were getting into and they'd faced death before, but poor Penny.... Deagan's heart sank. If only Doc were here, he thought. But he probably don't even know where we are.

At that moment Khan walked in, his swarthy features impassive under a scarlet turban. He carried a long roll of chicken wire and a large dagger. The blade was curved, like the coils of a snake and the handle fashioned from mother of pearl. Edgar motioned for Vernon to set the prisoners up. They arranged Deagan and Assante against the wall and dragged Penny in front of them onto a thick strip of carpeting, which was stained with dried blood. The hulking Sikh applied water to each of their faces until it became apparent that they were conscious.

"Is everybody awake now?" Edgar said. His lips curled back exposing a row of yellow teeth. "Good, because you're going to partake in a little intercultural exchange ceremony."

"Listen, there's no reason to hurt her," Deagan said. He felt the desperation edging into his tone. "She don't know nothing."

Edgar frowned, strode over to him, and kicked him hard in the shins and again in the gut. Deagan groaned, but didn't cry out. He glared at the Transcendental Prophet with a look of pure hatred.

"You will not interrupt me again," Edgar spat in clipped tones.

"Big man when you're pushing around women and men who are tied up," Ace said. "Just take off these damn ropes..."

Edgar's face reddened as he glared from Assante to Deagan. "Obviously this may require a more detailed interrogation than I anticipated," he said. "But that just makes things all the more enjoyable. Khan, begin."

The big Indian nodded and sliced the ropes securing Penny's arms. She struggled ineffectually as his huge hands stretched out her left arm.

"Let go of me, you creep," she said. Khan's fingers dug deeper into her flesh.

Penny attempted to bite his hand, but the giant merely cuffed her viciously across the mouth. She gasped and as her head was thrown back, the blood smeared her teeth. Khan grabbed her wrist and wound a portion of the chicken wire around her arm, immobilizing the elbow. A second wrapping of the coil made her flesh stand out between each loop of the mesh. Khan twisted Penny's right arm behind her back, then leaned forward, forcing her to the floor. After kneeling down to straddle her, he picked up the long dagger and began rubbing the point of the blade across her outstretched arm.

Penny screamed as a line of crimson welled up and flowed down her arm.

"Let her go, you son-of-a...!" Assante cried. Edgar's hideous laugh drowned out the rest of his words.

"It'll more interesting when we get to the other parts of her body," Edgar said with a wicked smile.

Khan flipped Penny onto her back, using his knife to slice open the front of her dress, exposing the swell of her breasts inside the lacy whiteness of her slip and brassiere.

"If I ever get out of this, I'll kill you," Deagan said gutturally.

"I'm afraid that isn't very likely, Mr. Deagan," Edgar said with a smirk.

Just then a haunting, whistled melody trickled from the heavy curtains off to the right side of the stage. Edgar and Vernon looked around, trying to pinpoint the source of the sound.

"More likely than you might think," a strange voice said. Edgar whirled just as the Wraith appeared, strolling toward them, his big forty-five outstretched. This time the bush hat was gone, and in its place was a black stocking cap, fitted over the same darkly translucent mask. Although the mask made him appear almost faceless, what features that could be discerned appeared horribly twisted.

"Ace, look," Deagan said. "It's the Wraith."

"Tell that big monster to get away from the girl," the Wraith said. "Do it now, or I'll put a bullet in you."

"Khan," Edgar said. The giant rose holding the dagger in one hand and the excess chicken wire in the other.

"Drop the knife to the floor," the Wraith said. When Khan complied, the Wraith told him to kick it away from him. Moving forward, the figure in black pushed Edgar and Vernon toward the big man. Momentarily turning his head, the Wraith started to say something to reassure Penny, who was crying hysterically. But as he did so, the huge Khan whipped the roll of chicken wire toward his gun hand, knocking the weapon from the Wraith's gloved fingers and onto the stage floor. The giant moved forward with incredible quickness for a man his size, but the Wraith suddenly stepped backwards, withdrawing a long, leather sap from his left jacket pocket, and smacked Hamilton Vernon across the temple with it. He threw the dazed prosecutor in the path of the onrushing giant, who stumbled slightly. Edgar made a quick rush for the fallen pistol, but with a shadowy flick of his arm the Wraith sent a long throwing-knife toward the scrambling prophet. The blade sank deeply into Edgar's right shoulder and he crumpled to the floor, writhing in pain. Both Ace and Deagan began frantically scooting toward him, their bodies writhing, snakelike fashion.

"Nice throw," Deagan yelled.

The enormous Khan reared suddenly to his feet and grabbed the shadowy figure in a bear hug. He lifted the Wraith off his feet, locking his powerful arms around the dark avenger's back. The Wraith cocked back his arm and smashed several hard punches to the giant's face, but they seemed to have no effect. Khan walked forward to the wall of the stage. Placing the still helpless Wraith against the wall, Khan began to bear down with greater force. Gloved hands frantically ripped at the huge Sikh's face, twisting the giant's lip and trying to tear open his mouth. The massive arms clinched tighter and each breath became successively harder to draw. Deagan was sure the Wraith's ribs were ready to break.

In desperation the black hands flailed about and caught one of the thin ropes that operated the curtain. The Wraith quickly looped the slack line around the giant's stovepipe neck and pulled. The big man's lips twisted downward into a jagged grimace. Kahn attempted to tighten his grip on the bear hug, but the line began cutting into the flesh and tissue of his neck. The Wraith's breathing was coming in hoarse pants now and it appeared his arms would fall uselessly to his sides at any second. Still, the gloved fingers twisted the knotted cord at the huge man's neck. Suddenly, the giant released him and seized the gloved hands twisting the cord. As soon as his feet were solidly on the stage floor, the Wraith's right knee shot up into Khan's groin. Sagging slightly, the giant released the Wraith's arms, and grunted. The dark figure sidestepped away delivering a powerful two-punch combination to the huge man's left side.

Khan ripped the cord from around his neck and glared at the Wraith, his mouth twisting into a hateful scowl. Arms outstretched, Khan lumbered forward, obviously intent on grabbing the shadowy figure once again, and tearing him limb from limb. But this time the Wraith nimbly sidestepped again and delivered a whipping kick to the big man's left thigh. As Khan whirled, the kick was repeated, this time delivered to the knee area, followed by a snapping punch to the giant's mouth. Khan's lips curled back in a feral grimace, his teeth glinting like a blood-covered flash of bone through an open wound. As the Wraith attempted to parry yet another rush by the powerful Sikh, the Indian was able to connect with a looping punch that sent the darkly clad figure reeling backward.

Sensing his advantage, Khan leaped forward with incredible quickness. The Wraith attempted to avoid the giant, but was again shaken by a powerful blow that dropped him to his knees. The gloved hands spread out on the floor of the stage, and before he could rise, the giant delivered a vicious kick to the Wraith's abdomen. The kick was so powerful it lifted the shadowy avenger completely off the floor and sent him rolling several feet. Khan rushed forward, intent on finishing his foe and raised his leg to execute a powerful stomping kick, but the Wraith somehow managed to stagger to his feet. Before he could straighten up and pivot away, Khan's immense hands seized the Wraith's throat. The look of rage was momentarily supplanted by a sinister smile as the giant tightened his grip, but a flash of dark limbs, followed by a frightening ripping sound caused Khan's sinister smile to sag somewhat lugubriously. The large hands seemed to linger at the dark man's throat only a moment more before falling away. Khan took a small step backwards and reached almost tentatively for the front of his tan tunic, which was now bright red, with the mother-of-pearl hilt of the curved dagger protruding from the center. Khan's incomprehensible words, spewing forth with red, frothy bubbles, continued as his lips drew back and he tumbled to the stage floor. The enormous legs twitched and kicked a few times, then he lay still.

"Good fight, brother," Deagan said. "Couldn't have handled that one better myself."

"We've got this one covered," Ace said.

The Wraith glanced around and saw that Assante and

Deagan had literally pinned the prone Edgar to the floor using their own bodies. Deagan raised his legs and dropped his feet roughly onto the back of the Transcendental Prophet's head with a resounding thunk. The thin blade of the Wraith's knife was still embedded in Edgar's shoulder.

"Good job, men," the Wraith said. "Forgive me, if I don't untie you just this minute, but I have some business with our eminent District Attorney."

He stepped over and retrieved his pistol, then went over to the supine figure of Hamilton Vernon, slapping the unconscious prosecutor's face slightly. After a moment Vernon blinked groggily and the Wraith pulled him roughly to his feet.

"Time is running short, Mr. Prosecutor," the Wraith growled in a low voice. "And this is your last chance for a reduced sentence." He rammed the muzzle of the forty-five against Vernon's nose. "Now, spill it."

"I–I don't have to talk to a hoodlum like you," Vernon sputtered. "I'm the District Attorney."

"As far as I'm concerned," the Wraith said, "you're just another two-bit hood in a three-piece suit. Right now, the only thing you are is a step away from singing soprano." In a darting motion he withdrew the automatic from Vernon's face and stuck it against the D.A.'s crotch. A roar of thunder and a flash of light made everyone in the room jump. Everyone except the Wraith, who readjusted the gun so it fit snugly against Vernon's private parts.

Deagan and Assante looked over in horror, and saw that although the bullet had gone low, the heat from the blast had only seared open the inseam of the prosecutor's slacks. The strong smell of urine filled the stage area as a puddle formed around Vernon's shoes. The Wraith said, "Talk. Now. Or I raise my aim."

"All right, all right," Vernon said. His voice quavered. "What do you want to know?"

"The Grantman kidnapping." The Wraith's voice was a low growl. "What's the set-up about?"

Vernon's mouth lolled open, his breaths as rapid as a dog's.

The Wraith's gloved fist tightened around the prosecutor's neck. "Come on, give."

Vernon's voice seemed to raise a few octaves. "The Grantman kidnapping–it was just a smoke screen. To fool the cops. Draw them away. The real hit's gonna be Congressman Marcantonio tonight at the fund raiser."

"You worthless coward," Edgar shouted. "Don't tell him anything. We'll only be held accountable for what they can prove."

Deagan raised his feet and brought them down hard on the back of the prophet's head again. Edgar yelped in pain.

"I'm beginning to get the hang of doing that," Mad Dog said.

"Vernon, keep your damn mouth shut," Edgar grunted. "Or you're a dead man."

Vernon's eyes flashed to the fallen prophet. "He's right. I can't talk. They'll kill me."

"Wrong," the Wraith growled. "Right now you're accountable to me," He pressed the muzzle further into Vernon's groin. "Talk. Now."

"K.C.," Vernon shouted. "He's got the gun right against my balls."

"Like you got any, you gutless wonder," Edgar managed to mutter before Deagan repeated his foot gesture.

"Give me the details of the hit," the Wraith said.

"It's gonna be when Marcantonio moves to the podium to give his speech," Vernon said. "Right after they show the newsreel. There's somebody dressed like you who's gonna shoot him."

"Who?"

"I can't say," Vernon sobbed. "Please. They'll kill me."

Another deafening roar sounded. Vernon jerked and nearly fainted, but when the smoke cleared it became obvious that the Wraith had only fired between the man's legs once again.

"Last chance, or I aim higher," the shadowy avenger said.

"It's got to be Ward Casper," Penny said. "I saw the outfit in his closet right before he chloroformed me."

"Is she right?" the Wraith asked.

Vernon nodded, the tears running down his cheeks. "Everybody knows he's authorized to carry a gun, so it won't be suspicious. After he does it he'll just ditch the costume. There's an old tunnel system that connects the hotel and the courthouse."

"Why is he going to kill him?" the Wraith said, easing his grip slightly. "And why try to pin all this on me?"

"We needed a fall-guy with a bad reputation. The city's almost bankrupt," Vernon sobbed. "All the labor strikes and everything. Marcantonio's voted against Taft-Hartley and has been opposing the plan to use state and federal funds to start the big highway project. It's the only chance to appease organized labor and get things moving again."

"By displacing thousands of poor people from their homes?" Ace said.

"Nobody cares about them," Vernon said nervously,

turning his head as if almost glad to address someone other than the faceless nemesis that stood before him.

The Wraith pulled the man closer. "What's Casper's connection to all this?"

"He's...he's been involved for a long time. Both of us have." He looked down. "It goes back to the War. Something we did when we were in the army together."

"What was that you and he were saying before about Ellen Casper?" the Wraith demanded, pulling Vernon's face back toward his own.

"Ellen...Ward's wife...she was killed," he said nervously.

"Don't tell him anything, you damn idiot," Edgar roared again. As Deagan raised his still-bound feet once again, the prophet made a snake-like move and rolled free of their confining legs. He rose suddenly and ran toward the Wraith pulling out the impaled knife from his shoulder as he moved. The Wraith whirled, twisting Vernon in between him and the advancing assailant just as Edgar slashed with the blade. Vernon screamed in pain and a thunderous report seemed to follow almost simultaneously. The Transcendental Prophet clutched at his chest furiously, then sank to the floor. The knife clattered on the planks beside him.

The Wraith checked Vernon's wound, a long gash across the chest. It looked bloody, but rather shallow.

"He'll be all right," the Wraith said, letting the prosecutor drop to the floor. "The wound's not serious. He just fainted."

"Certainly not a gold medal performance," Ace said with a grin.

The Wraith holstered his weapon, stooped to pick up his knife, then walked over to Deagan and Assante. He leaned over and cut Mad Dog's bonds, then handed him the thin blade.

"I'll see to the lady," he said. Walking over to Penny, he knelt beside her. The first thing he did was to help her to her feet. Her right hand went immediately to hold up her ruined dress. "I'm sorry, but this may hurt," the Wraith said. He began to carefully peel back the wire mesh, and Penny screamed in pain.

Suddenly in a flash almost too fast to be seen, Doc Atlas rushed through the rear of the stage area and grabbed the Wraith with his powerful hands. With a quick pivoting motion, Doc flipped the dark man over his shoulder. The Wraith made a heavy thud as his body crashed down onto the planks of the stage. He attempted to roll to his feet, but Doc was on him, delivering a tremendous punch to the masked temple. The Wraith careened over on  his side, but Doc still wasn't finished. He jumped forward and grabbed the Wraith's weapon, ripping it from its holster and tossing it behind him. Pulling the dark man to his feet, Doc seized the Wraith's shirt, bundling the black cloth in his left fist, while drawing back his right. Before he could deliver the punch, Doc felt Deagan's hand clutch his own.

"Doc, no," Deagan said. "Don't."

Doc's amber-colored eyes were ablaze as he glanced back at Deagan. He was not used to anyone questioning him, let alone one of his closest friends.

"Thomas, let me go," Doc commanded.

"Un-uh," Deagan said. "This guy saved our bacon, and I ain't gonna stand by and watch you smack him around no more."

"He's right, Doc," Ace said, struggling to feet. "He saved us all."

"But this man is a criminal," Doc said. "One positive act cannot cancel out the many crimes he's committed. Have you all forgotten that one of our goals in this mission was to bring him to justice?"

"I can no longer abide by this code of self-righteous vengeance you seem bent upon," Ace said.

Doc looked at him questioningly. "Meaning what?" he said.

"Meaning I can't stomach you cutting up his brain and making him into another one of your passive idiots." Ace shouted. His tone modified slightly as he added, "Doc, you're the finest man I've ever known, and you saved my life that time in Normandy. But aren't you putting yourself above the system, the very fabric of the law, that you've sworn to uphold?"

The words seemed to cut into Doc like a scalpel. Ace stared at him a moment longer, then made his way over to Penny. With a deft but careful move he peeled away the rest of the chicken wire. "As far as I'm concerned, Doc, if you want to do that, you can do it alone. I'm finished with you."

"That goes for me too, Doc," Deagan said, somewhat more gently. "In this case, anyway."

"Count me with them," Penny said, wiping the tears away from her bruised face. "This man's a hero. We'd all be dead if it weren't for him." She held her bloodied arm, the tears streaming down her face, and looked away.

Deagan felt the tension evaporate from the powerful golden arm. Doc's left hand let the dark cloth slip from between his fingers, as he released his hold on the Wraith, who had recovered somewhat in the interim.

"Bonnie Grantman's in the next room," Doc said. He added almost absently, "She's sedated, but appears to be unharmed."

"Doc," Deagan said. "We got to get back to the city. They're gonna assassinate Congressman Marcantonio tonight at that fund raiser across from city hall."

"I assumed something of the sort," Doc said. "The kidnapping of the Grantman girl was part of an elaborate subterfuge." His voice had recovered its resonance. He walked over to Penny and touched her shoulder. "You'd better let me check that wound."

"I'm okay," she said. "Thanks to him." She nodded at the Wraith, who was still standing at stage left. Then her fingers caressed Doc's hand and her lips curved into a slight smile. "Just get me to phone so I can call this damn story in."

Doc smiled at her bravery. She continued to look up at him, and then kissed him gently. Assante sighed and shifted his gaze to the floor. Doc took a tube of antiseptic cream and a spool a gauze out of his utility belt. He spread the cream over the torn skin on Penny's left arm, then he wound some gauze around the wounds.

"Make sure you keep this clean, until we can attend to it further," he said. He walked over to the fallen K.C. Edgar, who by this time had a large crimson puddle spreading beneath him. Leaning down to check the man's carotid pulse, Doc straightened a moment later and shook his head. He did the same for Khan, and then stepped over to Hamilton Vernon.

"This man appears to be wounded only superficially," Doc said. He removed a pair of handcuffs from his belt and secured them over Vernon's wrists. "When he comes to, make sure to tell him he's under arrest."

"It'll be a pleasure," Ace said, grinning slightly. "And I'll be sure to tell him I'm not available for the defense."

"Thomas," Doc said, "I'll need you to call Detective Roland at the following number." He jotted it down on the back of a card. "Tell him where you are and that you've recovered Bonnie Grantman. Do not mention my involvement at this time, nor should he tell anyone else that the girl has been found, especially Randolph Grantman."

Deagan nodded.

"So when am I going to be able to call in my scoop?" Penny asked.

"When the final act is complete," Doc said, glancing around the ironic setting. "There are still killers that need to be stopped." He walked over to the area where he'd thrown the Wraith's pistol and picked it up. Then he walked slowly across the stage to the darkly clad figure, and handed him the gun, butt first.

"Perhaps you would like to accompany me back to the city," Doc said. "We have an assassination to stop."

"We'll never make it back in time," the Wraith said, holstering the pistol.

"How did you get here?" Doc asked.

"I've got a motorcycle," the Wraith said. "A black

Indian,"

Doc nodded.

"I saw your unconscious friends being loaded into the back of a private ambulance in the alley behind the court building," the Wraith continued. "It looked fishy, and I decided to follow them. When they started going away from the city instead of to a hospital, I got real suspicious and tagged along."

"And a good thing, too," Deagan said. "But how did you find us, Doc?"

"As I told you before, I suspected Edgar's involvement," Doc said, staring at the obscured face of the masked figure before him. "Polly found this estate listed on the county tax records so I surmised that you might have been here. But principally, I tracked the frequency from your miniature radio transmitter."

Deagan grinned, reached in his pocket, and took out the fountain pen-sized device.

"You sure got here quick," he said.

"I took the Hermes," Doc answered.

"You flew the Hermes here?" Deagan said. "Wow."

"Yes," Doc said. Then, to the Wraith, "We can fly back to the city so we can apprehend the rest of these villains. You may pick up your motorcycle later. Thomas will see to it that it's stored safely in my warehouse."

"It'd be my pleasure," Deagan said, moving forward and extending his hand. "For saving our bacon."

After a moment he felt the gloved hand clasp his own as he stared at the twisted features, vaguely visible through the dark translucence.

"But why, Atlas?" the Wraith asked, turning toward Doc.

"Why should you want me to go with you?"

"So you can finally expiate the demons that haunt you," Doc said, softly. "And put Ellen Casper's ghost to rest."

17

Melody of Vengeance

ᛏᚺᛖ two men strode through some French doors and into the moonlit expanse of the mansion's sumptuous grounds. Doc rounded the corner of the house and continued up a long, crushed stone drive. The sleek frame and angular wings of the Hermes sat about thirty feet away. The bodies of two hoodlums lay on the ground between the house and the aircraft. Doc stepped over them nonchalantly.

"I see you've been a bit busy yourself," the Wraith said as he walked over the bodies.

"Once I was certain my associates were here," Doc said, "I wasn't going to let anything, or anyone keep me from rescuing them."

"I gathered that," the Wraith said, rubbing his jaw. If he smiled, it was invisible under the dark mask.

Doc watched the Wraith's expression as he saw the lightweight construction of the Hermes up close.

"You flew here in *this*?"

Doc was already beginning his standard safety checks. He nodded.

"And this can carry the both of us?" the Wraith asked.

Again, Doc nodded. He checked the fuel level and turned to the masked man. "How much do you weight? In your full regalia."

"Why?"

"I must calculate the probable fuel usage."

The dark man's head canted slightly. "Probable? I'm not sure I like the sound of that word." He told Doc how much he weighed.

"Then we should have just enough to get back to the city," Doc said. "Coming?"

The Wraith hesitated for only a moment, then moved forward "Atlas, what you said about putting old ghosts to rest.... Did you mean that?"

"Come with me and find out."

They wheeled the Hermes around so the nose faced toward the gate on the long drive, which Doc had used for a landing strip. In the impending darkness, Doc completed his final safety checks. He showed the Wraith to the passenger seat and demonstrated how to use the safety harness. Doc took the pilot's seat and pulled his own harness around himself. Before cranking up the motor, he retrieved two sets of goggles from the dash compartment and handed one set to the Wraith. "You might be more comfortable if you removed that stocking from your face, Counselor, and wore these."

The Wraith's head jerked toward him.

"You know who I am?"

Doc nodded. He slipped on his goggles, and began turning a series of knobs on the instrument panel. The Wraith peeled back the translucent mask, revealing features twisted under the sheerness of a nylon stocking. After a moment's hesitation, he rolled up the stocking and slipped the goggles over his face. Doc pressed the starter button, and the propeller began to do an incremental rotation. Within seconds the spin was transformed into a hazy blur, and the Hermes began to roll forward. They raced down the long drive toward the sculptured pillars of the front gate. Suddenly the fence appeared before them, but almost immediately began to dip from view as Doc pulled back on the stick and the craft lifted off. With the motor situated behind them, its noise was greatly reduced, making conversation possible. The Wraith glanced at the rapidly receding trees and bushes then stiffened slightly as Doc banked left for a turn.

"Do you intend to expose me?" the Wraith asked.

Doc considered the question, but did not answer right away. Finally, he said, "I hold the lives of those people you saved back there very dearly. However, I cannot condone the wanton killing that you seem to be intent upon committing. I find it especially peculiar that a man in your profession would undertake such a campaign of vigilantism."

"But you've killed people, too. Haven't you?"

"Only with good reason," Doc said.

They say in silence for a few moments.

"Have you ever been in love, Atlas?" Paul Milton asked, the British inflections returning slightly to his voice. When Doc didn't answer, the Wraith continued. "Ellen and I were sweethearts back before the War, but she came from a prominent New York family, and I was a lowly assistant deputy prosecutor." He sighed. "We intended on marrying, but her family was against it. Then, the War started in Europe and my parents were killed in one of the blitzes on London. I went over to settle the estate, saw how things were, and enlisted. I thought I'd lost Ellen already. She never answered any of my letters. I found out years later her father had managed to intercept them all."

As the Hermes shot through the darkening sky, Doc

scanned the illuminated dashboard lights and checked the altimeter.

"When I returned to the States afterward," Milton continued, "all I focused on was making money. I began my own practice, and it became quite lucrative. It didn't matter that I was defending some bloody low class goons with dirty money. And then, one day…"

"Ellen came back into your life?" Doc asked.

"Yes," Milton said, somewhat surprised. Then he chuckled. "This sounds a bit like a bad melodrama, doesn't it?"

Doc said nothing.

Milton continued: "I heard her playing 'Beautiful Dreamer' one day at an art gallery. It had always been our favorite song. I sat there transfixed, listening, and went up to her after she finished. Suddenly, it was as if we'd never been apart. So we…. She was married to Ward Casper, but she had come to realize that all he was interested in was her money and social standing. She was planning on divorcing him. Then she became pregnant. It put a new wrinkle on things, but she still intended to leave him soon after the baby was born."

"She was a very beautiful and talented woman," Doc said. "I can understand why you went after the men responsible when she was killed."

"That's not entirely accurate," Milton said. "Webber and Boggs were my clients, and they told me in confidence that they'd only used the explosion as a cover-up. Ellen and the baby were already dead when the car was blown up." He gripped the steel frame tightly as he continued. "They told me it had been arranged for them to take the blame. Once they were released on bond, they were supposed to be taken up to Canada to disappear."

"So you killed them?"

"No. They were supposed to meet a boat at pier sixty-six in the harbor," he said. "I knew once they left, I'd never find them again–never know who was actually responsible for Ellen's death. I was desperate, so I used some of my old commando gear to disguise my appearance, and went to intercept them. And whoever was supposed to meet them. I wanted to conduct my own interrogation. But when I got there, the men in the boat came up to the pier and opened fire on them. I returned fire and it developed into a small gun battle. The boat fled but Webber and Boggs were dead. Someone saw what looked to them like a ghost running from the scene. One of the papers turned that statement into the Wraith, and," His mouth twisted into a grim smile, "a legend was born. I've spent the past two years trying to track down Ellen's real murderer, but I've never gotten close. Then what started as a desperate initiative, developed into a war. Tyranny and injustice seemed to well up everywhere. It was like I was suddenly fighting a crusade." He stared at Doc again. "And now you say you know who's responsible?"

"I believe Ward Casper killed her," Doc said.

"Casper? But why?"

"The exact circumstances are yet to be known," Doc said. "But Casper was using his judicial influence to help the New York mobsters gain a foothold in local real estate by granting early foreclosures, and fraudulent purchases through dummy corporations. It's possible Ellen found out about his dealings and threatened to expose him."

"But what makes you think that he killed her?" Milton asked.

"He and Hamilton Vernon covered up a crime that was

committed by Randolph Grantman's son in Germany at the end of the war," Doc said. "The modus operandi was the same: an exploding car. That, and certain real estate records my secretary was able to obtain for me, show that Casper was slowly siphoning off his wife's family fortune by selling the estate and repurchasing it with figurehead corporations of which he was the president. His ties to Grantman from the Germany matter explain the mob's involvement, so it was never feasible that the gangsters would want to kill him. He was already secretly in their corner. Thus, the murders take on another significance. The bombing and the mobster retaliation against the judge were just ruses meant to draw suspicion away from the true killer. I'll know for sure once I'm able to interrogate the judge using hypnosis and sodium pentothal."

"No, dammit, it all fits," Milton said, clenching his gloved fist. "Ellen's parents were killed in an automobile accident shortly after they were married. That left her the sole heir to the estate. How could I have been so bloody blind not to have seen this before?"

Doc continued flying in silence. Finally, Milton asked, "So how did you figure out who I was?"

"That was a rather complex process," Doc said. "I used my prototypical computer to compute identity probabilities based on a myriad of factors. This gave me a basic list, upon which your name appeared. We were narrowing down the list when this Grantman matter interceded. But my ultimate conclusion was rather elementary: your use of the song, 'Beautiful Dreamer,' during the rescue of Maria Hernandez. It associated you with Ellen Casper and…" He let his voice trail off.

"I still don't see how you bridged the final gap," Milton

said.

"The birth certificate for Ellen Casper's son," Doc said. "I checked a photostatic copy of the original. She started to write your name in the space allotted for the baby's father, then purposely left it blank. Alexander Paul Casper was your son, wasn't he?"

The Wraith didn't answer, but he punched his thigh viciously with a gloved fist.

Just as the lights of the silhouetted skyscrapers were becoming visible in the distance, the engine sputtered slightly. Doc checked the fuel gauge and saw it was hovering just above empty.

"What's the problem?" Milton asked.

"We've used more fuel than I anticipated," Doc said.

"Do we have enough to make it?"

Doc's mouth compressed into a thin line. "I believe so."

"Dammit, Atlas, we've got to make it. I won't be denied now that I'm finally this close."

"Vengeance is often an unsatisfying aspiration," Doc said.

Milton turned to look at him. "I call it justice."

As they flew on in silence, the engine began to miss and sputter with more frequency. "We may have to glide in," Doc said, pulling back on the stick and causing the Hermes to climb higher.

Milton looked at him quizzically. "Is this wise?"

"I'm going to attempt to land on the building's roof," Doc said. "The street will be too congested."

"Is that feasible?" Milton asked.

"The fund raiser's in the Ambassador Hotel," Doc replied. "I happen to know the building has a capacious roof. Hopefully I'll be able to land within its confines."

"Hopefully," Milton repeated.

The Hermes continued to climb, its engine missing with greater regularity now. Then, as they reached the apex of their ascent, the sputtering stopped. The silence seemed deafening, as the wind tore at their faces and Doc began to angle the craft downward, toward the city lights below.

"Which one is the hotel?" the Wraith asked. Doc did not reply. He was devoting all of his concentration to the delicate banking maneuvers as the light aircraft swooped down in a precisely controlled spiral. They drew close to one of the taller skyscrapers and a sudden wind shear racked the Hermes like an invisible wave. Doc adjusted the pitch and continued his circular descent. They seemed to miss the white stone corner of another building by mere inches, then the Wraith saw the flat expanse of darkness of the hotel roof getting closer. Seconds later, the wheels hit the surface. Doc applied the braking device and gripped the stick. The Hermes bounced and rushed toward the parapet on the opposite end, coming to rest only inches from the wall.

"Perhaps we should split up," the Wraith said, taking off the goggles and pulling the stocking and mask down over his face again. He unsnapped the safety harness and jumped from the seat. Doc was already moving toward the stairwell doorway at the other end of the roof. His steps made crunching sounds as his heavy boots moved over the pebbled-stone surface. The door was locked, but Doc merely braced one hand on the wall next to it and gripped the knob in his other hand. The smooth muscles bulged in his forearm momentarily and the door sprang open. The sudden exertion caused a twinge of pain in his side and crimson blots began to stain through the tan fabric of his shirt. He glanced around to look for the Wraith, but the shadowy figure was nowhere to be seen. Doc glanced at the metal railings of the fire escape across the roof. Without delaying another second, he rushed down the stairs and into the top floor of the hotel.

A porter, who'd been bending down to pick up a used room-service tray next to a door, turned his head as he heard the noise of the golden avenger's rapid approach. The man's head bounced into the wall as he struggled to straighten up quickly.

Doc paused and stared straight at him.

"The political fund raiser," Doc said. "Where's it being held?"

"It's in the main ballroom, sir," the porter said, his eyes the size of small saucers. "First floor."

Doc glanced around. The doors to several elevators were down the hallway, but they were on the fifteenth floor. A wait for one of them to reach the top could mean the difference between life and death. Doc seized the porter by the upper arm, lifting the man onto his toes.

"Do you have a service elevator here?" he asked.

"It's over there," the porter said, wincing from the pain of Doc's grip. "But it's for hotel staff only."

"Show me," Doc said. He released the pressure on the man's arm and followed him as he scurried down the hall. A corridor extended between the last set of rooms near the back wall, ending at a heavy door. The porter fumbled with his keys and unlocked the door. It opened onto a small storage room and to the left were the open horizontal doors of a large freight elevator.

"Take me to the ballroom," Doc said. "Immediately."

"Yes, sir," the porter said, stepping inside the elevator and pulling down on the woven strap to shut the doors. Once they had slammed shut, he inserted a key into the panel, then gripped the lever and plunged it downward. The elevator descended with what seemed like interminable slowness, and Doc regretted not having tried a faster way down. He glanced around the inside of the cage, looking for something he might be able to use as a distraction device. Despite his expert marksmanship ability, he certainly did not wish to risk firing a shot from his revolver in a crowded ballroom. He reached up and unscrewed two of the light bulbs from the side fixture. The porter watched him, but said nothing. Finally the elevator came to rest and the porter pushed on the top door.

"Where exactly is the ballroom?" Doc asked.

"Down that way," the porter said, extending a trembling finger.

"Take me there," Doc said. He grabbed the man's upper arm again, and they did a quick trot down the corridor. At the end of the hallway, they entered a huge kitchen area. The floor was slick with grease and made walking a bit tricky. Cooks in white uniforms and restaurant waitresses stopped what they were doing as the oddly matched pair rushed through. Beyond the kitchen area was a laundry section, then a maintenance shop. The porter tugged at Doc's hand and scuffled his feet.

"It's in there." He pointed. "In there."

The wall had a single door in it. Doc released the porter and turned the knob. As he pulled the door open he could see there was a small room that was separated from the main area by some heavy curtains. Doc pulled one of the curtains aside carefully. The ballroom was immense, and filled with at least four or five hundred people. After scanning the assembly, Doc saw a raised speaker's platform standing at the front of the room, perhaps thirty feet to his left. A man with heavy jowls stood behind the lectern, speaking into the large chrome microphone: "And now, it gives me distinct pleasure to introduce the honorable Congressman Vito Marcantonio."

He stepped back to lead the applause as a heavy-set man with black hair, wearing a double-breasted blue suit, began to walk up the steps onto the stage. The Congressman fumbled with some papers from his inside jacket pocket. Doc's eyes scanned the room, then he saw a slight tremor in the curtain directly behind the stage. Flinging himself into the room, Doc hurled one of the light bulbs directly at the podium. It shattered with the quick pop of a report, and the people in the front rows stopped applauding and quickly looked at Doc. He hurled the second light bulb directly at Congressman Marcantonio's head. It exploded on contact with his left temple, the fine spray of glass making a momentary halo-like appearance. The Congressman fell to his knees, just as the curtains in back of the stage were ripped apart and a darkly clad figure stepped through holding a chrome forty-five.

"Oh my God," someone yelled. "It's the Wraith!"

At the sight of the masked intruder brandishing a pistol, pandemonium broke out as people began to run for the exit doors, crashing into one another and cramming together like a herd of panicked sheep.

Doc reached the fallen Marcantonio, literally plucked him from the stairs, and stowed the Congressman under the platform. He instinctively ducked as the figure in black extended the auto-pistol and fired. As the flame shot from the barrel, more screaming broke out in the ballroom. The sound of chairs being overturned mixed with the screams as the throng of humanity continued to clamor over each other to get to the doors. The ersatz Wraith fired another shot at Doc, who by this time had his own revolver out. Doc pointed his pistol at the assailant and squeezed off a round. The masked figure jumped back into the curtained area behind the stage. Doc knelt down and spoke to the congressman, who had overcome his slight disorientation.

"I'm sorry I had to take such extreme measures, but an assassin was lurking nearby," Doc said.

"What?" Marcantonio said. "Who?"

"Remain here and you'll be safe," Doc said. He stood and leaped onto the stage. Moving to the last area where he had seen the would-be killer, Doc extended the muzzle of his gun and ripped back the curtain. Behind the hanging cloth was another expansive room, with a door on the rear wall. Suddenly, panicked screams and more shots emanated from behind the wall. Doc jumped down and ran for the door. He reached it in seconds and quickly went through. It opened into the same long service hallway through which he'd come with the porter. Each crevice and doorway seemed an ominous hiding spot.

The shots seemed to have echoed through the building, and even these back corridors were empty now. The body of a porter, his white jacket stained with two crimson holes, lay twisted on its side. After checking the man and confirming he was dead, Doc moved to the center of the hallway and, gun extended, walked toward the kitchen area. In the center of the floor lay a crumpled black coat. Doc paused to pick it up, then scanned the area ahead of him. Farther down he saw a dark hat, then the corridor seemed to extend into a series of recessed doors. He knew the killer could be hiding in any of them.

Doc zig-zagged down the hallway, moving from one

doorway to the next, trying each door he found. Several
opened up into the kitchen area. Others were locked, and still
more of them opened into the serving areas of various other
ballrooms. As he progressed toward the next doorway, Doc
detected some movement in one of the recesses across the hall.
Thrusting his revolver out in front of him, Doc leaped across
the hallway and grabbed the figure by the arm, pulling
outward. It was a woman in a maid's uniform. The inertia of
Doc's movement had thrown her into the middle of the hall.
He crouched down, trying to keep her quiet.

Doc raised up to guide her back into the recession from
which she'd come when her eyes widened and her scream
seemed to die in her throat. He glanced in the direction of her
gaze and saw a darkly clad figure pointing a forty-five
semiautomatic pistol at them. Just as he managed to throw the
woman to a position of relative safety, flame roared from the

automatic. The round whipped by Doc's head and he began to bring up his own weapon when he heard a grunt behind him. Turning, Doc saw another Wraith, this one bareheaded and jacketless, bending over clutching his abdomen, his big pistol slowly rotating in his grasp. A piercing whistle trilled out the first few bars of "Beautiful Dreamer," the melody of vengeance. The hatless figure's face contorted viciously under his mask, and he made sudden attempt to bring the pistol up and aim it at Doc.

A second shot sounded and the hatless Wraith curled forward and fell to the floor. Doc stepped over, kicked the forty-five from the fallen man's limp fingers, rolled him over onto his back, and peeled off the dark mask. The face of Ward Casper, a trickle of blood leaking down from his mouth, his eyes glazed over and sightless, seemed to glare back at them. Doc stood and faced the real Wraith, who was perhaps ten feet away, leaning against the wall, holding his smoldering semiautomatic pistol at his side. The wail of sirens sounded in the distance.

"Is the Congressman all right?" the Wraith asked.

"Yes," Doc said.

"I'm glad you could save him. At least I won't be blamed for that one too," the Wraith said. His features were once again indistinguishable under his mask, but Doc thought he detected a note of wry humor.

Doc glanced toward Casper's body. "It seems I owe you my life as well."

"It looks like you've been hit," the Wraith said, pointing to the blood-soaked left side of Doc's shirt.

"A previous wound," Doc said. "And one of the reasons I won't be able to pursue you as you beat a hasty retreat." A slight smile traced over his lips and he leaned back, resting against the wall, and holstered his revolver. "Whoever you are."

The Wraith holstered his pistol as well, and touched the fingers of his gloved hand to his stocking cap in a salute of respect to Doc. In another moment he was gone.

"So did you ice this one too, Atlas?" Detective Hal Roland asked, bending down to pulling off the mask of the prone figure of Judge Ward Casper. "Excuse me, your honor," he added sarcastically.

"No," Doc said. "I did not."

He was shirtless and leaning slightly against the corridor wall as an ambulance attendant taped a large bandage against the ruptured wound on Doc's side.

"That's hard to believe," Roland said, fingering the mask. "The way you been piling up bodies lately, you're giving the real Wraith a run for his money."

"You really should get this re-sutured as soon as possible, sir," the attendant said.

"Well, Atlas, you want to go to the hospital before you come down to the precinct house to make your statement?" Roland asked.

"The hospital can wait," Doc said. "I'd rather apprehend the last perpetrator in this affair."

"Oh yeah? And who might that be?" Roland asked. He stepped toward Doc, took out his pack of Chesterfields, and grinned. "Cigarette?"

Doc shook his head.

Roland placed one of the cigarettes between his lips, but didn't light it. "So tell me, Atlas, who we going after?"

"The man responsible for the assassination attempt, the kidnapping of Bonnie Grantman, and the death of Ira Bloom," Doc said. "As well as the deaths of those four police officers at the Lexington Hotel."

Roland's lighter paused in front of his face, the light from the flame dancing over his cheeks, but he capped the lighter before holding it to the cigarette and asked Doc to explain.

"Randolph Grantman," Doc said. "He orchestrated the kidnapping of his own daughter, then ordered the thugs to kill Ira Bloom at the hotel. He was also behind the plot to kill Congressman Marcantonio."

"Huh? How do you figure that?" Roland asked, the unlighted cigarette bouncing as he spoke.

Doc slipped on his vest and shirt and cocked his head for Roland to follow him. He walked down the hallway at a brisk pace. The cop motioned for one of the others to take over the crime scene and moved into step with Doc.

"Grantman owns quite a bit of stock in the various construction companies that are poised to begin this highway project," Doc said. "He stands to lose a lot if the project is blocked."

"And that's why he wanted old Vito out of the picture?" Roland asked. "It makes sense, but why did the judge do what he done?"

"Casper owed his judicial appointment to Grantman," Doc said. "He also helped Grantman cover up a crime committed by Warren Grantman while he was in the military in Germany. Casper used that favor to obtain Grantman's assistance in covering up the murder of Ellen Casper and her son."

"Hey, Atlas," Roland said, removing the unlit cigarette from his mouth. "Slow down a little, will ya?"

"We don't have time to move slowly," Doc said, as they neared the exit. "We have to get out to Grantman's estate before he realizes we're onto him and escapes."

"All right, all right," Roland said. "Just lemme call Efrem to meet us out there with a couple of State guys, okay? I'll be a little bit out of my jurisdiction."

Doc stopped and said with a slight grin, "And I know how serious those jurisdictional problems can be."

When Roland's unmarked squad car rolled up in front of the Grantman estate, the long driveway was ablaze with flashing crimson lights. In front of the house sat two ambulances, as well as a State Police car and the blue sedan of the FBI.

"Somehow I don't like the looks of this," Roland said, driving over the lawn and parking near the fountain. Its gurgling streams were colored by special lights.

They walked up to the front door and Roland flashed his shield at the uniformed state cop stationed there.

"I'm sorry, sir," the cop said. "Crime scene. No unauthorized personnel."

"Look, sonny, I'm about as authorized as you can get," Roland growled. "And this is Doc Atlas. You ever heard of him?"

The young policeman's eyes widened as he glanced at Doc, but he said nothing.

"It's all right, Griffin," a voice said from over the young cop's shoulder. "They can come in."

It was Special Agent Efrem. He was standing just inside the door, looking very haggard. Roland and Doc stepped inside.

"What the hell happened here?" Roland asked, looking around.

"Looks like a murder/suicide," Efrem said. "Apparently Warren Grantman snapped. It appears he shot his father, and then took his own life." He bit his lower lip. "I hope the Bureau doesn't come off looking too bad in this one."

"He wasn't no saint anyway," Roland said. "We got him figured for being behind this whole kidnapping thing."

Efrem looked startled. "You're joking."

"Not hardly," Roland said, jerking his thumb toward Doc. "The big guy here figured it all out. We been sorta working together on this." He smirked. "It's a jurisdictional thing."

"Well, I'd be very interested in hearing about that," Efrem said, looking at Doc. "Would you like to sit down, sir?"

"Unfortunately I have a gunshot wound that I sustained earlier and it must be attended to," Doc said. "But Detective Roland can brief you on our entire theory. As he said, despite several jurisdictional problems that have arisen, he and I are in total agreement on the case."

Roland turned and caught Doc's quick wink.

"Isn't that correct, Detective?"

"Sure is, Atlas," Roland said with a grin. "I'll have one of the uniforms drive you back to the city."

18

Tabula Rasa

"AND so the kidnapping case of Bonnie Grantman comes to its disturbing and bloody end. While the whole incident was steeped in tragedy, the successful rescue of Miss Grantman at least lends a fragile hope that some good was, in fact, salvaged. We should remember this as a tribute to the brave souls who perished, both police officers and innocents. If we can emerge as a people tempered and stronger, then their sacrifice may not have been in vain." Deagan stopped reading and pawed at his eye. "This is really good, Penny," he said.

"Will you finish it up," Ace said irritably.

Deagan scowled at him and continued. "And, on a personal note, this marks my last column for the *New York Daily Guardian*. I wish to thank all my loyal readers who have followed me throughout my career here."

Deagan tossed the copy of the newspaper onto the tabletop in Doc's study and turned in surprise to Penny. Ace and Polly, who were seated on either side of her, looked on in astonishment also. Doc, who was standing by the window staring outside, remained impassive.

"You ain't really quitting the newspaper business are ya?" Deagan asked.

"Relax, Mad Dog," Penny said. "I've already been offered a job with the *Daily News*, but I want to take a couple of weeks off." She held up her left arm, which was still swathed in bandages, and smiled as she looked at Doc. Assante's eyes followed her gaze, then went back to her face. "Besides, the pulp magazine is certainly going to expect me to write this one up," she added. "I've even got a great title in mind."

"Oh yeah?" Deagan said. "What is it?"

"Melody of Murder," Penny said.

"Hmm," Deagan said. "Not bad. What do you think, Doc?"

"How about Melody of Vengeance?" Doc said.

"What I still don't get, Doc," Deagan said, "is how you figured Grantman was behind it all?"

Doc turned and smiled benignly at the group.

"My first suspicion arose after the two hoodlums killed Ira Bloom and those police officers at the Lexington Hotel," Doc said. "Detective Roland had stated that no one knew where they had sequestered Bloom. He made a telephone call to the hotel just before we left Grantman's. That was the only way the thugs could have known our destination and beat us there." He walked around the table and placed a hand on Penny's shoulder. "Grantman's previous anti-Semitic remarks about Bloom alerted me to this. Then there was the matter of the tapes. On the two messages recorded by Grantman that were purportedly from the kidnapper, the recording started prior to the first ring of the phone. But as I discreetly observed Grantman, when Diana called from the office, as per my instructions, he answered the phone first, with his fingers poised on the recording switch. This led me to hypothesize that he was expecting the calls from the alleged kidnapper." Doc smiled broadly. "And of course, the customarily excellent work of Polly, gathering the financial clues to Grantman's private holdings that tied him to the public works project, and ultimately to organized crime, cannot be minimized either."

Polly blushed as Deagan rubbed her neck affectionately.

"So was his son a loser, or what?" Deagan said. "A real looney toon, too."

"Actually, Warren Grantman was a very disturbed young man," Doc said. "However, it's also entirely possible that some of the unscrupulous people with whom Grantman had dealings saw the plan was falling apart and decided to eliminate them both as a potential loose ends. But that will be up to the police to prove."

"Wow," said Penny, her eyes widening. "That sounds like something that should be looked into pronto."

"You were going to take some time off, remember?" Ace said. "After what you went through at Edgar's you deserve it."

"Yeah, that's for sure," Deagan added. "Hey, Doc, what about the Wraith? We still going after him now? After him saving us, and all?"

"I've decided that perhaps we should give him *tabula rasa*," Doc said.

"Huh?" Deagan said. "What's that mean?"

"It's Latin for blank slate," Ace said.

"I knew that," Deagan said, "But what I meant was, did you ever figure out who he really is?"

"I did," Doc said slowly," but do you really want me to tell you?"

No one in the group spoke. Finally Deagan shifted in his chair and said, "Aww, hell. I guess not. The guy saved my bacon, so I guess the least I can do is give him his privacy."

"Now I'm really starting to worry," Ace said. "Deagan and I are starting to agree on things again. The next thing he and I will be listening to Frasier Clark and *The Shadow* together."

Everyone laughed. Doc went over to the blackboard at the front of the room. He pulled up a silk curtain hanging in front of the slate. On it was a detailed drawing of a map.

"Now that we've officially closed the case of the Wraith," he said, "I'd like everyone to consider a new prospect. There are documented reports of some sort of jungle man living in this area of the African Continent. If we could fly into Cape Town and embark on a safari to here," he pointed to the map. "We could investigate these sightings and evaluate their veracity."

Doc paused, looked at the attentive group, and went to the wall switch that controlled the fans. He flipped it on and said, "Go ahead and smoke if you wish. The fans and hood will do their work adequately enough." He smiled slightly. "One of the things this case did was make me realize tolerance for one's peers is a virtue worth cultivating."

Ace raised his eyebrows, removed his cigarette case, and looked at Deagan and Polly. They were both following Doc's presentation with rapt attention. He placed a cigarette between his lips and brought out his lighter, but before he could ignite the wick, Penny brought her lighter up. She winked at him and smiled gently as he placed the end of the cigarette into the yellow flame.

Meet the author:

Michael A. Black holds an MFA degree in Fiction Writing from Columbia College, and has been a police officer in the south suburbs of Chicago for the past twenty-eight years. His short stories have been published in a variety of anthologies and magazines including Ellery Queen and Alfred Hitchcock's Mystery Magazine. Mike's other novels include A Killing Frost, Windy City Knights, and A Final Judgment, featuring private investigator Ron Shade. He has also written two standalone thrillers, *The Heist* and *Freeze Me, Tender*.

Tim Faurote, whose illustrations appear on the cover and inside this book, is a commercial artist and lifelong fan of the pulp magazines. He lives with his family in Decatur, Indiana.

For more on Michael A. Black visit

www.michaelablack.com

Coming February 2007

From Echelon Press

The Diva Fool

By Silvia Foti

Book One

Turn the page for
Chapter One

Overture

The doorbell tinkled as I entered, but The Wizard acted as if he hadn't heard it. I wasn't offended or surprised–I'd gotten used to his moments of focused concentration. He lifted the woodsy perfumed broom, its knobbed handle gleaming, and swept about three to six inches above the floor, leaving crumbs and dust behind. He remained intent on finishing his task, whistling a gleeful melody as he brushed the air with a whoosh to right and left. After observing him for several moments, I still could not figure out why he swept in such an odd fashion.

Gemstones, herbs, incense, and Tarot cards crammed the studio's shelves. Cinnamon spice laced the air from a fat, red candle flickering in the corner next to the blazing fireplace. The place held an aura of high-mindedness mixed with whimsy, and I loved the incorruptible way it made me feel.

Slowly, methodically, The Wizard swiped the space above the well-worn wooden floor. Absorbed in his work, over and over he sang in a deep tone, "Be gone…away…fly…leave." When he had swept the last corner with a curlicue swirl, he approached the center of the room, lifted the broom waist-high, parallel to the floor, and rotated his body, eyes closed, muttering a prayer.

Suddenly, his eyes popped open. "Alexandria Vilkas," he cried. His joy charged me like a mug of steaming tea. "Come in, come in."

"Hello, Master." I stepped forward and quizzically looked at him.

With indigo eyes and a snowy beard trailing to his heart, he wore jeans and a thick ivory wool sweater. Dots of perspiration rimmed his brow, and when he wiped his clammy forehead, he mussed his stiff, white hair. He upended the broom, holding it like a pitchfork. "It's the New Moon, time to clear away the detritus from the last cycle and usher in our new desires. Your timing is impeccable–I've just cleared away the negativity."

I smelled dust bunnies. "Cleared away the negativity?"

"From clients, mostly. Dump every problem! By the end of the moon cycle, it's an astral mess." Breathing deeply, he spread his arms and looked around. "Much better, isn't it?"

"If you say so."

Looking me over from head to toe, he lamented, "You are a wet undine, aren't you?"

My hands flew to my hair, drenched all the way down to my waist from the heavy snow outside. I could imagine how terrible I looked, but I shoved those thoughts aside to talk about this momentous occasion.

"It's March 4th," I said. "The big day."

"Hmmm."

"Please, you're not going to put it off any longer, are you?"

He motioned toward the leaping flames in the brick fireplace that engulfed two crackling logs in an orange blaze. "Very well. Take off your coat and dry it by the fire."

Once we settled on his zebra-patterned couch, he showed me his new ten-inch crystal ball set atop a pewter stand that an artisan had sculpted into a trio of jesters.

"Oh, how beautiful!"

"Ordered it by catalogue."

From my past year of studying with my master, I knew the crystal ball did not contain any magical properties. All the hocus-pocus, if you want to call it that, came from The Wizard's mind, trained with rigorous study and capable of sustained concentration.

I nodded, regarding the folds of a black velvet, hooded cape hanging next to a wall-mounted sconce of a dragon. The Wizard had added those to the decor since my last visit seven days ago. He always added something new…last week he hung ornamental flower fairies in front of the window. The week before, he rearranged his essential oils into a pyramid.

"It's March 4th," I said again, as if that would make The Wizard hurry.

"You must be patient. Tell me all you have learned this year."

I could tell he was fishing for a certain answer by the way his forehead creased like an accordion; but I had no idea what he wanted to hear. "We've been working with Tarot cards, their aspects of astrology, elementals, symbolism, numerology, colors, reversals, dignities, and correspondences–what they mean individually, and how they interact with each other in a spread."

"And what else?"

"We've covered ritual work and meditation, fortune-telling versus divination, and path-working. You also had me shooting guns and picking locks."

The Wizard folded his hands together and looked me over. "I'm sorry, but I don't know that you're ready."

What did I say wrong? "But you promised!"

"Initiation is not an exact science. It's true that we've been studying together for 365 days, but you are not ready. Not yet."

He may as well have pricked my hope with a needle and deflated it until it crumpled into a rubbery puddle. "What else do I need to do?"

The Wizard massaged his chin. "You must pass a test."

The acids in my stomach whipped my breakfast of Baltic rye bread and farmer's cheese into an acrid soup, but I swallowed hard because I trusted my master. He would give me a test I had a chance of passing. "What sort of test?"

"Tell me about the story you are working on."

He often assigned me spiritual exercises that applied to my occupation as a journalist. As a reporter for *Gypsy Magazine*, a bimonthly in Chicago, I covered paranormal happenings such as haunted houses and ghost sightings. I'd had this job for three years, and I had earned a challenge. "'Tarot Cards and the Celebrities Who Use Them.' Is this story going to be part of my test?"

"If you are ready to live a life of service."

Our lessons always came back to the topic of service and helping others. I knew this. Why did he repeat himself?

"The story is always more than just about your byline, Alexandria Vilkas. It is about how readers will benefit from the information. By the same token, entering the Order of the Tarot will not make your life easier. Your own needs and wants must be subjugated for the betterment of someone else."

I heard only "The Order of the Tarot." "The Order of the Tarot? That's the first time you uttered the name of the secret society."

The Wizard nodded. "It goes by many names, but that is the one you will know it by."

"What does it do? How many members does it have? Are you going to let me join today?"

The Wizard held up his right hand. "All in good time. First, you must pass the test. Oh, and there's one more thing."

"What's that?"

"Since the Order of the Tarot is a secret society, you are not to discuss it with anyone, not your mother, not your friends, not your boss, not your boyfriend. No one. Do you understand?"

I nodded, wondering if he weren't being a bit overdramatic, but I swore to keep my promise. "I don't have a boyfriend."

"Never mind that."

The Wizard glanced at his crystal ball, polished it with his sleeve, and picked off an imaginary piece of lint, perhaps one that contained my negativity. Then he leaned in, as if pulled by an invisible force. "Oh, my," he gasped and he looked at me in awe.

"What? What?"

I focused on the three jesters holding the crystal ball,

as they stood frozen in their dancing positions.

"Your test is two-pronged. Do you want a reading on what you can expect?"

"Yes, please."

The Wizard smiled. "Very well."

He reached into a nearby wooden cabinet and pulled out a deck of Arthurian Tarot cards wrapped in a black silk scarf. He made a big show of unveiling the cards…shuffling, whispering a petition, and asking me to cut them into three piles using only my left hand. With a flourish, he flipped over the top cards from each of the three piles onto the black silky folds.

The Page of Swords (The Adder) appeared first, followed by the Ten of Spears (The Green Knight), and the Three of Cups (The Dressing of the Sacred Spring). From my previous year of studying the Tarot, I knew the meanings of these cards, but I was curious to hear my master's interpretation.

"After this story, your life will never be the same," he announced. "You will become a servant to those in jeopardy of malevolence…supernatural and mundane. Shall I continue?"

Gulping, I nodded.

The Wizard drew his eyebrows together and proceeded in a clinical monotone. "You are the Page of Swords, an inconspicuous witness to important events, a clever spy to make sense of unexpected plot twists, an active person with a sharp mind and a gift for learning secrets. You endure a ten-day struggle, an awesome task of life over death that demands courage and diplomacy. During that time, a handsome married man seduces you, presenting you with an item as a gift. If you suppress personal desires, you will be positioned to help victims of cruelty, immorality, and ruin. When your mission is complete, pay homage to the spirit of the spring."

Despite the warning I sat back and grinned, like I'd just discovered a special present on my lap left, by one of the flower fairies hanging near his window. The Wizard had been grooming me for this moment all year long, and now I hovered on the threshold of enlisting into the elite, secret society that fought supernatural evil forces. I'd heard rumors about it shortly after I started working for *Gypsy Magazine* and made it my mission to find out more so I could do a story on it. I remembered being surprised to hear The Wizard admit he was in a position to help me gain entry into the clandestine organization, but that I could never write about it.

"Wow! Sounds like the story is everything I've asked for. And for ten days!"

The Wizard studied the spread, gazed into his crystal ball, and shook his head with a "*tsk, tsk*."

"Do not underestimate your attraction to the married man. You have known him in a previous life; that is why his pull is so strong."

I inhaled sharply, now beginning to appreciate the test that lay ahead. I knew exactly which married man he was foretelling–that's what filled me with dread. Bruno Scavoro, a trustee of *Gypsy Magazine*, had enough magnetism to flip-flop the earth's poles. I just hoped he didn't have the capacity to derail me from what I wanted most–membership in the Order of the Tarot.

"You said this test was two-pronged. What did you mean by that?"

"Earning the degree of the Fool involves two

challenges. The one with the married man is the easier of the two. The other you will recognize when you see it. See me after it manifests itself."

Echelon Press

Publishing

Echelon Press Publishing

Celebrating

Unique Stories

For

Exceptional Readers

WWW.ECHELONPRESS.COM